Caliostro

Tale of the Lyvirten

Publisher: Under The Veil Publishing
Illustrated Cover by: Dusan Markovic
Edited by: Brian Paone & Aaron Bear
Formatted by: Elysian Formatting
ISBN:

This book is dedicated to my family. Thank you for always believing in me. Shido, the best man I know and my soulmate, thank you for letting me bounce my ideas off you and for brainstorming with me. My beautiful daughter, you make my soul shine; you make the long days of writing have a peaceful and happy end. My mother, thank you for always being a front-stage mom and for reading my fiction even when you don't read fiction.

Prologue

Mahaven Forest, AD1261

Light broke through the forest trees. Charred tree bark and corpses of small and large animals graced the sight of the young boy on his knees in the center of the woods. "Mother? Why was I born like this?" he asked, panning from his open palms to the damage he had caused.

His mother knelt and placed both hands on either side of his face.

His crystal-blue eyes met her silver ones.

"My love, it's how you were born. Embrace it, control it, and never question why. You were born as you should be." She pulled him into her embrace. A forlorn smile spread across her face.

Tear-filled eyes gazed at his father standing behind them as they both sighed.

BLUE EYES

In the hazy moonlight sat alone figure, quite unlike the rest of the Mahaven Mountains inhabitants. Sounds from near and far filled Caliostro's senses. Creatures of all kinds lurked in the darkness. Many centuries had passed while sitting on that very balcony each evening, yet he still listened. He found each swish, drip, click, and even the occasional scream soothing. His back relaxed into the high-backed chair; a sad smile spread across his face with the awakening night, his mother's past words echoing in the back of his mind. *"My love, it's how you were born. Embrace it, control it, and never question why. You were born as you should be."*

Her words faded when the distinctive sound of someone drowning broke through his musing. The gurgling and rising heart rate was close by. *How did someone get on my land without me knowing?*

Caliostro stood and hopped onto the balcony's edge but stopped just before leaping off the railing into the air, listening closer. A frown creased his smooth forehead. *Human?* He leaped and landed below. No sound emanated nor were any indentations left upon his landing. In one fluid movement, he dashed toward the lake.

The human's heart rate was now racing beyond its capable speed.

Soon it will give out. Caliostro reached the lake's edge, dove beneath the surface to grab the sinking human form, and his nostrils flared to life. Yes, the undeniable scent of a female. Her energy, though low, sang to him. Fire burst to life under his skin, and the feeling of magic dancing all around brought light once more to the darkness within him.

Water from the lake erupted around their intertwined bodies as they left the icy depths. Her soaked form appeared lifeless, pressed against him. Light snow fell,

2

echoing the human world season. Though it was a facsimile of true snowfall, it was still bitterly cold.

He surveyed the surroundings and found a grassy patch under a tree a few feet away that snow had not yet touched. Before he rested her there, a Dagaru Worm feasting on a lost human soul made itself known. The sucking sounds grew louder in haste to finish its meal. Its six-foot-long body pulsated, covered in slimy soot, accompanied by a mouth filled with razor-sharp teeth and no eyes to see. Unaware of its audience, the creature slithered and coiled around the last essence of the human soul. He ignored the creature and jumped over the lake to another tree. Studying her gave his heart a sprint to an invisible finish line, but the blue tint to her full lips sprung him back into action.

Kneeling, Caliostro leaned forward and pressed his warm mouth to her cold one. A whitish blue light flowed between their interlocked lips. The blue and pale tinge faded; blood flow had returned. Her heart rate normalized until her lids lifted. Heat ignited between them as their eyes locked. Glowing blue fire of his gaze reflected off her Emerald Lake orbs. His brow frowned, and the temples at his hairline lifted in silent confusion.

Her eyes widened and her heart raced, yet she didn't shrink from him.

"Who are you?" He was still a breath's length away, but their lips were no longer touching; he had released them upon her awakening.

She attempted to sit upright, but his large hand pushed her to the cold ground.

"It's best if you don't move on your own just yet."

She complied, resting back on the grass.

"How did you end up here?"

She shook her head.

"What's your name?"

Her brows furrowed before she cast her eyes down.

"Do you not know who you are?"

She shook her head again, which prompted a shiver to run through her.

A knowing look spread across his face. Her warmth took precedence over her identity, which made him slide one arm under her legs and the other under her shoulders.

"Wait. I think I—"

"It's okay. I'm going to lift you now." With a firm grip, he stood. "Can you put your arms around my neck and hold on?"

4

She answered by securing them around his neck.

"Close your eyes."

She glanced up at him and stilled.

"You can trust me. I have no interest in hurting you."

With eyes squinting, she looked away, then closed them after a moment.

The left corner of his mouth arched upward, before looking skyward. The black leather of his dress boots dug into the ground as his suit crinkled with the movement to stoop. Their clothing undulated when he leaped into the air. A shiver rumbled through the woman, making him clutch her closer. Blue wing-shaped lights spread from his back as they flew toward the manor.

Moments later, the surrounding air stilled. The faint scent of cedar, jasmine and a mixture of two more smells wafted under his nostril, stopping him mid descent, before they could land on the balcony below. His brow wrinkled and perked as he beheld her face.

With eyes still shut, she squirmed in his grasp, and the crinkles on her eyelids deepened.

That scent ...

A tremor from her ended his musing. The soles of his dress boots eased onto the balcony that held a tall table and two chairs. Holding her tight to him, he strode toward the double glass doors. Both swung open as he neared, clearing the way for his entry.

"This is my home." Caliostro passed a large vanity that held an oversized mirror with lights around its frame. He noticed her eyes remained shut. "You can open your eyes now."

Inch by inch, her lashes lifted, until the full view of the room filled her vision. Her green eyes reflected the soft light of the massive room as they moved from one side to the other.

This was a mistake …

The ends of her dark hair grazed the back of his wrists and hands.

Clearing his throat made her look up at him. "Can you stand?"

"I think so."

Caliostro lowered her to the floor but held on until the strength in her legs firmly planted her. The pull on his senses overlapped. He held his breath and stepped backward. Taking the opportunity, he approached a dark gray door trimmed in white. A light illuminated around his frame once he entered. Moments later, he returned to the room, and their eyes met.

"Who are you?" she asked.

He smiled. "Did it just dawn on you to ask that?"

Blood rushed to her cheeks. She scanned the room, and her gaze landed on the king-sized bed. "No, but—"

"*But*?"

She glanced at him. "I was in shock, and then, how we got here …"

"Caliostro," he answered in a clipped tone, ignoring her last words. "Here's a towel and bathrobe. That's the bathroom. I'm sure you figured that?" He pointed to the dark gray door. He stepped nearer to her and placed both items on the bed. He didn't react to her shrinking from him, but he took note of it. "Please feel free to use anything you need in this room."

She hugged herself, running both hands up and down her naked arms, while watching him.

He caught the slight quiver of her bottom lip. "You should get changed. I will leave you to it." He bowed his head.

She eyed the glass doors, then the only other door besides the bathroom.

When his head raised, the enticing sight of the side of her neck was his undoing. There, under soft, tanned skin, protruded her life's energy, making him desire a taste. *What's wrong with me? I've never had such desires.*

She faced him, but his back was to her.

"Once you change, I will return to speak with you."

With speed her eyes could not hope to follow, he was gone. The sound from the door clicking in place was the defining evidence he had been there.

***

She stared at the closed door, recalling details about her savior. His smell lingered, but she couldn't place the mixture of scents. He was tall, well-built, and moved with an air of confidence. He wore a three-piece suit with the collar undone. *He must be some sort of businessman.* Around his neck he'd worn a light-colored stone necklace. Then it was his face—high cheekbones, a long-bridged nose, and those intense blue eyes that had laid against soft olive-colored skin. Everything about him made her heart race just by remembering.

To calm her fierce heartbeat, she looked out through the glass doors, but it was pitch black. She pulled on the doors. Neither would budge, locked. *No, no.*

The wet ends of her dress tangled around her calves in her haste to check the other door. She tripped and stumbled into it. She gripped the knob and turned it every which way. She banged on the door with one fist, then two. "Hey! Let me out! What's going on?" She kicked the door, which gave her a stubbed toe.

In pure frustration, she hopped to the bed and sat in quiet anger. "Why don't I have shoes on? Why am I even here? And what is this place?"

After rubbing at the offended toe, she calmed down, then sneezed. *I should get dry. No point in being sick and locked in.*

She entered the bathroom, and her mouth dropped. Gold and white porcelain was everywhere, with cream-colored marble floors. A couch rested against one wall. A wardrobe closet and coatrack stood in the short hallway at back. The space was vast. *Who is this guy?*

The full-length mirror standing next to the couch caught her eye. Once in front of it, the reflection that stared back was a stranger. She placed two fingers under her right eye. "Who am I?"

Her gaze fell on the door reflected from behind her. *I better lock it.* She turned the lock and shook the knob for extra measure. She surveyed her attire. *Where was I going, dressed in this?* Damp sections of the white evening gown clung to her. It felt soft and woven of delicate lace.

Her hands slid down the gown and gripped it. In one motion, she pulled it up and over her head. The lace pooled next to her in a heap. White panties and bra followed. Back in front of the mirror, she spun around but turned back when she spotted a long scar on the center of her back. The redness and freshly grown skin spread from the long gash like claws. Her brows furrowed, the reality of her situation sinking in. Step after step became trudged.

She turned on the hot water and let the steam fill the surrounding space. *Where did I get such a scar? Who am I, really?*

***

Caliostro knocked on the bedroom door and waited a few moments before leaning closer to it. "I'm entering now." His hand waved over the lock; it clicked and released. He entered, closed his eyes, and listened intently.

The shower was running, and her heart rate boomed.

His eyes opened. With a heavy sigh, he crossed the room and waited by the hearth.

***

The water ran cold before she turned it off. Upon exiting, she recalled the towel and bathrobe Caliostro had left on the bed. *I could run out really quick and grab them, but what if he's back?*

With her mind made up, she gripped the doorknob, then recalled the cream-colored wardrobe from earlier. A moment later, she pulled the double doors open and found fresh towels and more bathrobes. Once she'd dried off and wrapped in the plushie feather-light robe, another door caught her eye. She stepped towards it, but a sharp pain shot through her head, causing her to lose interest.

With the sharp pain still lingering, she stumbled to the double sinks and turned on the left one. Steam rose from the hot water, fogging the mirror. A second shock of pain shot through her head, making her grab it.

An unfamiliar voice calling a name flashed through her mind. *"Do you understand, Alioson? Don't fail."*

Blinking several times, she focused on her reflection. "Alioson. Am I … Alioson?"

She towel-dried her hair while gazing at herself in the mirror. *Alioson* ... Still toweling her hair, she unlocked the door and returned to the bedroom.

***

Caliostro sat in one of two upright chairs adorned with cream and tan floral patterns. Carvings decorated the bottom, and detailed moldings donned the legs and back. He crossed his legs and interlocked his fingers under his chin. Thoughts filled and overflowed with the unknown woman in the shower.

Every nerve ending was alert enough to know when she had stepped from the shower and that her name was possibly Alioson.

***

She was shocked to find him there. She surveyed him, but her gaze landed on his full head of coal-black hair straining the edges of his hairline from being arranged in a high ponytail. *Hmm, it had been lying freely below his shoulders before.*

He turned and met her gaze, and she froze. Before she could blink, he was on his feet, striding toward her. The hair she had been drying with a small hand towel lay forgotten over her stilled hands.

Once he reached her, nothing could stop the boiling anger. "Why did you lock the door? Am I a prisoner here? And I understand it's your home, and I am grateful to you for saving my life, but could you please knock next time?"

"Of course, I will keep that in mind. As for the lock., it was a precaution."

"A precaution? If I wish to leave right now, will you let me?" She approached the glass double doors.

"Yes, if you wish. You are not a prisoner."

She pulled on the door handle to prove her point.

At once, he was next to her.

She jumped back and peeked to where he had been.

Caliostro turned the doorknob, which opened with little effort.

She gathered the robe at the base of her neck. "How did you do that?"

The doors swung open, and he faced her. "Like I said, you are welcome to leave any time you wish."

"Are you going to answer my question?"

He closed both doors and sat in the seat he had occupied earlier.

"If you will not answer, at least tell me where we are."

"I will answer if you would sit."

13

She released her grip on the robe and meandered toward the chair opposite him.

"This is my home."

"Yes, that much I figured. I want to know where we are." She leaned forward in her chair.

"We are on the border of Gertin but on the other side of the veil. This place is the Mahaven Mountains and the Moors of the Veil."

Her eyes widened. "I'm sorry," she said with a chuckle. "What are you talking about?" She leaned back, readjusted in the seat, and looked from side to side.

"This may be too much information for you in your current state. We can discuss it more later." He stood and straightened the front of his suit.

"Wait!" She jumped, grabbing his arm.

Caliostro eyed the hand on his forearm, then regarded her.

"Please, I need to know. I must know who I am and how I came to be here." Her voice quivered, but she let no tears fall.

He rested his hand over hers for a moment, then removed it from his arm. "If you would sit."

She complied.

14

"I only know what you know. I'm afraid to inform you. As you know, I found you in my lake two hours ago, and now, here we sit." He crossed his right ankle over his left knee, reclining in the seat, and sought her eyes with his.

She squirmed under his watchful gaze but also leaned back, trying to relax. Holding herself close, she shut her eyes.

Caliostro stared at her. *She is very bizarre. I have never met a human like her before. I'm not sure how she's here and alive. It makes little sense. I will need to keep my guard up. No living human can cross the veil, but somehow ...*

She opened her eyes to see him staring at her with a drawn brow and tightened jaw. "What is it? Why are you watching me like that?" She rubbed her hand through the damp hair resting on her left shoulder.

Caliostro caught sight of small yellow bursts within her eyes. He stood, inclining his head.

"Forgive me. I didn't mean to stare. It's just you are ... an oddity to me, and I don't get many visitors here."

"Oddity? You think I'm the one who's peculiar here?"

He squinted one eye and raised a brow. "Are you implying I'm peculiar?"

"Well, besides the fact that you're secretive and appear to do some nonhuman things and tell … interesting stories …"

He laughed. "To your mind, I guess I am peculiar; however, that doesn't change the facts surrounding you."

"Yes, I have no clue who I am nor how I came to be drowning in your lake. And let's not even talk about how I'm in Gertin." She plopped onto the bed with a huff but jumped right back up.

"Near Gertin," he murmured. "At any rate, it's best to leave the rest of your questions until tomorrow, as it's already rather late. I shall leave you to rest. I will send up Duncan with some refreshments for you if you would like." He headed toward the exit.

"Who's Duncan?"

"The only other living being who resides here."

His answer was so vague and clipped, she let it go. "I don't mean to act as if I'm blaming you for not knowing how I came to be here, Cali… Caliostro. Truly, I am grateful you saved my life. Thank you." She placed her hand over her heart, smiled, and approached him.

16

He raised his hand to stave her off. "Think nothing of it. Please excuse me." He left, closing the door behind him.

She ran to check if he'd locked the door. Shock filled her to find it unlocked. *I should find something to put on.* She returned to the bathroom and checked the armoire's drawers first. She found extra sheets for the bed in the first drawer. The second drawer held female undergarments in sizes from small to large and in many colors, all brand new, with tags intact. In the next drawer, she found t-shirts in just as many sizes and colors. The next two drawers followed suit with skirts, pants, leggings, and more.

"What's with this guy? Does he entertain so many women that he keeps new multiple sizes stocked?" Sighing, she grabbed underwear, a black t-shirt, and a pair of black leggings.

Once dressed, she returned to the main room and sat at the cream-colored vanity. Its craftsmanship brought a smile to her lips. "Beautiful, vintage Victorian." *Why do I know that?* She gave it a once over and pressed a switch on the side of the mirror, which illuminated a dozen lights around the entire frame. "Wow." She opened the first drawer to the left, which held a gold brush and comb set.

"I see these haven't been used either." The next drawer held every kind of hair accessory one could imagine. The rest held various beauty items. She removed the comb, detangled her damp hair, and brushed it to help it dry faster. She turned her head left, then right, giving herself a once over. *Not too bad.*

She stepped onto the balcony through the glass doors and searched the night sky. "What in the world?"

The moon's color emanated from red ombre to gold, casting the night sky in strange colors.

"I've never seen a moon like this."

"On the other side of the veil," Caliostro's words echoed in her head.

A knock at the door made her forget her train of thought, and she stepped inside to approach the bedroom door. "Yes?"

The door opened to a tall, older man with short silver hair and silver eyes, wearing relaxed khakis and a black-knitted cardigan. His slim build was fit, and he was calm and very focused. "Miss, I have your meal." He entered the room with a covered tray and a tote bag.

"Yes … umm. Thank you. You must be Duncan?" She stepped out of his way.

He approached the table between the two chairs in front of the fireplace and placed the tray and bag on it. He faced her with as smirk, which was more chilling than kind. "Yes. Will you be needing anything further this evening?" He scanned the room before resettling on her face.

"No, thank you. Would you thank Caliostro for his hospitality, please?"

"I will do that. Have a great … rest, miss." He left with a resounding click of the door.

Her stomach growled in response to the smell that wafted through the room from whatever was under the tray. She hadn't realized how hungry she was. In a famished daze, she rummaged through the white tote bag Duncan had left next to the tray. Inside was a bottled soda and two bottles of cold water. Lifting the tray revealed pot roast, potatoes, and green beans.

Upon finishing her meal, she tied her hair back and spied the inviting bed. She thought about the door and wondered if Duncan had locked it. A quick check confirmed her thoughts. Anger flared. *If he wanted to hurt me, he could have by now.*

She turned off the tall lamp that stood in the corner and crawled into bed. As soon as her head hit the pillow, layers of dreams claimed her consciousness.

WHAT ARE YOU?

There was no sound, yet she awoke with a start. She went to the balcony doors and pulled, relieved to find them unlocked. A dull light hit her eyes, but the sky was bright and clear, mirroring what she'd viewed last night. Above her, the sun beat down, yet its light was pale and faded. Not knowing what to think, she peered over the balcony's edge to the garden just below and miles of green fields. The lake glistened in the distance.

Darkness surrounded her, and water filled her mouth. Alioson shook her head, stepped inside, and entered the bathroom. She splashed water on her face, leaning her weight into the sink, and stared at herself in the mirror.

Sighing heavily, she moved into the bedroom and sat at the vanity as the name Alioson danced about in her mind. *Alioson ... Alioson ... Ali ... o ... son.*

She cocked her head to the right, twisted her lips to the left, then returned her face to normal. "Do I feel like an Alioson? Well, it's better than no name, and why else would I recall it?" She shrugged. "Alioson it is."

A knock sounded, bringing her to attention. She hastily checked her hair for loose strands. Pausing mid inspection, she chastised herself. *Why should I care what my hair looks like?*

"Come in," she answered.

Caliostro entered, carrying a large tray and smiling. "Would you like breakfast?"

Before she could answer, Duncan entered with another tray, and they both went onto the balcony and set up everything in record time. Duncan returned and bowed his head before disappearing through the door and closing it behind him.

She found Caliostro waiting at the balcony doors. "I didn't really get to say yes or no. Also, why was my door locked again?" Anger was apparent in her tone.

He placed a glass of orange juice next to a full plate of scrambled eggs, bacon, and fruit slices. "Yes, well, you are still a stranger in my home, and I have enemies, so one can never be too careful."

Alioson watched him set up for another moment, then stepped onto the balcony. "Please don't lock the door. It makes me feel like a prisoner, and I want to believe your words from last night."

"Forgive me. It's not personal. However, I felt the need to protect my domain under the circumstances." He stopped working on the breakfast placement and looked up. "Please have breakfast with me. I'm sure you're famished and have many questions as well." He proffered an inviting hand to the chair opposite his.

Her gaze left his face, as difficult as she found that, and landed on his outstretched hand of invitation. She took the seat.

"Thank you," he said, sitting as well.

After she had sampled everything on the plate, she noticed him scrutinizing her. "Why do you stare at me so?"

"Because I find you very … interesting. I don't think you have any clue how much."

23

"First, I'm an oddity. Now you think I'm interesting?" She chortled as she ate. "Yes, I'm a stranger here, and I don't know who I am or where I'm from, but other than that—"

"Well, what question do you have for me?"

"Where are we? Truly?"

"I told you last night. Did you forget?"

"I recall. And it sounds as nuts now as it did then." She snickered. *Not sure why I'm laughing. Maybe I'm losing it, along with my memory.*

"Nuts or not, it's the truth." He took a sip of orange juice.

Their eyes met over the table for a silent moment, and she knew he believed all he told her. "So, we are behind … the veil, as you call it?"

"Yes."

"And this veil is what, exactly?"

"To put it simply, it's the door to a world for the nonhuman to live when not walking among you." He gauged her reaction, leaning back in his chair.

She laughed. "Okay, if that's true, then how are we both here?" She cocked her head, raising both hands, palm up.

"That's a good question. It explains how I'm here but not you. You, I haven't figured out yet." The corners of his mouth curled upward.

"What's that mean? Are you saying you're one of the nonhuman beings who live on this side of the veil?"

"I am. And I'm saying if you are human, that's even more interesting than any other possibility."

"And why is that?"

"Well, if you are, in fact, human, you would need to be dead, and you don't appear dead."

Alioson was at a loss for words. *He must be messing with me, or he's completely insane.* She stood. "Look, I'm very grateful for you saving me, but you can't expect me to believe any of that. I mean, it's crazy." Her heart was beating so fast she was sure he could hear it.

Caliostro stepped toward her. "I'm afraid it's completely the truth, though it's up to you whether you believe my words."

Alioson moved backward. "I think I want to leave now."

His smile turned into a hard line. "You're not my prisoner, to be sure. I don't believe in taking prisoners."

Still, he advanced, making her back up farther to the balcony's edge.

"W-well, I …"

"I need you to come with me. There's something you need to see." He grabbed her around the waist and leaped into the air.

She screamed, thinking he meant to throw them both over the balcony to the ground below. A memory of the night before hit her—wind and air pulled at her wet frame; Caliostro carried and flew with her. She stared at him now, his arms about her waist. The speed with which he flew pulled and whipped her hair around her face. Alioson hid close to his chest, her heart hammering.

Minutes later, they stopped, and he released her.

She looked around, disheveled and confused. "We just flew. Is that what happened last night when you carried me? What are you? What …" She stumbled back a bit.

"Breathe, I will explain later. I've brought you back to the lake because this is where you appeared. Do you recall how you came to be here, now that you've returned?" He straightened his black suit jacket and stalked around her.

She turned to the left, then the right, not recalling a thing. She tried to think and conjure memories. Anything would be better than the darkness that covered her mind. The name Alioson flashed in her mind again. *How can my name be the only thing I recall?*

Caliostro clapped his hands together in front of her, startling her into focus. "Are you still going to tell me you recall nothing about how you ended up on my land and drowning in my lake?"

"What do you want me to do? I want to know who I am. All I can remember is my name—Alioson—but nothing more. And there's you, who's what? An alien?" Her tears choked her as she fell to her knees in the dewy grass. The snow had melted around the lake, with the sun beating down.

Caliostro listened to her heart for any signs of lies. He found none. While listening to those beats, her energy and blood called to him yet again. A hunger he had never felt before plumed ever so softly.

Alioson noticed his eyes glowed a bright inhuman blue, and his look was that of pure hunger and something else underlining it she could not place. She felt unease at his stare, which made her rise and step away from him.

He turned and walked a few paces until his senses calmed down. Once he felt more himself, he approached her. "I brought you here to show you the truth of my words." He grabbed her wrist to lead her through a line of trees.

After walking about a mile or more, he stopped at an open field. "It's here." He gestured with his left hand, releasing her wrist.

Alioson saw nothing. "What's here? I don't see a thing."

"Stand here … and feel." Caliostro placed a hand on either of her shoulders.

She tensed.

"Relax. I'll show you," he said each word at a slow pace. He released her, moved behind her, and leaned down to whisper in her ear, "Just reach out your hand."

He waited for her to reach, but she didn't move. Her heart hammered in his ears, and her scent disturbed his senses. He took her hand and lifted it in front of her.

On her fingertips, light burst with little sparkles all around, and a haze of smoke hovered across her fingertips. Alioson's entire hand faded through a wall of mist that now formed across the entire field.

Caliostro moved from behind her and watched from the side.

Tingling rose in her hand, and little cracks inched up her arm. Alioson jumped back, as if in pain.

Caliostro placed both hands on her shoulders. "Are you okay?"

Tears filled her eyes. "What the hell is going on? What is this?" she yelled, pushing away from him. She turned and ran back the way they had come. Branches whipped at her, ripping her clothes. She reached the lake and fell to her knees.

Caliostro stood behind her, listening to her heavy breathing.

"W-what … is that?" she asked, trying to catch her breath.

"The veil, it's one of many walls, if you will. It separates this world and the human world."

"This is insane." She looked across the calm lake. "Why am I here?"

"The better question is, what are you? If you are human, you have come here through some unknown circumstances. If you are a being of this world, we know how you are here. However, you are human from all I have seen, and yet, here you are … alive." He moved to stand in front of her, making her look up. "As a human, you should only be here to pass through to your final destination."

Her faraway gaze seemed to stare through him.

"There isn't much I can do to help you figure out why or how you came to be here, but you may stay at my manor until you regain your memories or until we figure out a way for you to return through the veil." He moved to take her arm, but she scooted back and stood.

"Are you saying I can't just step through or whatever?" She hugged herself, as if to stop herself from falling to pieces.

"What did you feel back there when you connected with the veil?"

"I'm not entirely sure. I felt tingling, little sparks, then pain shot up my arm."

"Since you are alive, you cannot just step through. That's why you felt those effects. If you attempt to step through, your energy will deplete, and death would follow."

Alioson's eyes cast down, and her shoulders dropped. "So, what? I'm trapped here?"

"Yes and no."

She glared at him. "It's either yes, I am or no, I'm not."

"I believe you are trapped here, though you are welcome to try going through the veil as you are." His hand gestured toward where she had run from.

"Yes, I want to try. I must. None of this makes sense."

Caliostro grabbed her, and before she could blink, they stood once again in the field. "Please, proceed," he said, waiting.

Her steps were unsure. She walked until she felt a light tingling. Frozen in place, she gazed back at Caliostro, who watched in silence. Faced forward again, she took a big step, then couldn't move. A pull of energy had forced her to stop, and it brought her to her knees. Her vision blurred, and darkness claimed her.

***

Caliostro watched her sink to the ground but caught her as she fell. He lifted her into his arms and inspected her. Shadows from long eyelashes fell over high cheekbones. The sunlight kissed her tanned skin, and her long dark hair fell over his arm in silky sheets. *No human has ever affected me, yet why do I crave a taste for the first time?*

Bloodlust was foreign to him, and energy lust was even more so unknown to his senses. Caliostro spied her exposed neck. Shaking his head, he took to the skies with her limp form pressed against his chest.

***

She lay unconscious against the soft silk sheets.

He glanced at the fireplace, which sprung a fire to life, illuminating the room in a soft glow. "Who are you really, Alioson? If that is truly your name." He watched her uneven breaths. He sat on the bed next to her when he noticed a loose lock of hair resting across her eyes. Before he could stop himself he dashed it away. "I must share more of my energy with you, or you will be damned to your current state."

He hesitated, but throwing caution to the wind, he leaned down toward her. Their lips hovered an inch apart, and a blue light transferred from his parted lips to hers.

Alioson's eyes shot open, and they stared at each other for a moment. To his utter shock, she didn't push him away but clinched her eyes and waited.

Caliostro's gaze fell to her awaiting lips a moment before he took them, their hearts beating in synchronicity. The energy that passed between them grew stronger. Caliostro's blood surged to life as electrifying heat coursed through his body. The feeling that permeated through him was a level of mind-altering allure he had never experienced before.

Her arms snaked around his neck, pulling their bodies closer together.

Caliostro could taste her humanity, yet something underlying hid within her. *I took the risk of bringing you here. Please don't make me regret it.*

Her consciousness slipped as he released her lips. She fell into a deep sleep, and he watched over her all night.

***

Alioson awoke the next day in the room she'd occupied before Caliostro had taken her to the lake. A quick glance under the covers confirmed she was still wearing the same clothes. In confusion, she sat upright and looked around. Shadows cloaked the room, yet she spotted Caliostro seated by the hearth, their gazes locking. She threw back the covers and planted both feet on the floor. An explosion of pain pulsated through her

33

head. Instinctively, her hands covered either side, and she shut her eyes. They shot open when a disturbing memory accompanied the pain.

Flashes of splattered blood, two figures fighting, and a dark alley where a man watched her passed through her mind. *Am I recalling who I am?*

Once the pain subsided, she lifted her head to see Caliostro standing in front of her.

His brow creased with worry, and his lips drew a hard line. "Are you okay? Are you feeling dizzy?"

Alioson's hands dropped to her sides as she looked past him to the glass doors. Orange, red, and purples with a touch of darkness dimly lit the sky. She refocused on him. "Not dizzy but some kind of headache and …" She glanced away.

"And …?" With both hands in his pockets, he leaned down so their heads were level.

Alioson leaned back into the mattress, then jumped up from the bed and moved around him. "And other than that, I feel fine. Did you stay here while I slept?" She wrung her hands together.

Caliostro followed her every movement. His eyes hadn't missed a single tick she displayed. "I thought it best, though I would have felt your distress had I not been here."

"Felt my distress?"

"Yes."

"Okay, hold on a second." She paused and dragged both hands down her face. "I know you can … umm, fly apparently, so you can also, what? Read minds or feel my emotions?"

"I can feel your emotions because I healed you with my energy more than once. We are connected through that sharing of energy."

Her mouth opened, closed, then opened yet again. "What are you, exactly? What is this place, really? Was the world always like this, and I just don't remember? What … *energy*? Did you do something to me?" She hugged herself, nearing hysteria.

Caliostro didn't answer, waiting for her to calm down. "I will explain everything to you, but it will be a lot to take in, for a human. Not once have I led you to believe I was a human. I do not need to hide what I am and will share all I know with you." He approached her, causing her to step backward. "Please, this way." He indicated with his hand, taking the lead.

A tremor ran through her at the thought of what he would say next. *It's better to know the truth. Being in the dark is worse.* She gathered her courage and followed him.

***

They entered a long, dim corridor that held floral carvings all along the walls. Everything was painted in ivory and rustic colors with undertones of gold. They soon reached an extraordinarily wide staircase. The stairs were also ivory and trimmed in gold, like the rest of the house.

Alioson watched Caliostro's back as he descended stairs. She still wasn't sure what to make of all he'd told her, and even more so, what to make of him.

His ponytail swung in rhythm with his even steps. With one hand in his suit pants pocket, he gave the air of a relaxed and cool demeanor.

Alioson followed him through a massive foyer. with vaulted ceilings and a low-hanging crystal chandelier, catching the last rays of hazy sun streaming in the tall glass windows facing them. She stood gawking until he called her name.

"Alioson?" Caliostro stared from an archway a few feet away, half turned toward her.

They stared at each other, and she recalled her arms snaking around his shoulders, the kiss, the heat, and blue light. She gasped aloud, her hand covering her mouth.

Caliostro walked back to her, both hands sliding in his pockets. Cocking his head to the side, his right brow raised in confusion. "Is something wrong?"

"Did I … Did we?" Her eyes lowered, and heat filled her cheeks.

"Did we, what?" His gaze landed on her mouth.

After a moment of silence, she looked up to find him staring. Her tongue darted out to moisten her lower lip.

He moved in so close and leaned down. His breath mingled with hers. Caliostro's eyes blazed with blue fire.

The intensity of their glow made her stumble backward. "Your, your eyes." Her hand raised toward his face, making him turn away.

"This way, please."

Alioson's hand dropped to her side as she followed him in silence.

***

They walked through the archway and entered a large dining hall. In the center was a long table covered in a silver and white tablecloth and dishes to match. Chamber wall lights lit the room on both sides, giving it a romantic glow.

They reached the far end of the table, and Caliostro stopped and placed his hand on the back of a chair next to him. He slid it out and stepped aside. "This is where we will dine."

Alioson nodded and took the offered seat.

He pushed it in for her as she scooted in place. "Excuse me for a few moments. I will return soon."

Before he could move away, Alioson gripped his forearm.

Caliostro arched one brow and looked at her hand, then at her. "Yes?"

Alioson removed her hand. "How soon will that be?"

"Soon." He left through a door at the end of the dining hall and met Duncan. Caliostro acknowledged him with a glance but kept traversing the carpeted hallway until he reached his office.

Duncan followed him, closing the door as they entered.

"Ask," Caliostro said, going to one bookshelf near his desk.

"I think it would be best to leave my words for later." His silver eyes followed Caliostro's every move.

Caliostro stopped his search to focus on Duncan. "Oh, really? That's unlike you." He homed in on what he had been looking for. Thumbing through a few pages, he turned toward Duncan. "You followed me. Why?"

"Your grandfather contacted me."

A sigh escaped Caliostro's lips. "That can also wait till later." Caliostro moved past him, the door swinging open before he reached it. He didn't bother to close it as he headed down the hallway the way he had come.

***

Several minutes passed before she heard the door open and close.

Taking the head seat next to Alioson, Caliostro pushed a book toward her.

"What's this?" She eyed the book titled *Theory of the Veil*.

"This is a book from a human perspective that I think will help you get an understanding to a degree."

She turned it over and opened to the first page.

Some will choose to believe me, and some will laugh at me, but I must share with you my time on the other side of the veil. You may ask, "What is the veil?" To put it simply, it's another world within our world. A place where we humans pass through at our death. How do I know this? I, myself, died and am now writing about all I experienced. I died but returned, and now I wish to share with you, the reader, all about ... the veil.

Alioson looked up as the door opened, and Duncan entered, carrying a tray with two covered dishes. After placing one in front of each of them and wine glasses, along with champagne and ice, he left them alone again.

"Can I ask you something?"

"Go on," he replied.

Without looking at him, she asked, "Why did you save me? Why are you helping me? We don't even know each other."

"I heard you drowning. Your presence intrigued me ... and then."

"Then?"

"Then once I held you in my arms, it was as if … no, your life's energy called to me. I had to save you, and I did." His eyes locked with hers on the latter of his words.

"Why did you kiss me?" Her heart raced.

Looking away, he took a bite of his steak, put down his fork, and wiped his mouth. "I presume you mean after you encountered the veil?"

"Was there another time?"

"Initially, I didn't intend to kiss you. I was healing you, as I have done before, and you kissed me, but it wasn't unwanted." He smiled. "I told you I have shared my energy with you, and that has connected us. That sharing was a mouth-to-mouth exchange; I intended nothing more."

She couldn't recall who had kissed whom first, so she let it drop and moved on to finding out more about him. "Well, besides that, if you're not human, what are you?" Her right hand resting on the table fisted the cloth and shook in anticipation.

"Ah, the million dollar question. I'm a mixture of multiple types of beings." He took a sip of champagne.

"You can fly. You can heal others with your energy."

"Yes. As you know."

"What else can you do?"

The corners of his lips curled into a knowing smile. "Many things."

"How old are you?"

"Old enough to have tasted too many centuries." He laughed bitterly, looking down. "I feel a bit put out, seeing as you can ask me any facet of my life." He beheld her face. "I cannot do the same to you." His brows furrowed as he gave an icy stare.

Alioson fidgeted in her seat and glanced away from his lowered glare. "I feel I should apologize, though I didn't mean to make you feel uncomfortable." She refocused on him. "As you know, in my current state, sharing isn't an option."

"No need to apologize. You must forgive my conduct. I'm not used to company." He stood. "We can talk more tomorrow. I will bid you a good night. Duncan will escort you to your room once you have finished dining."

At the sight of his back as he left, a nervous feeling centered in her belly, and her heart festered. Emptiness spread and solidified without his presence. She chuckled. "What's wrong with me?" Alioson shook her head, then focused on eating, but after a few more bites and a sip of the wine, she slid her chair back.

Duncan entered the room, as if on cue. "I'm here to escort you, miss."

"Oh, I'm sure I could find my way." She stepped around the chair.

"I have orders from Lord Masterson," he said, cutting her off.

"Who?"

"Lord Caliostro Masterson."

"Oh, so that's his last name." She grabbed the book that had lain forgotten during the latter of her meal.

Duncan inclined his head. "Shall we?" Taking the lead, he strode through the archway.

Her steps slowed upon reentering the foyer, still in awe at the beauty of the manor. She noticed the lights from the dining hall go out, making her turn.

"Miss?" Duncan inquired, stopping on the fourth step up.

"Oh, sorry. It's just the lights going out suddenly startled me," she answered, following him again.

"All the lights here are remote controlled." He held out a white remote to the side so she could see while they ascended.

Alioson was so enthralled with just looking around she didn't notice Duncan had stopped until she bumped into his back. "I'm so sorry."

He peered over his shoulder and met her apologetic expression with cold eyes and mouth set in a hardline. "It's all right, miss. We have arrived. I shall bid you a good night."

She entered her room, turned to close the door, and saw the hallway lights go out and Duncan fade into the darkness. With so much on her mind, she eyed the book Caliostro had given her. "How did I get here?"

She set the book on the vanity, laid across the bed, and soon slept.

When she awoke, the sun was coming in from the balcony doors. She didn't move to rise but stayed in bed. Time ticked away while her mind asked question after question. Who was she? How had she come to be here? Where was she from? And who was Caliostro? She wanted to know the latter just as much as who she was.

Her pondering ended when she heard the glass doors open. Before she could move to see who had opened them, someone was on top of her with one hand over her mouth, and another hand held her wrists above her head. A muffled scream escaped her. Frantic to be free, Alioson arched her back and squirmed, but the assailant held firm.

"It seems Caliostro has dropped his standards these days."

Still trying to break the hold, Alioson couldn't discern much of the assailant other than they had a woman's voice. She turned every which way, but the woman would not budge from her straddle position.

Growing tired of Alioson's struggling, she tightened her grip, pushing her farther into the mattress. "You do smell a bit off, but still edible." She leaned toward Alioson's neck.

Alioson cringed when she felt the flick of a tongue run over her pulse. *What is she? Caliostro, help me! I need to fight!*

***

Caliostro's wings extended behind him as he flew toward the manor. He'd felt a flash of distress from Alioson; he was sure of that. Their connection was stronger but not strong enough to have a lasting effect. The manor came into sight when Alioson's voice screamed in his mind.

Caliostro's teeth clenched and both sides of his jaws spasmed as he pushed at full speed. The water from the lake beneath him parted from his velocity. Trees and bushes upheaved as he passed them. He slowed once the balcony was in sight, a familiar scent hitting him.

***

Alioson screamed behind the hand once more and pushed with all her might. One of her wrists came free, and she fisted it in the woman's hair.

The assailant's eyes opened wide and stared pointedly at Alioson, then darted toward the balcony doors.

***

Caliostro's hand wrapped around the female's throat and slammed her into the far wall. The room vibrated from the sheer force. He glanced to see how Alioson fared.

On the other side of the bed, she kneeled, gasping for air. One hand massaged her neck, and the other made a fist in the sheets.

He sighed, concentrating on the woman snarling and hissing at him.

Her glowing eyes were the same blue as his yet dimmer. She kicked at him, which he caught with his free hand, holding it to his side. "Are you really fighting me over that flesh bag?" She swatted at the hand holding her by the throat.

He released her, stepping backward. Straightening his suit, he stood between her and Alioson. "Why are you here? You haven't darkened my door for over a decade."

Her eyes panned from Alioson to him.

He knew she wanted to get at her. *"If you try, it will be the last move you ever make,"* he sent telepathically.

The woman smiled and stepped closer, her face within an inch of his.

He remained still, their eyes staring through each other.

"I came to this dreadful place to see you, and you're treating me like this over a meal." She glared over his shoulder at the now standing Alioson, who rubbed at her wrist "I'm sure she's not nearly that tasty." She laughed.

"Leave. Now, Dalidah, before I lose my patience."

She made no move to leave.

"There is only one reason I have never destroyed you, and you know it well." He stepped close to her once again.

"Caliostro, my love," she purred, resting her open palm against his chest. "Sweet brother, you know I've always let you win, but don't let it go to your head." She chuckled, running her long fingers through the black hair that rested below her bare shoulders.

"You only draw breath at this moment because of our past, but don't push it. We both know I am much stronger than you."

Her smirk died. "Keep your snack, then. I only wanted a taste." She pouted her red-painted lips like a child that had not gotten their way. "You are so selfish these days, brother, but I will continue to darken your door." And with that, she sped away.

The scent of rosemary and vanilla swept by, and the curtains at the balcony doors swished in her wake.

Caliostro faced Alioson, who sat on the edge of the bed, staring off, and came to stand in front of her. "Are you okay?"

"Am I okay?" she scoffed. "That woman was your sister? And what is she?"

"Dalidah is what humans call a vampire."

"And you are also a—"

"No. I'm not a vampire. I am much more." Seeing the mixture of confusion and fear on her face, he felt the need to reassure her. "I won't hurt you, Alioson, and she will not come near you again. I will make sure of it."

She jumped to her feet. "That monster got in here without your knowledge, so how do you plan to stop her a second time? She seemed rather determined, you know, to just eat me!" Her arms lifted on either side of her and slapped against her thighs. Alioson scanned the room, hugging herself, as if Dalidah would reappear from the closest shadow.

Caliostro grabbed her shoulders and eased her to sit on the bed. "I promise you now, she will never enter here again, nor will she bring harm to you." He reached an open palm behind him and made a fist. Both glass doors shut and locked to confirm his statement.

Alioson looked to the balcony, then at him. "Are you going to tell me what you are?"

"I don't think you really want to know that answer. The info may be a bit much for you to handle right now."

"Let me decide that. I think, with all I've seen, I can handle it." She looked him square in the eyes. "My memory loss seems based on personal stuff, but I still have knowledge of things I've learned. I have read about vampires and werewolves in novels, so is it all true?"

"Yes, well, let's say most things have a truth to them, fiction and otherwise."

"I see. And you're what, exactly?"

"In time, I shall tell you."

"But you're not a vampire like your sister?"

"Dalidah's not my proper sister. We refer to each other in that way, because of our life together in the past. We have shared blood in the way vampires do, so being called mother, father, sister, or brother is normal. I was given her blood hundreds of years ago."

Alioson's eyebrows lifted, and her eyes widened.

"I have lived a long time, and my history is complicated. But more importantly, have you recalled anything?"

"No, nothing yet."

His brow raised. "Really?"

She stood and attempted to pass him, making him notice she hadn't gone untouched in the struggle with Dalidah.

He grabbed her wrist and stopped her, their eyes meeting.

"Your eyes are glowing," she said, so mesmerized she couldn't look away.

He pulled her closer and leaned in.

She didn't fight him but moved with him.

Before his lips touched hers, he said, "Your wrist is bruised. Be sure to tend to it. You can find what you need in the bathroom." He released her and moved away.

Clearing his throat brought Alioson back to her senses as well; she hurriedly turned away.

"We can finish our chat tomorrow. Dinner will be served in a few hours. When you hear the bell, please come to the dining hall." He left.

***

Alioson stood watching the door he had left through moments ago. She absently touched her bottom lip. "Was he about to kiss me? Caliostro, what are you, really?"

Doing her best to shake the thoughts running through her mind of kissing him, what he was, who she was, and much more, she attended to her bruised wrist. In the bathroom, she found a first aid kit in one draw. Applying an ice pack to the bruise stung at first but quickly soothed the soreness.

A few hours later, she heard the dinner bell, which made her startle even though she knew it would sound at some point. "Get yourself together!" She had changed into a black maxi dress and was barefoot. Leaving her hair down, she headed to the dining hall.

***

Caliostro stared into the fireplace as the newly lit flames roared to life. It wasn't as if he needed the warmth, but the movement of the flames comforted him. A knock sounded, but Caliostro was so lost in his thoughts it went unnoticed. *Why do I feel this hunger for her, for her life's energy, of all things? I've never once had lust for it. Why now, why her?*

Finally, the knocking at the study door brought him from his wayward thoughts. "Enter."

Duncan entered and closed the door behind him.

"Have you heard anything from the magic guild? Any disturbances of the veil?" he asked Duncan, sitting behind the desk that consumed more than half the wall space.

"Yes, I spoke with Sorceress Vandrah."

Caliostro's eyebrows raised. "Really? I did not know you had those types of connections. Few speak with the guardian of the veil."

"Yes, well, she seems to think there was a breach of the veil."

"Meaning?"

"Someone used some type of magic, more than likely to bring a human through, and the timeframe seems to coincide with your guest's arrival."

"I see. Keep me updated on any other findings. Something doesn't smell right to me."

WHEN THE PAST WAS BORN

Once in the dining hall, she knew going barefoot had not been the best option. Though the manor was warm enough, the marble floors throughout did not hold the same warmth. Alioson walked to the far end of the long dinner table, where two placements were set. Silver and white dishes held fruits and cheeses, accompanied by delicate pastries. Everything smelled amazing. A silver cloche sat before her place, making her wonder what was under it.

Alioson lifted the lid as Duncan entered but quickly replaced it upon sight of him.

"Allow me." He removed the lid, and her eyes widened at the fresh vegetables and what looked to be duck with some sort of orange sauce covering it. "Enjoy your meal, miss." He turned to leave before she could stop him.

She frowned and sighed. After waiting a moment, she covered the plate and rose from the table, the urge to find Caliostro pushing her through the door after Duncan.

***

Why am I doing this? I should make her leave. It would be so much easier if I did. Her energy and scent are overwhelming. And her heart. I'm sure there was something different in its sound, yet she's just a human—

Caliostro felt Alioson's energy outside his office door. A knock came upon the door and in popped Alioson's dark head of hair. Caliostro stood in front of it an instant later. "Can I help you find something?" He held the door from opening farther.

She noticed his one arm blocked her entry.

"Are you lost?" He stepped closer to her.

She ducked under his arm and into the office.

Caliostro smirked, closing the door.

"I was looking for you, actually."

"Oh, well, how can I be of assistance?"

"I was wondering why you were late for dinner." She glanced at him, then moved to the right side of his desk, eyeing the shelf of books.

"Ahh, I had work to attend to." He followed her. "Were you waiting for me?"

"I hate to eat alone, and it felt odd to sit at that large table with no one else present."

Caliostro smiled. "Please forgive my lateness. Shall we eat?"

Alioson nodded and led the way.

They ate in silence, Caliostro watching her. He knew she could feel his eyes on her.

Every so often, she regarded him, and her heart rate rose.

How could he stop when the desire to taste her was driving his senses mad? He reached toward her, but the office door opening stopped him.

"Lord, you have a call," Duncan said, holding the door open.

Caliostro glanced over his shoulder, knowing full well there was no call. "Will you excuse me, Alioson? Business calls, so I will bid you a good night."

"Caliostro."

He stopped but didn't turn.

"If you have time, I would like to go out tomorrow."

Duncan glowered at her request. *"It would be ill-advised to allow her to go traipsing about the grounds, or anywhere. We can't trust her,"* Duncan shot the thought at Caliostro.

He acknowledged Duncan, then returned to Alioson. "That wouldn't be the best idea currently. Dalidah is possibly nearby, also some beings here tend to … show interest in your kind."

Her eyes widened. "I see. Then, when do you think I can leave? Is there even a way?"

Never, echoed through his mind. "I'm working on helping you find a way back to your world, rest assured." He left, Duncan shadowing him.

They walked down the dim hallway to Caliostro's office, but Caliostro stopped a few feet before reaching the door and faced him.

Duncan mirrored his movements, stopping on a dime.

"Duncan, I don't need you to intervene. I don't repeat my mistakes." Caliostro's words were clipped and forceful.

"Yet you left after my interruption."

Caliostro stood toe to toe with Duncan in total frustration. His blue eyes bore through him like a laser beam.

Duncan held his ground without faltering. "Remember, Lord Masterson, though I am your friend and follow you, I am your watcher first."

"Don't worry. I'll never forget why you are truly here." Caliostro walked ahead and entered his office without looking back. He leaned against the door, his memories attacking him from all sides. *Alioson will never be another Catherine. I won't let anything like that happen again.*

His memories took him back to her.

***

1819 Mortal Society

The night filled with mist, and the moon was high. Caliostro crouched, his gloved hand touching the dewy ground beneath his feet. He inhaled deeply and caught the scent of the rogue werewolf he hunted. The Lycrian was from the Monster Hunters Guild and, while on a mission, had disappeared. The guild had contacted Caliostro to take care of the problem, even though he no longer did that kind of work. It had been at least three centuries since he had officially stopped working for them. Yet here he was, still cleaning up their messes.

Caliostro wore all black, head to toe. His hood covered his long hair, pulled back by a leather cord. He ducked into a dark alley that smelled of stale urine, spoiled food, and blood. He had picked up the wolf's scent again at the village entrance. Caliostro hoped to catch up to him before a place like this became involved.

The village was too quiet. All the residents were inside their homes. Even though it was sundown, it was still too early to be that quiet. A woman's scream rang out in the chilly night.

Caliostro turned toward the sound and made haste. The scent of freshly spilled blood burned his nostrils. Approaching closer confirmed the Lycrian's presence. The blood-soaked body of a young woman lay lifeless in a shallow ditch. Upon closer inspection, he saw torn flesh hanging from her neck. She reeked of the Lycrian's stench, as did the surrounding grounds. He had to be nearby. Thunder split the sky above him, and raindrops fell.

Caliostro looked up. "Dammit, the scent will become masked."

A rustling sound to the left of the house caught his attention. A petite, young girl, with long pure white curly hair that fell past her waist and gray eyes stumbled and fell, then took off running.

She must have seen something. He tracked her to a tavern as the rain beat hard all around him. He entered the dirt-covered wooden door to his left and located the girl.

A man stood over the frightened girl. He slapped her hard across the face, and she hit the floor. The bar held a few people who watched but didn't intervene. "How many times do I need to tell you it's dangerous, and that a young woman shouldn't be wandering the streets at night alone!"

The young woman said nothing and bit into her bleeding lip. "Why do you care? I hate you and this stinking town!"

The man's eyes grew larger, and his nostrils flared. He yanked her up by her hair, either to drag her to the back or continue beating her on the spot, but Caliostro chose not to wait for either outcome. The man's hand came down like a hammer, and the young girl braced herself for the blow, when Caliostro caught it in his iron grip. The man turned to see who had grabbed him and found himself face to face with Caliostro's blazing blue eyes.

"You will release the girl," he said calmly.

The dazed man nodded and loosened his grip without pause or thought.

"You will return to the bar and forget she went out tonight."

The man eyed her, and Caliostro's gaze followed as he released the man's hand.

Caliostro pulled his hood back to not frighten her further. "May I have a word with you?"

She surveyed the establishment of blank faces, then regarded Caliostro. Though shaken, she nodded in agreement.

He gestured for her to lead the way to a table, and she followed.

As they made their way, the burly man passed the bar, then quietly disappeared through a back door, still feeling the effects of Caliostro's glamour.

Caliostro and the young woman sat at a nearby table. She looked in the man's direction who had disappeared through the door, then at Caliostro. Her eyes transfixed with fright.

Watching her cheeks redden made Caliostro wish he had chosen a different course of action for the bartender. "I need to speak with you about what you saw."

Her eyes grew so large they almost swallowed her face. She trembled as she looked around nervously again. "Nothing. I saw nothing." She attempted to stand, but he grabbed her wrist. "Let me go!" She pulled away so fiercely he was left holding only her glove.

Her bare hand revealed black markings scrawled across knuckles, an infinity symbol on her middle finger, while crescent moons were etched in the others. All sigils of the Magic Guild.

While Caliostro contemplated the magnitude of his discovery, she dashed for the exit without another word.

You know far more than you are letting on.

***

Present Day

Caliostro's mind returned to the present. Sighing heavily, he stood erect and got some much-needed business done. For the next hour, he focused on ledgers and paperwork from his hotel chain that required signing.

A rapping came at the door. He was very much aware that Duncan had been waiting there all along. "Enter."

Duncan stepped in and gently closed the door behind him. With his arms neatly folded behind his back, he approached the desk.

"Do you have something to report?" Caliostro asked without looking up.

"While checking the perimeter, I picked up a few unfamiliar scents."

Caliostro stiffened. "How many? Type of being? Location?" He looked up from the paperwork that had become far less important.

"Four. Two Lycrians, a low-class vampire, and I'm unsure about the fourth. Close to where the lake meets the wood line. They were fading, so the beings were gone long before I arrived."

Caliostro stood. "Well, it's been a while since the Monster Hunters Guild attempted to sniff me out. Perhaps I should pay them a visit." He smiled to himself.

"I would advise against it."

"And why is that?" He grabbed his jacket from the chairback.

"I'm not convinced they are sniffing *you* out. Your guest—how long will she be staying with us?" he asked, eyebrows raised.

"Why?"

"She is in a living human state. They are likely catching *her* smell and may not be a part of the guild." Duncan locked eyes with Caliostro as the tension in the room thickened.

Clearing his throat, Caliostro put on his suit jacket. "Duncan, you know I will do as I wish in this." He laid his hand on Duncan's shoulder.

Duncan's gaze landed on Caliostro's hand, which was fast becoming a grip.

"You would do well to remember who and what I am." He smiled through his statement, then passed Duncan.

"And you would do well to recall I'm on your side."

Caliostro strode to the main foyer and stopped at the large painting of a frozen lake. He slid his hand along the gold-rimmed bottom and heard a click and the sound of dragging. He waited patiently as the wall moved forward and slid open. With focused steps he entered the darkened passage, and lights lit as he descended the curved staircase. The gray stone walls trapped a smell of sandalwood and sage.

He reached the bottom where the scenery mirrored the modern look of the rest of the manor. Caliostro stopped at a maroon door at the end of the short hallway and entered a five-digit code on the gold panel to the left. He crossed the sill and paused to behold the surroundings.

White, red, and yellow sheer fabric draped all three walls. Illuminated wall lanterns peeked from between the layers, and lush cream-colored carpet covered the floors. In the center of the room was a king-sized canopy bed draped in white lace.

Caliostro sauntered to the end of the bed and stared at the figure who slept in the center. "Hello, Catherine."

Her lips were a rose pink, and her long lashes lay still against her defined cheekbones.

Caliostro walked around the bed and stopped at her side. He watched her chest gently rise and fall. "You're still with me?" He smiled sadly, knowing she couldn't answer.

***

Alioson stared at the moon from her balcony seat. She stood, ready to head back in, when she noticed a figure engulfed in a light rush by below. "Caliostro?" She watched until the light faded in the distance.

A knock at the door caught her attention. She stepped inside to answer. "Yes?" she said, approaching the door.

"It's Duncan, miss. I've come to check on a few things."

She hesitated but realized if he wanted to enter, he could. She opened the door.

"Thank you. May I?"

"Umm, sure." She stood aside, allowing him to pass and enter.

He strode onto the balcony. She heard rustling, then a bright light flashed. He returned inside, closed the doors behind him, and headed for the exit.

"Excuse me! But what just happened? What was that light?"

"It was for your protection. So please feel at ease while Lord Masterson is away," he said, never breaking his stride.

"Wait! I'm not at ease. If you would answer my question directly, I may feel less nervous."

Duncan's eyes closed as he inhaled, then reopened on the exhale. "I mean no disrespect, miss. But even if I attempted to explain, you would likely not comprehend."

Alioson looked down and away, massaging her left temple. "I'm honestly tired of hearing that and being kept in the dark." She peered at him. "It makes me uncomfortable."

Duncan's aloof demeanor turned dark. "It would be in everyone's best interest for you to ask as little as possible during your stay."

Alioson's mouth opened, then closed, and her eyes tightened.

"If you'll excuse me," he said, striding through the open door.

In frustrated anger, she gripped the doorknob, posed to slam it, but gently closed and locked it. Although he had told her she was safe, her nerves were on edge with news of Caliostro's absence. Alioson sat on the bed, hugging herself, and pondered her situation. A desire to be in the open air tugged at her senses.

***

The Hunters Guild (Mortal Society)

Caliostro inhaled deep, then scrunched his nose. "It seems a short time away has weakened my tolerance of this world's stench," he said, straightening his suit. The land of mortals mimicked the realm of the veil, with similar cities, broad land masses, and segregated communities. The major difference was the passing of time. That, and the many hidden inhabitants shielded from humans. The Monster Hunters Guild had always kept residence in the human world against the recommendation of the guild's high council. To human eyes, the guild building looked like a standard four-star hotel.

Caliostro entered and approached the front desk.

A woman with long brown hair and jade-colored eyes greeted him. "How may I help you, sir?"

"I'm here to meet with Durian."

"Sir, I'm sorry—"

"You will be if you don't call him. Now." Caliostro leaned over the counter. His eyes beamed, illuminating her form.

She stepped backward and picked up the phone. "There's a …" She paused, looking to him for his name.

"Caliostro Masterson." He smirked straightened a cuff that was already in place.

"Yes," she answered, then hung up the phone. "This way, Mr. Masterson." She came around to escort him, but he stopped her mid-stride.

"I know the way." Caliostro passed the woman and headed down the pristine corridor of the main lobby. He rounded the corner and stopped in front of an elevator that read STAFF ONLY above it. He entered and pressed number seven and waited as the doors slid closed.

The elevator stopped moments later.

A man with silver eyes, short spiky black hair with white tips, and a pale complexion greeted Caliostro as the doors slid open. His sunken eyes stared, and his lips clenched tight. He wore an all-black three-piece suit, the jacket falling past his knees and fitting loose. "It's been a while, Cali." He stepped backward to allow Caliostro to exit the elevator.

"I don't recall saying you could call me Cali, Durian." He passed three closed doors and stopped by the fourth. The door swung open. He entered and sat on the nearest couch.

"Still showing off, I see?" Durian closed the door behind him.

"When the occasion calls for it." He leaned back to unbutton his suit jacket.

Durian chuckled, then his face became serious again. "To what do I owe the pleasure of this visit?"

"Let's not play this unaware game, okay?"

"That's too bad. I love games, *Cali.*"

"Your guild should know better by now to leave me alone." Caliostro's relaxed tone became stern and direct.

"Not sure why you're telling me. You know I have a boss, like everyone else." His smirk returned.

"Keep your hunters off my property. That's the only warning you will get." Rising, he re-buttoned his jacket, then eyed Durian. "If you're looking for something and it ends up on my land, you had better wait until it runs back off. You get me?" He walked to the door.

Durian cracked his neck from left to right. He slowly got to his feet and walked around his desk. "We all do what we must." He watched Caliostro walk out before the smirk died on his face.

***

The Manor

Caliostro was gone for over a week. She had no computers at her disposal, nor calendars for her to confirm. She measured days by the rising and setting of the sun. During his absence, she explored the enormous manor. The first floor also had a vast library that held thousands of books. She found a gentleman's parlor, a massive chef's kitchen, and a large empty room she couldn't determine its purpose. Floor-to-ceiling mirrors covered one wall, and the floors were comprised of a rich tan tile with a lacquer finish, while another section of the floor had a soft cushion-like mat.

She rubbed her bare foot across it, then she noticed another wall in the back of the room had racks of weapons. An echo of metal against metal rang in her ears. A sharp pain shot through the center of her back, the trauma bringing her to both knees. She bellowed, the sound ricocheting off the walls.

Once the pain subsided, Alioson eyed the weapons rack. No concrete memories were attached, but the room evoked a feeling she could not define. Her thoughts hazed over, and her vision blurred. She rose and ran from the room.

Alioson returned to the main foyer. A painting of a frozen lake caught her attention. She stared at it for a moment until she realized it was of the lake Caliostro had rescued her from. She reached to touch the golden trim, but she felt someone standing just behind her.

Before she could turn, a powerful hand grabbed her wrist and spun her around. "What are you doing?" his deep voice boomed in her ears.

The anger she heard made her heart race.

His eyes softened, yet the glow within them sharpened. He stared down at her parted lips, as if he meant to devour them. Caliostro moved in closer, gently pressing her against the wall beside the painting. A trapped breath escaped a moment before his lips pressed against hers.

Alioson's eyes widened in shock, then they drifted close. *I missed him. How could I miss him?*

A sudden explosion went off in her brain, and her free hand fisted in his collar. A fire was set in the pit of her stomach and rose to burst under the skin of her lips. Her eyes closed when his tongue sampled her bottom lip, then slipped it into her mouth.

He released her wrist, and she coiled her arms around his neck, leaning into the kiss. They held nothing back as they delighted in each other.

The clearing of a throat brought them back to reality, but their ignited passions did not cool. Duncan cleared his throat a fifth time before they tore themselves apart.

"What is it?" He placed his forehead against hers, still staring into her eyes.

She didn't remove her arms from around his neck and stared back. Her eyes glazed over with unquenched desire, labored breaths escaping her parted lips.

"Hunters on the perimeter."

An exasperated sigh left Caliostro as he pulled from Alioson's embrace. He faced Duncan, allowing Alioson's arms to drop to her sides like rags.

She gently fell against the wall, now her sole support, as she tried to gather composure once more.

"Thank you. I'll take care of it. Please escort Alioson to her room."

"Of course." Duncan approached the foot of the stairs to wait for her.

Caliostro noticed she looked everywhere but at him. "I have to take care of some unwanted visitors, but when

I return, we should speak." He stepped backward, making her look up at him. He smiled, then disappeared.

CONNECTION

Caliostro flew to the perimeter line near the lake. The putrid stench of the hunters enveloped him. In the distance, he spotted the party and laughed to himself. *So, they slithered into my domain even after my warning.* Caliostro swiftly crossed the open plains of his holdings, skimming the veil's barrier, and landed. He stepped into view.

They waited.

"So, you're the famous Caliostro?" one of them said, scrutinizing him. "You don't look like much to me."

Caliostro grinned, watching them size him up. "You all must be new, huh? I guess you haven't lived up to the boss's expectations since he sent you here, to die."

"Who the fuck is this guy?" the one to the far right asked.

"Who cares? Let's just end him and be on our way," another said.

The leader stepped forward, drooling at the mere sight of Caliostro. He was built like a tank, with short spiky brown hair. The hunger in his yellow eyes was easy to interpret. They all ached for a fight, and he was more than happy to oblige. "You should know, there will be no escape!"

Caliostro rolled his head in a full circle. "You took the words right out of my mouth."

Three encircled him, while the other four succumbed to the transformation. The sound of muscles wrenching and reforming echoed across the empty clearing. They howled as fur commandeered bare skin, and bones stretched until their massive beastly visage was all that remained.

"I knew I smelled wet dogs," Caliostro said as two of the creatures were ready to pounce.

Their deformed snouts dripped with mucus, and long, sharp fangs salivated as their senses grew stronger.

They will have to go first. Lycrian are such troublesome beasts. Caliostro flipped from the circle and landed amid the four Lycrians. He summoned his blade forth. The opal pendant around his neck disappeared as a hilt made of the same stone appeared in his right hand, bluish white light spilled from it in the shape of a blade. It melted the claws of the first two beasts as they swung for him. Caliostro twisted, then thrust his sword, moving beyond their speed.

The other three hunters moved to strike.

Caliostro vanished.

"Where the hell is he?" one yelled, its fangs dripping saliva.

Caliostro came from above. His blade swung, taking the creature's head. Blood sprayed through the air as he severed bone from flesh. Moments later, the Lycrians were dead. Caliostro refocused on the three remaining hunters.

They charged.

He pushed back the hair from his eyes and sneered before he approached them. The black strains flew in the hazy sunlight as surely as his blade seared their flesh.

***

"Caliostro!" Alioson jerked awake. She rubbed the sleepiness from her eyes and scanned the room. *What was that?* Alioson walked to the large floor lamp and switched it on. Her hand froze below the pull chain as she recalled the frightening images of Caliostro fighting a group of monsters.

She glanced toward the glass doors. *Is he fighting those things right now?*

Alioson patted herself on either side of her face. "Get a grip, Alioson." She placed her hand over her heart. "I've got to stay alert. I hadn't even realized I'd fallen asleep."

She opened the balcony doors and stepped outside. *It should be fine if I get some air for just a few seconds.* Her eyes shifted around nervously. "See, no Dalidah," she said but backed toward the door.

A sudden crash from the right drew her attention. Before she could think, dust and debris flew at her. Alioson crouched, shielding her face, and braced herself.

Nothing. She lowered one arm, then the other, and opened her eyes to find Duncan standing before her.

***

"Caliostro!" Alioson's voice echoed through his mind. His concentration waned for a split second, barely dodging a flaming sword. Only he and the three hunters stood in the open field. He had to end this fight soon and return to the manor.

"Destroy him! Now!" the leader commanded.

The female of the group chanted, and a gust of stale air swirled around him.

An Enchanter! She needs to die next. Caliostro readied his sword.

A younger boy with spiky hair and dark baggy clothing stepped forward. The winds blustered and rushed across the clearing.

"A second Enchanter?" Caliostro grimaced. "Why am I surprised? They never fight fair." Caliostro squared his right foot and waited.

The leader bared fangs and claws. His eyes glowed green, and a rancid stench wafted from them. Onyx wings of mist burgeoned from his back, lifting him into the air.

Caliostro had never seen such a creature, nor could he afford the time to ponder. Mirroring its movements, he flew swiftly from beneath him in a serpentine fashion, then hovered above the creature's head.

It dodged by flying backward.

Caliostro faced him and charged before the beast could hope to recover. Staving his sword through his middle, he quartered the creature before it could react. Caliostro landed, looking up at the shocked expression on the leader's face, then the carved pieces of his body fell to the ground.

The boy summoned a cutting wind of fire that encircled Caliostro and filled his head with a deafening chatter.

Closing his eyes, Caliostro stilled himself and silenced his mind. His wings expanded on either side, followed by a burst of light dissipating the firestorm. He opened his eyes as another wall of fire attempted to assail him. He rushed through the flames, his fiery blade halving the boy's head, then slashed the body in two. Caliostro focused on the female Enchanter attempting to flee. "There will be no escape." He pursued her.

She brought forth the roots of trees to shield her as she fled.

Caliostro swooped in front of her, stopping any farther advancement. "You come on my land …" he said, stepping toward her.

She stumbled and fell over the very roots she had summoned.

"And now you think to escape?" He snickered and crouched in front of her as she leaned back, her hands digging into dirt. He held the tip of his sword under her chin, forcing her head to tilt. After a moment, he stood, then turned his back.

The female seized the opportunity to call forth an earth spell, but before the words left her mouth, Caliostro twisted, removing her head.

Blood drenched his suit, but he didn't care. He took to the air to return to the manor.

***

"Are you okay?" Duncan asked.

"I think so," Alioson replied as she surveyed her surroundings.

Duncan leaped off the edge of what remained of the balcony so fast it was barely a blur and grabbed something huge and hairy.

Alioson ran inside and closed the door behind her. The door clicked, and a shield of light flashed, then dissipated. She backed up until her legs touched the bed. An unbridled battle raged just below her. She sat, needing to be content with waiting, but ached to see, to know more. *Why do I care what happens to him? Why?*

Curiosity overshadowed the fear that should have been present and accounted for. "Caliostro ..."

***

Caliostro navigated to the manor. He landed in the rubble of Alioson's balcony. He dispersed his sword, causing his ivory pendant to return to the chain around his neck. Being thoroughly covered from head to toe in the blood and gore of his kills, he removed his jacket and used it to wipe clean as much of it as he could. Bits of rubble dropped from above, making him peer up. He closed his eyes and sensed she was unharmed but frightened. He discarded the jacket, pushed his hair from his face, and leaped in a single bound onto the balcony's edge.

A moment later, the door slid open, and he entered. "Alioson."

Tears of joy and relief filled her eyes at the sight of him. She ran to him but stopped short.

"I apologize for all the commotion."

She laughed. "You call that commotion?"

"Well, it's usually not this lively here, at least not so often."

"I'm not sure I want to know who was attacking, but luckily, Duncan came when he did."

Caliostro responded with a nod. "Stay inside. I need to check the perimeter to ensure there aren't more of them."

She stared after him as he leaped over the balcony's edge. The doors closed, and the light emanated once more. She hugged herself. Both hands absently rubbed her arms. Flashes of her dream of Caliostro and the scrimmage on the balcony ran through her mind. Question after question bombarded her. *Can I die here? Am I already dead? Caliostro assured me, but what if?*

"Stop it." She sighed and closed her eyes. "I need to clear my head."

83

She went into the bathroom and threw cold water on her face. *Don't think, don't think—*

The door across from the wardrobe caught her attention again. She opened it and discovered a massive closet filled with clothing. "This place is ever filled with surprises." She browsed the various garments, and an emerald-colored silk-sleeved dress, still with its tag, caught her eye. She could not resist the urge to try it on, so she carefully removed the tag, undressed, and slipped the dress over her head. It fit as though it had been made for her. Alioson admired the way it accentuated all her curves.

A knock on the bedroom door gave her pause.

"Miss?" Duncan said from the other side.

Alioson ran from the bathroom and opened the door to greet him.

"Lord Masterson has asked if you would come down to the foyer."

"Yes, I can. I'll be down in a moment."

"As you say." He turned to leave, but she grabbed his arm to stop him. Duncan eyed her hand, then her face.

Sensing her forwardness, she let go and stepped backward. "I wanted to thank you for protecting me before."

He turned to fully face her with an icy glare. "It wasn't for your sake. It's my duty to the lord of this manor." With that, he moved down the corridor.

"Even so, thank you!" Alioson observed him until he rounded the corner. She shut the door and sat at the vanity to pull her hair into a messy bun. She slipped on a pair of cream-colored silk slippers and felt her knees wobble. "Why are you nervous?"

Her gaze fell to her mouth. The sensation of his kiss returned to the forefront of her mind. Without realizing it, her fingertips lifted slowly to trace her bottom lip back and forth. "It was just a kiss." She sighed, her heart still beating fast. She dropped her hand and clenched her fingers together. "This is not the time to think about that."

She braced herself, then headed to the foyer to face Caliostro.

***

Caliostro waited for Alioson at the bottom of the stairs. Anger filled him. They could have hurt her during that fight, and he wasn't completely sure she couldn't die here. The scent of cedar and vanilla announced her presence. He looked up and regarded her as she descended the stairs, unable to lower his gaze.

Alioson stopped in front of him.

Caliostro stepped forward and took her hand, then led her to the back terrace. A large stone table with five cream-colored cushioned chairs around it sat in the center of the terrace. Around the edge of the terrace were brick pillars and stairs descending to the grass. To the far left were more chairs and a fire pit. Fire-lit lanterns sat all around, providing a warm glow.

The moon colored the sky in a hazy blue-white light. Alioson gasped at the scene it created.

Caliostro had his back to her, both hands in his pants pockets, as a breeze caught the ends of his long hair.

Her eyes softened as she watched him.

"When I pulled you from the lake, you were near death." He turned to face her, his blue eyes glowing like beacons. "I transferred part of my energy—or rather, my inner force—to save you, which creates a bond of sorts."

She hugged herself. "What do you mean, 'bond'?"

"I can … sense you. Even at great distances. I'm sure by now you can feel me as well. We are permanently linked."

"Why? Why did you do that? I mean, saving me—someone you didn't know—in this strange realm where I obviously don't belong."

Caliostro moved forward, unsure of how much to share and how much to hold close. "When I heard your heartbeat, the need to save you devoured my reason. I knew I had to save you."

"You had to save me?"

He felt exposed but found his composure once more. "I have only shared my inner force with one other person, and it did not go well. Even knowing that, I was compelled to take a chance."

"None of this makes sense. I don't understand how I even ended up in your lake, in another world. And why do I feel like I haven't just met you?"

"It's true. There's something here." He waved his hand back and forth in the open space between them. "Once I heard your heartbeat, I had to save you, and now …"

Her heart raced. "And now?"

"Now"—he stepped toward her—"I feel other things I shouldn't."

They both stood frozen in place, locked in one another's gaze.

Caliostro could hear her heart throb.

She moved closer, cautious and yet compelled.

Caliostro removed his hands from his pockets and waited. The bolder she became, the more his inner force stirred.

She rested a hand above his heart and tipped her head back.

His gaze fell to her mouth.

Alioson raised herself onto her tiptoes to gain better access and pressed her lips against his. An essential battle ensued. He rapaciously took her into his embrace, pressing her against the nearby brick pillar, and Alioson moaned into his hungry mouth.

"This is too dangerous." Caliostro recoiled, his breathing labored, and eyes glowed brighter.

"I don't care." Alioson placed her arms around his neck and kissed him again.

He surrendered, delighting in her willingness. He pressed his forehead against hers, pushing himself away. "If we keep going, I cannot stop."

"I've decided I want to know it all, so please don't push me away." She held him tightly, eyes pleading.

Caliostro cradled her back against the pillar. He leaned in, his moisture-laden heavy breath grazing her neck. "You don't understand what you're asking."

"But you do, so show me what I don't understand."

He kissed her again, even more passionately. His mouth dominated hers. She parted her lips, and Caliostro obliged. A surge of energy from within her flowed between them.

Alioson felt an extreme jolt of pleasure as her inner force poured into Caliostro and his into her. She moaned, but his mouth captured it.

He leaned into the kiss more, slowly closing his mouth over her tongue. His eyes were ablaze. Their light almost bursting from the sockets. He held her tight as she cradled the back of his neck.

A sudden flash hit him hard, causing him to falter— an image of a little girl, afraid and hiding. She screamed as a hand reached toward her. Caliostro shook his head to clear it and opened his eyes to find Alioson crumpled on the ground. "Alioson!" He lifted her into his arms.

Moments later, he laid her on top of her bedsheets.

She didn't move, but her heartrate and breathing were normal.

Caliostro contemplated while she slept. The hours ticked by. She was so peaceful it scared him. He waited, barely blinking or breathing.

Little beads of sweat formed on her brow, and her eyes rolled under her lids; she was dreaming.

***

"Mommy, I'm scared," the little girl cried out.

"It's okay, my sweet. There is nothing to fear. Mommy just needs you to stay in this closet, no matter what, unless I come get you. Okay, my love?" Tears welled in the eyes of the woman with long dark hair.

The little girl nodded in agreement.

"I love you." She quietly closed the folding closet door.

The little girl gripped her yellow flower sundress in her small hands while squeezing both eyes shut against the darkness. Minutes ticked by, then the sound of her mother's voice raised in anger reached her ears. Against her mother's wishes, she opened the closet and tiptoed to the stairway. In the living room below, through the railing, she saw a man in a black suit with long dark hair holding her mother against the wall.

"Do you honestly think you can hide her from me, Ayina?" He chuckled. "You still don't understand what I am? Do you?"

Her mother tried to free herself, but her efforts were futile. She strained to speak against his grip. "Please, just let her be."

"My dear, that is not how it will happen. I will have her. It is what we agreed on."

A lamp flew off a long wooden table behind him and crashed into the side of his head.

"Really?" He snickered, throwing his head back, tightening his hold. "Why would such a thing work? Your minor powers will do you no good today, witch."

The little girl watched the man bite her mother's neck. Blood sprayed everywhere when he ripped away her flesh.

Her mother's screams echoed through the house.

The girl also screamed.

The assailant turned his gaze on the child and bore into her. His eyes glowed a bright blue. Blood covered his mouth and chin, dripping onto his white shirt under the suit jacket.

She ran just as he dropped her mother's lifeless body onto the floor. Hidden back in the closet, she shut the door behind her. She stooped to duck behind a basket of laundry and tried as hard as she could to be quiet and still. She saw his shadow from under the door enter the room.

"Come out, little flower. I won't hurt you."

The door swung open, and the child screamed as his hand reached to grab her.

***

Alioson awoke screaming just like the little girl in her dreams.

"Alioson! What is wrong?" Caliostro stood over her, brow furrowed.

She looked at him and through him at the same time. Languorously she sat up and held her head.

"It was just a dream or … a nightmare?" he said, hoping his words brought calm.

She leaned forward, turning slightly from him. Her equilibrium tilted as she scanned the room in a daze, the experience still fresh in her mind. "What happened to me?"

"You passed out on the terrace, so I brought you here to rest. You've been out for some time."

Alioson languidly raised from the bed. "Did I pass out because of our kiss? I remember …"

"You remembered something?"

"No. I remember kissing you, then passing out." She didn't know why she lied, but she knew she wasn't ready to share the pure ecstasy she had felt.

Caliostro sensed uncertainty and dread in her. "Exactly what I was afraid of happening has happened. We exchanged our inner force. I knew I should have held back." He looked away from her, unwilling to share the concern clearly etched in his expression.

Alioson could feel his pain. She didn't know from where it came, but it overwhelmed her, then it disappeared just as quickly as it had hit her, leaving her alone with only her thoughts. It was all too much for her to handle at once. "Caliostro."

He faced her once again, his mouth set in a hard line.

"I know very little of you, very little of myself, but in this short time, I have developed feelings for you—

feelings I know you are aware of." She watched her hands tightly wringing together.

He nodded.

She took an uneven breath and paused. "I know you don't know me either, but I hope to remedy that soon. I would like to know your story if you're willing to share it with me, to trust me."

Caliostro sat next to where she stood. He took her hand in his, urging her down beside him.

LESSONS LEARNED

"I was born in the Mortal Society to a farmer and his wife."

"I thought you were born here?"

"No, I was introduced to the realm of the veil much later. We led a calm and simple life, though my parents were anything but simple." He smiled. "My mother's name was Deita. She was a Lische being.

"A Li-sh-ah?"

"Yes, mortals from your realm refer to them as angels. She was my father's guardian before she became his wife." His eyes misted over, as if he was slowly slipping into the past.

"My father's name was Dragus. He was a Lycrian. Simply put, a werewolf to mortals. He was the grandson of the oldest Lycrian known to our kind. When I first showed signs of more of my mother's powers, we surmised that her blood must have altered the cursed blood of my father somehow." Caliostro stood and walked to the hearth. He snapped his fingers, and a fire roared to life.

Alioson followed and sat in one of two chairs, staring into the flames. "It's amazing you can do things like that. To my eyes, you appear human."

"Well, many believe so, but this body"—he looked down at himself—"holds secrets even I have yet to discover. My mother and father always were forthcoming about themselves. But she cautioned me, when around humans, that I should keep these facts secret." He smiled to himself, recalling his mother's words. "At the time, I didn't understand why I needed to, but soon I understood all too well." Caliostro sat across from her. His eyes were aglow with anger, pain, and defeat. "I still remember the day they died."

***

AD1264

"Mother! Father!" Caliostro pushed through the flames that flanked him. He reached the hallway that led to his parents' bedroom. He saw a tall, solid form standing still within the thick smoke.

His mother shrieked in pure panic.

"Mother!" Caliostro charged forward just as a body knocked him through a window. He pushed the body from him and rolled to his side.

A creature with a beak, fur, and four arms lay lifeless beside him.

Scrambling to his feet, he stared at the gruesome thing. Glass breaking on the other side of the house made him turn away. He attempted to move toward the sound, except something grabbed his ankle. He peered down to find the creature barely alive. Caliostro yanked his ankle free and ran around the side of the burning house.

He found his father laying in a pool of blood. His long black hair practically covered his entire face. Caliostro's heart sank in his chest as he ran to him. He dropped to his knees, afraid to touch him, afraid not to. His torso was ripped open, and one eye slashed through.

"Father!"

"Caliostro?" He slowly turned his head toward him. "Urgh. Run. Get … out of … here," he said with his last breath.

"Father!" Caliostro grabbed his father's shoulders and pulled him against his chest. The fear of harming him was no longer a concern.

His mother was mid-flight when a pure-light arrow struck her. Her eyes widened with surprise as she fell to the ground with a loud thud.

"Mother!" He knew he had to get to her. Caliostro rested his father on the ground, then ran to his mother. He scooped her up and held her to him as tightly as he could without hurting her. The arrow that had pierced her dissolved into her slight frame, as if it never existed. "Mother, what's happening? Why aren't you healing?"

Blood poured from her wound and mouth when she tried to speak. Her hand slowly reached for his face. "I'm so sorry, my sweet boy."

Caliostro shook his head, tears escaping the corners of his eyes.

"There are … so many things … I haven't told you. You must … get away from here. Run. You cannot fight … now."

Caliostro shook his head. "I will not run. I will—"

She grabbed the front of his shirt. "You must!"

"I won't!" From the corners of his eyes, he saw movement from the tree line. He sensed many more beings moving in on them. "I will not leave you, Mother. I will stay and fight and kill whoever has done this!"

As the roof of their home caved in, four shadows emerged above the canopy. They drew their bows and trained them on him.

Caliostro lifted one hand in their direction, but before he attempted an attack, a beam of light rose and surrounded him.

His mother pushed a small object into his hand and rolled away from his embrace.

When he opened his eyes, he found himself at the foot of a waterfall in a vast clearing that stretched as far as the eye could see. He came to his feet, searching for her, only to discover he was alone. She had not transported with him, like they'd done so many times before.

Directly behind him was the portal she'd opened, though it was collapsing. He watched her come to her feet on the other side, about to face the four figures eager to end her. They all appeared to be human. She meandered toward them. Hazy blue light surrounded her feet, and wings of light sprang forth and draped her back.

Caliostro attempted to cross through, but an invisible force prevented him. He begged, screaming for her. "Mother! Mother!"

She glanced at him and nodded, then smiled just as the portal closed.

He fell to the ground, tears streaking his soot-covered face. He beheld the item she had slipped into his hand—the opal pendant she'd always worn. Rain soaked him to the bone. Caliostro closed his eyes and listened. First, he could only hear birds chirping, then branches falling, the animals running through the nearby woods, then the crackling of fire and fighting. He opened his eyes and took flight, determined to get back to her.

It felt like an eternity before he returned to his homestead. The rain doused most of the fire. He went to the spot where he had last held his mother, only to find burned grass and dismembered bodies scattered all about. When he finally discovered her, it was clear she had not survived the battle. A mixture of mud and blood covered her white dress, ripped beyond true recognition.

***

Caliostro dashed away with unshed tears and stood. "It would be best if I left you now."

Alioson leaped to her feet, grabbing his wrist. "I know it was a long time ago, but I'm sorry for your loss."

He rested his palm over her hand, then gently removed it. "Thank you for saying so." He left, softly closing the door behind him. He traipsed his office and locked the door. Seated behind his desk, his mind crept to the past once more.

***

"Hello, young one." The woman smiled at him, stepping forward.

"Pardon?"

A sinister grin graced her full lips, masking her beauty, revealing her true nature. Caliostro's hand gripped his sword.

Her eyes followed his movement, and her smirk diminished. "Do you plan to cut me down, fierce Caliostro?" She laughed, stepping closer still.

"Why have you been stalking me? How do you know me?" He stepped backward, hand still on his sword.

"Don't concern yourself with the minor details." She sat on a crumbling brick wall. Crossing her leather clad legs, she bent to dust the dirt from her knee-high boots.

Caliostro watched her but did not come closer.

"What if I said I had information on the ones who killed your parents?" Her hooded eyes gleamed as she found her smile once more.

He drew his sword and pointed it centimeters from her face. "If you have such information, speak it now!"

She laughed. "Go ahead, run me through. Risk never learning the truth."

"Who are you, and what do you want?" Caliostro let the point of his blade graze her skin.

Her eyes widened, and his sword flew from his hand. An uncontrollable fit of laughter claimed her as Caliostro drew his second sword and held it under her neck. "You're no fun, you know that? I see I have my work cut out for me." In an instant, she appeared behind him.

He turned, slashing at nothing.

Her laughter echoed in the night air.

His eyes rolled once realization hit him. "Vampire," he mumbled. He sheathed his sword.

"Are you done? Ready to listen? Or should we play some more? I'm game for whatever." She reappeared in her seat on the brick wall.

"Speak, demon." He cautiously faced her.

"Did you enjoy the sight of their dismembered parts? Sadly, I arrived after they had killed your mother." She waited for her words to sink in.

Caliostro's eyes widened in shock. He stood erect.

"Yes, now you understand, my sweet. Though those hunters weren't delicious, I still enjoyed killing them." She threw her head back with laughter.

He stood stiff, glaring at her, while she casually explained the carnage of her deeds, as if it were a normal event.

She put her arms around his neck and placed her rosy lips next to his ear. "I know you want revenge, and I can give it to you. Of course, everything has a price."

"What do you want?"

"Your blood."

He pushed her away and stepped backward. "Why would I agree to such an exchange with no proof that what you say is true, demon?"

"What a cynic you are for someone so young. Tsk, tsk, dear boy. Our exchange will be advantageous to your cause, I assure you." She grasped his face in her hands and breathed him in. "My blood will strengthen you. Trust me, it will be worth the sweet taste of revenge, so give in to Mistress Dalidah.

***

The scent of roses wafted through Caliostro's senses. "Dalidah," he said, glancing out his office window.

She stood just a few feet away. Their eyes locked as she beckoned him with a leading crawl of her fingers and disappeared.

Caliostro went onto the terrace and stopped at the top of the steps when he spotted Dalidah.

Dressed in a long red gown that trailed behind her, she seductively glided across the grass and up the few steps.

"Why have you come again? You know you are not welcome."

"Oh, dear Caliostro, why are you so mean to me?" She lifted both gloved hands, followed by a shrug of her delicate shoulders. "Isn't it obvious I've missed you? And this is how you treat me?" She chuckled, sashaying to a nearby chair.

Caliostro's eyes followed her. "I don't wish to do this with you. I have far too many things on my mind to deal with right now." Caliostro walked back the way he came.

Dalidah stood in front of the entrance, baring his way. "You act as if I'm not one of those things on your mind. Were you or were you not just thinking of me?" A smile formed on her ruby red lips.

"Dalidah, leave."

She glanced to the side, then threw her arms around his neck. "I see you still have leftovers," she whispered in his ear.

Alioson came into view, shock and fear clear on her face.

Caliostro curled his fingers around one of Dalidah's arms and swung her away from him. He stepped inside, the doors to the terrace slamming shut behind him. "It's fine. She can't enter any longer," he said, looking over his shoulder.

Dalidah stood fuming, staring at them through the glass doors. She tossed her hair over her shoulder and disappeared into mist.

"You two still seem close. I don't really want to step in between anything."

"Our history has long passed. I won't lie or pretend I felt nothing for her. In time, Dalidah revealed her true nature, and I no longer wished to be a part of her. The only problem is, because of our blood bond, we are forever linked."

"Forever? Like—"

"Yes, like us but different. Her and I are bonded through blood sharing. But enough about her, just know I will not allow her to harm you."

Alioson stepped closer and traced a finger under his left eye. "Do you know how often I've seen your eyes glow this intense blue? Why do they do this?" Her delicate fingers gingerly traced the peak of his cheek.

The glow of his eyes intensified.

It startled her, and she withdrew her hand.

Caliostro growled, grabbing her wrist suspended in midair. "When you touch me in such a way, it is difficult for me to squash the urge of my response."

"Then don't."

He kissed her, and she followed his lead. They embraced fully, clenching each other. Light swished and flowed between their moving lips, giving and taking each other's inner force. Caliostro changed the angle of his head to take in more of her when he caught the glimpse of an ominous figure leering at them in the far corner of the foyer.

Caliostro placed his hands on her shoulders, keeping her at arm's length. "We need to stop. Your body can't take another exchange so soon." He stepped backward and tried to shake off the sensations. He spied the far corner again; nothing was there. "I know this may scare you, but I'm constantly craving your inner force, craving you. I have never, in all my existence, craved anyone in such a way."

Her eyes searched his face, but she did not approach him. "Have you ever hurt anyone by draining their energy, their inner force?"

He looked down, then back at her. "I think we should stop for now, and you should get some more rest."

Many emotions danced across her face and stopped on a glower expression. "Why do you keep doing that? Every time I ask for just a little more, you pull back. Keeping me in the dark won't help me or anything else!" She stormed past him and up the stairs.

"Alioson!" He watched her round the corner and out of sight.

***

Alioson slammed the door behind her and threw herself on the bed, then quickly set upright, scowling. She grunted in annoyance, letting herself fall back again. "He's so frustrating," she said, grinding her teeth. Alioson's eyelids became heavy. She tried to blink away the sleepiness that filled her, but she lost the battle as the world of dreams claimed her once more.

***

Alioson's words echoed in Caliostro's head. *"Keeping me in the dark won't help me or anything else!"*

Caliostro entered his office to review some paperwork. *"Duncan, I need to speak with you now."*

A few moments passed, and Duncan entered. "You called, Lord Masterson?"

"Yes, I have business to attend to on the other side, as I'm sure you know." Caliostro refocused on his paperwork. "I want you to watch over Alioson while I'm away, anything she needs, et cetera."

"Of course. And how long will your business take?"

"I won't be away long." He raised an eyebrow at him.

Duncan cleared his throat to prevent himself from voicing his disapproval—a futile effort given Caliostro's abilities.

"Wipe the worry from your face, Duncan. She and I are linked. I'll know if she is in danger."

"Sir, about that—"

"I do not need you to remind me. It's of no concern to you."

"It *is* a concern of mine. I am your watcher appointed by—"

"Again, I'm aware of our truths. Did you move her, as I asked?"

"Yes. Everything was taken care of following the attack."

"Marvelous. You are dismissed."

"As you say, Lord Masterson. Do have a safe trip."

Caliostro left the office and shambled to the back terrace. When he reached the foyer, he stopped, looking at the upper level where Alioson rested. *"Alioson, I will return soon."*

He stepped onto the back terrace and took flight.

THE EFFECTS OF MEMORY

The City of Pardus (Mortal Society)

"How are you, my sleeping one?" Caliostro whispered to Catherine. "You seem well. I have said this many times before, but please forgive me for what has happened to you." He kissed the back of her chilly hand. "I know the Magic Guild wants you in their possession, and it's possible you would not be opposed to that, but you are my responsibility until you awaken."

A knock at the door drew Caliostro's attention. "Come in, Daloren."

A six-foot-four man, with long curly red and unkempt hair and golden-brown eyes, entered the bedroom. His skin tone told stories of the many deserts. "*Pravi cuna da*?" he inquired in the Pardus dialect.

"The same. I thank you for accepting my request on such short notice." Caliostro kept his eyes trained on Catherine. "And how have you been? I was unaware you had studied the Pardus language. When did that occur?" He glanced in his direction.

"Still the same old me, half-assing my studies." He chuckled. "I only know a few greetings so far, and it's been years."

Caliostro shook his head. "You say that, yet you do rather well in your field."

"Eh, I have to be good at something." He shrugged. "By the way, Grandfather asked after you."

Caliostro rolled his eyes and rested his gaze on Catherine. "Not sure why he'd ask *you*. He has Duncan for that."

"That's true. So, what prompted the move?"

"I have a human woman staying at my manor, and she's alive."

"Wait. Your location on the other side?"

Caliostro nodded.

"How is that even possible?"

"Good question. Some Hunters Guild members were found trespassing. I believe they sniffed her out."

"More than likely. So, that's why you moved her here?"

"Yes and no." He stepped from the bed to serve the room.

"So, is she pretty?"

Caliostro glared at him.

"Hey, it's just a question." He raised his hands in mock defense.

"I know where your line of questioning leads." He opened a drawer of a nearby dresser. "I came upon her by accident. That is all."

"You haven't … you know, fed from her?"

Caliostro remained silent.

"So, you have?"

"First, it's called withdrawing inner force or energy, not feeding. We have exchanged, and the connection has been entrenched."

"You don't waste any time." He hung his head and chuckled.

"It has nothing to do with time. I saved her, and I was drawn to her. The need to exchange was the strongest I have ever felt, and she wasn't opposed to it, to be clear. Also, it's for the best that we're connected in that way. Dalidah returned."

"She's back again?" He checked Catherine's eyes by opening each.

"Yes."

"Well, lucky you." He picked up the chart hanging at the bottom of her bed, made a note, and replaced it. "Anyway, there has been no change. Of course, I'm sure you knew that."

"I did expect otherwise."

"Look, I understand you're being cautious, but I honestly don't think there's a need. I'm a doctor who cares for humans, and it's clear to me she's no longer that."

"You think I am unaware? How many times have you spoken those same words to me?"

"Countless times, yet you still feel the need for her to have a human doctor on hand?"

"Human doctor or not, you're a Lycrian, my kin, and one of the few I can trust. That's why I have you checking on her from time to time. Also, I wish to treat her as a human, even if I caused her to lose her humanity."

"I don't know why you take the blame like that. She played a fair part of being in her current state." He watched Caliostro from the corner of his eye.

"With the hunters attacking my manor, I didn't want to take the chance of the Magic Guild finding her location. I had her at the manor long enough; here in the human world, it is safer in some ways."

"Do you honestly believe they are still looking for her?" he asked while checking the circulation in her legs. His left hand rested under her right foot as he made small circles with her ankle. He completed multiple rotations on one, then the other.

"I do, though it has been quiet as of late."

"How long do we need to use this location?" He placed Catherine's legs under the covers.

"Until it becomes compromised."

"You actually think that will happen?"

"It's entirely possible. We need to be prepared for that." He spotted a stack of files next to the bed. He rummaged through them and discovered they were background checks. "Are these—"

"They're possible candidates, watchers in the medical field from our clan, who could be helpful to Catherine when I can't."

Caliostro nodded. "I still prefer if it were you."

"I'll do my best. So, what's your plan for the Hunters Guild?"

"I paid them a visit and took care of the unwanted company. That's enough for now." Caliostro regarded Catherine once again.

***

The Hunters Guild

"Enter," a deep voice said.

A six-foot-two male wearing an all-white suit, with white and green catlike pupils, and shoulder-length snow-white hair entered the room.

"Report."

"Sir." The male bowed his head very low. An invisible force knocked him to the ground and slid him into a wooden cabinet over six feet away, breaking it.

"So, you come here to report nothing." He stood from behind the enormous cherry oak desk.

The man gathered his senses, getting to his feet. He bowed his head again. "Forgive me, Master Cordaglen. The entire team was wiped out." Blood dripped from the wound on his left temple. He didn't dare wipe it away.

Cordaglen sneered while staring out the eight-foot glass window at the city. "Well, it's just as I thought it would turn out." He faced the hunter. "You feel wronged, apparently? If I knew this would happen, why would I send the team, and then reprimand you?" Cordaglen laughed deeply, throwing his head back, then sobered up. With blinding speed that the human eye couldn't see, he stood directly in front of the hunter, who hadn't moved an inch. "After your time here, one would think you'd learn to train your thoughts, to silence them around me."

"Forgive me, Master Cordaglen." The hunter trembled in fear, waiting for another blow or death.

Cordaglen laid his hand on the hunter's shoulder. "Don't worry, Kurick. I always have multiple plans at the ready. But know, when the desire arises, your end may be near." He tightened the grip on Kurick's shoulder.

"As you say, Master Cordaglen. May … I be excused?"

"Yes, of course." He released the man's shoulder. "Oh, send in the woman waiting on your way out." He waved away the hunter.

"Yes," the hunter replied, looking relieved to get away.

As he attempted to leave, a woman dressed in a red floor-length evening gown sashayed past him. She smiled at him, and he scowled back. A snicker escaped her when the door closed. "Well, I'm here. What is it, dear Cordaglen?" she asked impatiently, holding her hand in front of her to eye her blood-red nails.

"Have a seat, Dalidah." He indicated to a chair. "And don't get an attitude with me. You know very well my temperament."

She sat without another word.

"Now tell me, how is my dear old friend Caliostro doing?"

Dalidah rolled her eyes. "Oh, please, Jerrick. Your humor is still rather lacking, but if I must say, he's just fine." She crossed one leg over the other and leaned back into the couch. "I was watching him, until I was thrown out and barred from his home, twice." Anger laced her tone. "We fought over his new toy."

117

"First, I'm not sure I like my first name on that tongue of yours. Second, how pathetic have you become to be barred from any location?"

Dalidah rolled her eyes again. "Caliostro and his manservant's powers are beyond my own, so there's nothing I could do." She shrugged, flicking one nail under the other.

"So it would seem, and this new toy?"

"A human who has broken the laws of the veil and somehow entered that realm while alive." She shifted in her position, uncrossing and re-crossing her legs. "No doubt he'll use her for feeding at some point." She smirked.

"That doesn't sound much like him."

"Well, what else would he do with her?"

"Just keep watch on him … and his new toy."

"What for?" she shouted, jumping up.

He gave her one look, and she was seated again. "Just do as I say, and you will stay on this side of extinction."

She pouted but said nothing more.

***

The Manor

Alioson lay awake despite her attempts at sleep. She glanced at the light streaming in from the glass doors. Not sleeping had become her new habit over the last three weeks. She had found pen and paper in one of the vanity's drawers right after Caliostro had left a few weeks back. A thirty-day calendar now rested near the mirror, helping her keep track of the passing days. Her days had been boring, but she did her best to stay busy by reading books and touring the manor. The rooms were unused on the upper floors. Three other bathrooms sat off the main hallway, all like hers. She hadn't returned to the empty room on the first floor but would eye it whenever she'd pass it.

The evening meal was to be served in the dining hall. Alioson decided that would be when she'd ask Duncan if he'd heard from Caliostro. No fresh memories had surfaced, so she kept replaying the dream that was a memory.

"That was my mother. What was her name ... Ayina? Who was that man ... no, he wasn't a man?" She recalled the blood on his face. A sharp pain shot through her head, and she grunted. "Why can't I remember more? It's taking too long." She recalled Caliostro's kiss and her waking after the dream.

119

"Caliostro." She remembered how she felt when he withdrew her inner force and the exchange of his entering her body, like floating on a cloud, and little shocks of electricity had fired throughout her. It had felt so amazing. "Caliostro's the key." She hugged herself, realizing the room had grown cold.

She got up from the bed and went to light the fireplace as a knock sounded at the door. She knew it was Duncan. "Come in."

"Did I wake you, miss?" He carried a silver tray as he entered.

"No." She rubbed her dry eyes. "Sleep hasn't really been on my side."

He gave her a once over before passing her.

"Thank you." She followed him to the table in front of the hearth.

Duncan set down the tray and lifted the cover to reveal a bowl of freshly cut fruit, a glass of what looked to be cranberry juice, and assortments of meats and cheeses.

"I'm rather hungry, thank you."

For the first time, he didn't excuse himself right away. "You're now connected to Lord Masterson, so I'll also watch over you. Please rest easy and know you're safe here."

"So, you know about that?"

"Yes. I'm aware of everything that's occurred."

"Everything?" she asked, blushing.

"I don't mean to be overly forward, miss. As you know, I came upon you and Lord Masterson in the foyer on that one occasion."

Alioson's brow lifted, and her eyes dashed side to side. "Yes, that's true."

"So, yes, everything." He stepped closer to her.

"I guess you and Caliostro are that close. I mean, that makes sense."

"You could say that." He moved within a hand's length of her. "I need you to know that if you betray his trust, there will be no escape. He is important to many."

She leaned back, stumbling a bit.

He caught her right arm in an iron grip before she fell.

Alioson frowned up at him, pulling her arm away.

He released it.

Alioson studied him as he straightened his dark forest-green vest that rested over a crisp white dress shirt.

"Do we understand each other?" He locked his hands behind his back.

"Sure, though I'm positive it's me who's in more danger." The scowl on her face deepened.

"As you say, Miss Alioson." He seemed ready to say something more but faced the glass doors just as she did; they had both felt Caliostro's presence at the same time. "I will excuse myself then, miss." He exited the room before Caliostro knocked.

Alioson quickly opened the door, revealing his form to her hungry eyes. Her heart raced. "Caliostro." She said his name as if it were a prayer.

He smiled.

"Where have you been all this time?"

"Is everything all right?" His gaze darted around the room. "I felt your distress, and why are you not sleeping?" He noted the slight dark circles forming under her eyes. He stepped inside, making her back up a few inches. His gaze rested on her in silence. The breeze caught his hair, blowing it toward her, enveloping her like a veil.

She stood stunned at how beautiful his loose hair was and how soft it felt waving against her face. She closed her eyes to its caress. *I missed you.* Her lids lifted to find Caliostro staring down at her.

"What a surprising thought," he said, putting his hand on her cheek.

She covered his hand with her own, letting the truth come forth.

"Caught that thought, did you? You know it'll be harder to be around you, knowing that."

He smiled, leaning in, and she knew what was about to happen. "Have you eaten?" he whispered in her ear.

A blush rose from her cheeks to her temples. "No, but Duncan brought me food just before you arrived." She stepped backward so he could pass.

Just as she made to follow him, he turned back, crowding her.

She closed her eyes, and her back touched the glass door he had closed a second before she would have fallen through it.

"Alioson? Open your eyes." He stared into them as he moved closer. "I missed you as well." His mouth rested softly against hers before he teased the upper lip with the tip of his tongue.

Her eyelids languidly closed again. Heat trickled throughout her body, and a trimmer pooled in her belly in anticipation.

Caliostro lifted her, hugging her to him.

Alioson's feet dangled as she pushed into the kiss, wrapping both arms around his back.

He spun, putting her down. "You should eat something." He pulled back and leaned his forehead against hers.

"I'm not that hungry." Her stomach rumbled, proving her a liar. "Okay, maybe a little."

Caliostro laughed, released her, and straightened his suit jacket. "You eat, and I'll see you later."

After he left, Alioson ate her fill, showered, and changed into a pair of black jeans and a white t-shirt. She pulled her hair into an upward ponytail and sat at the vanity. Her thoughts drifted to the dream. The man's hand was so big in her memory, and the room was dark. She could still feel how scared she had been. *If only I could recall his face ...*

Alioson closed her eyes and tried to conjure it to no avail. Her head dropped and rested on her forearm atop the vanity in pure defeat.

***

"Duncan, I need you on the terrace." He stood with his back to the open doorway, looking at the hazy sunlight as it glazed over his olive-colored skin.

"You called, Lord Masterson?" Duncan asked, standing in the doorway.

Caliostro closed his eyes and scanned Duncan's mind. The memory of his threat and iron grip on Alioson's arm played out. Caliostro had him by the throat, hanging from the air an instant later.

Duncan didn't grab for the hand that held him but looked down in silent defiance at Caliostro and his now glowing eyes.

"I'm sure I made myself clear, but I will state it clearer. You are not to worry about the relationship between me and Alioson. Do your job and protect when I say so. Move when I say, and do as I *say*!" He dropped a coughing Duncan and resumed gazing at the hazy light above, hands resting in his pant pockets.

Duncan watched Caliostro's back as he rubbed his sore neck. "I will protect you even when you can't see my reasoning, Lord. It's my purpose."

"I don't need your protection. If you have ever thought of us as friends, never violently lay your hands on her again. Is that clear?"

Duncan bowed his head and disappeared inside without another word.

Caliostro sighed. His anger cooled with the sound of Alioson's bedroom door opening from above.

***

Alioson descended the stairs. She saw the terrace doors were open but headed for the empty room with the section of padded floor instead. Upon entering she searched for a light switch. After blindly feeling around near the door, her hand found it. Ceiling lights and a chandelier illuminated the space. Windows lined the three walls with gold trim beneath them, accenting the room to match the rest of the manor.

She moved to the padded part of the floor and stopped to remove her slippers before stepping onto it. Closing her eyes, she conjured the memory of her mother and the man with blood on his face. All she could hear was her own breathing bouncing off the walls as she focused. After several minutes, nothing new came to her. Sighing aloud, she opened her eyes and fell to a sitting position on the floor.

Leaning back on her hands, she spotted the weapons rack she had noticed on her first visit here. She approached the rack and pulled a mid-sized broad sword from its resting place. She swung it out to her right side, but the blade halted.

"Caliostro?"

His posture was relaxed, even though he had stopped a blade with his bare hand.

"I see you felt inclined to exercise." He released the blade, and she placed it on the rack.

Pulling off his jacket, he walked to the padded floor, then rolled his dress shirt sleeves before facing her and waving her over. "If you want to exercise, I'm more than happy to assist you." He smiled, resting a hand in his pocket.

"I don't see why I'd need help with exercising." She folded her arms. "The need to jog my memory brought me here. I felt something when I was in here before."

"Oh, is that so?" he asked, giving her a once over, then circled her. "You look able enough. Should I show you some basics and test what you know?"

She followed him with her eyes. "I guess I'll try almost anything to get my memory back."

"Okay then, let's try a few things, shall we?" He stopped in front of her.

She nodded in return.

Caliostro threw a straight punch at her face, slowing the speed and impact.

She dodged, smacking his wrist in the same movement.

"Not bad," he said, the left corner of his mouth lifting. Next, he threw a kick and back fist at her, which she defended rather easily. He noticed she wouldn't allow him to get behind her. *Oh, she has been trained.*

She was sweating lightly, but obviously sparring or fighting wasn't new to her.

"Okay, let's stop. I think it's safe to say you have training." He bent to retrieve his suit jacket.

She sat on the floor with her legs folded. "But I still don't recall where I would have learned how to fight."

"Or why," he said, more to himself than her. He studied her, still unsure of who she was.

"I've been wanting to ask you something. I just don't know how to say it."

He waited, but she said nothing. Caliostro stooped in front of her, the hems of his dress pants rising with the movement.

Alioson's nails dug into the palms, and her knuckles protruded.

Caliostro kneeled and grabbed both her hands before she could correct the action. He lifted the open palm of each to his lips and blew. His gaze locked with hers a second before she looked away. "You can tell me, whatever it is. There's no need to be nervous." He released both hands and sat next to her.

Alioson followed his movement but glanced down and away for a moment. "I wanted to talk about the"—she wriggled her fingers and looked about the room— "exchange and inner force thing."

Caliostro stretched his legs in front of him. "Of course, we can talk about that. What would you like to know?"

She faced him, took a deep breath, then exhaled.

Caliostro stared back, not breaking contact, which prompted his usual glow to show itself.

Alioson blushed at the implication. "So, exchanging …" She wrung her hands together.

"Whatever you need to ask, there's no wrong way to do so. Please speak freely." He lifted a hand in invitation.

She leaned forward. "Does it work like the way vampires drinking blood works?"

"And how much do you know of vampires?"

"Just about what most people know, I guess. Memory loss is an odd thing. I can't recall where I lived or the people I knew, but I recall my education but not where I received it or the things I've done. Anyway, I'm not sure what's correct."

"Well, to answer your question, it's not really like vampire feedings or blood exchanges. It's a stronger connection and more permanent, you could say. As you know, it occurs differently than drinking blood." His gaze fell to her lips.

"Don't stare at me like that, Caliostro. You're making this harder."

Caliostro exploded into full-on laughter.

Alioson's eyes widened in shock. "What? What's so funny?"

"More of your thoughts have leaked through." His laugh ended in a light chuckle. "Also, I cannot do as you command. I find it difficult not to feed my sight with you."

Alioson's body heated. "How can you just say that to my face without batting an eyelash?"

"Hiding my attraction for you has proven difficult. But if you wish, I could try harder."

"I didn't say that," she whispered, holding her head down. She looked back up to see his eyes held unrestrained hunger, and the glow had intensified. "Caliostro, I need to know who I am, and I know you're somehow the key to that."

"Am I? How did you come to that conclusion?"

"When vampires and or supernatural beings feed on blood or inner force, can there be a connection through memories?"

"From what I know, yes, there can be. A vampire may see memories from the human they have fed from, and if blood is exchanged, then some vampire's memories can pass to the human."

Alioson nodded.

"Why do you ask?" He leaned toward her.

"After we had the exchange on the terrace, I believe I had a memory return." She looked anywhere but at him. When she refocused on him, his eyes had dimmed.

"Though it came to me as a dream," she said, trying to center attention on her own words and not his eyes.

"And you think what?"

"I think I remembered it only because you exchanged with me."

"It could be possible, but you could have simply remembered because it was time."

"I don't buy that. It seems connected, and I want to test the theory."

"I'm not sure I understand what you're trying to say. I need you to say what you want, whatever, this theory of yours is." His eyes exposed his arousal, and his breathing changed in anticipation of her next words.

She stood and stepped in front of him. "Caliostro, I need you to help me remember who I am. Please, I need to know who I am, where I came from, where I was going, and why I'm here, and ..." Tears streaked her face.

He was on his feet, wiping them away before they could touch her chin.

She grabbed both his wrists and stared into his gaze, her hands shaking. "I need you to kiss me, exchange with me. I think it's linked to unlocking my memories somehow."

"Alioson, you ask a very dangerous thing, though I'm not opposed. I've only exchanged with you and one other person in my existence." He pushed a few loose strands of hair behind her ear. "And to do so, however many times, to recover your lost memories, I am unaware of the potential effects it could cause."

"Can't we at least try?"

"Listen, the not knowing is the part I don't like, and …" He looked over her head.

Alioson grabbed one of his hands to make him look at her. "I need to know. I can't just stay here, never knowing. What if I never remember on my own? It's not like I can see a doctor here."

"Even if your memory returns, how will you pass back through the veil"

"Maybe if I can remember how I got here, I can figure out how to return home!"

"I understand, but you are asking—"

"I know what I'm asking. It's my decision, so please, can you try for me?" She clung to his hand. "We haven't known each other that long, but I feel our connection, and I believe you want to keep me safe. I feel you want to help me."

The light of his blue gaze intensified. He gripped the hand holding his and pulled her against him. They both stood still, staring into each other's eyes. He felt her heart thumping against his chest.

Alioson's lids drifted close.

Their pulses beat in sync as he took her mouth, first gently, then feverishly. *"I wish to protect you. You're being etched deeper into my heart, though it's as if you've always been there."*

Tears escaped the corners of Alioson's eyes, and her heart wrenched at the gentle words.

Caliostro took his time kissing her. He wrapped his arms around her waist, changing angles of the kiss, and sucked in her lower lip.

Alioson took the cue and wrapped both arms around his neck, holding on to him. Her feet came off the floor as he lifted and tightened his grip. A whoosh of air had her back pressed firmly against the far wall. Alioson gasped into his mouth, arching her back. She moaned aloud, licking and nibbling his bottom lip, then abruptly broke the kiss.

Caliostro's eyes fluttered open.

"Did the exchange start? I didn't feel the pull like last time," she questioned, looking confused.

Caliostro chuckled. "No, you wouldn't have. When it's not life threatening, I like to take my time." He paused, sliding the pad of his thumb across her swollen lower lip. "But I still don't think we should. It's just too risky." He released her and glanced away.

Alioson tightened her grip, halting him. "And I think we should, and I don't care about the risks."

"I can't let the same thing happen, not again." He pulled down both her arms and stepped backward.

"Caliostro," she began, moving toward him, but he was gone. Alioson leaned back against the wall and slid to the floor. She cradled her knees and sighed in frustrated defeat.

DESIRES OF LOSS

Caliostro decided that distance between them would be for the best. He returned to his office to pack important documents into his black leather briefcase. Once completed, he sat and fell into deep thought. *I need to be away from her, but she may be in danger if I'm gone too long. Our connection is much weaker on the mortal side. I just don't know.*

A knock came at the door.

"Enter."

Duncan came in, shut the door behind him, and bowed his head in greeting. "Lord Masterson."

"What is it?"

"I'll be leaving this evening for a few days."

"And you're informing me, why?" He scoffed.

"With the recent attacks and your sister showing herself as of late, I figured I should inform you of my whereabouts."

He spun in his chair to peer out the window. "Do what you must."

Duncan stared at the back of Caliostro's chair a few moments before turning to leave.

"Do well in your report to my grandfather," Caliostro said before he heard the door close.

Well, there goes my thoughts on leaving, at least till he returns. I still need to stay clear of her as much as possible.

Over the next few days, Caliostro found any reason he could to avoid Alioson. One evening, he heard light footfalls on the foyer stairs as he was coming in from the terrace at dusk. He stood frozen in the doorway.

The hazy sunlight cascaded overhead, and a dusting of the light illuminated her tanned skin. She wore a short flowing ice blue miniskirt and a matching off-the-shoulder body-fitting top. Her hair hung loose around her shoulders, and she was barefoot.

When she reached the last few steps, he dashed away to enter the manor again from the kitchen. Once in his office, he reviewed documents for his trip that he planned to leave for upon Duncan's return.

***

Alioson saw the terrace doors open and went to see if Caliostro was about. She stepped through the doorway. Seeing no one, she went to the dining hall. Upon entering, she saw a placement had been set for her. *Still avoiding me, I see.*

Alioson sat and waited. On the table were two silver buckets, one with ice and one with chilled wine. After a few moments, the door at the back of the hall opened. Alioson's eyes widened in shock as a young woman wearing a black pair of relaxed dress pants, white blouse, and a serving apron approached her with a tray in hand. A strange blue hazy light surrounded the woman.

"Hello," Alioson said in greeting.

The woman placed the tray in front of her, smiled, bowed her head, then turned to leave.

"Wait!" Alioson grabbed for the woman's arm. Her hand passed through, unable to make contact. She screamed, pushing herself backward to escape their proximity. Her chair fell over with her in it.

"Ow."

The young woman continued toward the exit.

Alioson looked at her hand, then at the open doorway. A chill ran down her spine as she watched it close.

***

Caliostro sat, organizing budget spreadsheets, when he heard Alioson scream. He dropped the paperwork and rushed from his office toward the dining hall. He spotted Duncan's corporeal summons heading toward the kitchen at the far end of the hallway.

Caliostro found Alioson righting a fallen chair. "Alioson? I heard you scream. Is anything amiss?"

"Do you have ghosts here? I swear I saw a ghost or something."

"That was a corporeal summons Duncan left to take care of the manor while he's away."

"Well, that explains it." She laughed nervously and rolled her eyes. "Just a corporeal summons, sure."

"I'm sorry I hadn't had time to inform you of that. You may see a few more about the manor until he returns."

"Everyone here sure has interesting abilities. So, is Duncan also a vampire or …?"

Caliostro took the chair at the head of the table as she reclaimed her seat. "No, Duncan is a Mystrelk."

"A what?"

"His kind is born of magic; they have attributes like vampires, but they aren't vampires."

"Okay then. Well, back on topics of things I can understand. Why have you been avoiding me?" She leaned toward him.

"Because it's for the best."

"So, you just decided that for me?"

He sighed. "I'm trying my best to protect you."

"What are you protecting me from? You? You're not what I need protecting from."

Caliostro's eyes went cold, and his lips formed a hard line. "You know nothing. You don't know what I'm capable of, nor my past transgressions." The silence of the room was deafening as his eyes bore into hers.

"And whose fault is that? You are the one who disappears and leaves me hanging. You!" Alioson pushed her chair backward and marched toward the foyer.

Caliostro grabbed her wrist, making her fall against him. "Are you sure you won't regret it?" He placed her free hand over her own heart. "It's racing and laced with fear. Don't try so hard." He released her and stepped past.

Alioson took hold of his wrist to stop his retreat and narrowed her gaze at him. "Regret is a part of life and something I can't predict. And I think you can tell the difference between fear and want."

Caliostro clenched his teeth in frustration, grabbed her to him, and claimed her lips. *Damn my weakness.*

***

Alison fell into the rhythm of the kiss, giving into the heat of his body. His hand cradled the back of her head, then one hand slowly slid down the side of her neck as their kiss changed direction. They both moaned in synchronicity, their tongues battling feverously. The exchange began. Caliostro slowed the kiss, and she followed his lead. With each gentle sweep of his tongue against hers, a small amount of their energy sapped equally.

Alioson soon lost herself in the ecstasy of it. The slow build of tingling that had begun in her belly now rose to her chest and pooled behind her eyes and reversed at the same time. Neither of them could think as the exchange went into full effect.

***

Caliostro felt the pull of her inner force deepen. The exchange was powerful as he let his own force flow into her. He lifted her onto the dining hall table, not breaking the kiss.

Alioson took the cue and wrapped her legs around his waist, making her dress gather at the hips.

I must stop. His grip on her tightened, nails digging into her waist. The draw and give of their inner force increased with each passing moment. A shockwave of electricity slammed into him.

Her back arched forward, and her head fell back, breaking the kiss. Alioson's full upper body fell back over his forearm, and her gaping blue pupils glowed.

Another wave hit him, accompanied by flashes of Alioson, making him stagger, but he held onto her.

Alioson's body jerked in his arms, then stilled, her eyes falling closed.

"Alioson!" He shook her.

No response.

Caliostro rested his head on her chest and ground his teeth in anger. He carried her to her room and lay her atop the sheets. He sensed multiple energies on the edge of his property. *More hunters lurking.*

Caliostro shucked from his suit jacket and threw it across the nearby chair. He pulled open the balcony doors and glanced at her before shutting them and taking flight.

***

Darkness filled her vision, and a smell of stale urine and waste turned her stomach. A rustling sound on the right made her startle. Her small hands pushed into a cold wet puddle at her back, and she wiped them on already soiled clothes. "Anyone there?"

"Shh. It's best if you just stay quiet," a raspy voice said.

Alioson slid her bottom backward until her back touched a wall. "Where is this?" The image of the man with scary glowing eyes hurting her mother replayed in her head. "Mommy," she whimpered.

"Be quiet. Look, I know you're new here, but you had better get with the program, and fast," the same voice whispered closer to her.

Alioson turned toward the voice but couldn't decipher their face in the dark.

A light shined from an arched opening some feet away. A taller boy with shaggy hair stood near her. Through the opening stepped a man holding a flashlight, illuminating parts of the room as it swung back and forward, searching.

Alioson saw a lot of other kids, all different ages. Some were huddled in corners or curled up on the wet floor. The walls looked like stone, and pieces of old wood furniture were thrown about with lumps of cloth here and there.

"Come, little one. It's time for you to be tested. And, you!" The man pointed at the boy who had spoken to her. "Come along as well! And don't give me any trouble."

Alioson shrunk more against the wall as the man turned to lead the way.

The boy grabbed her hand to pull her along.

"No! Let me go!" She tried to pull her small hand from his grasp, but he was quick to silence her.

"Shut up. What have I said? Just do as you are told and you will live, okay?"

She stopped fighting him and wiped at the tears staining her small chubby cheeks with her free hand, smearing her face with even more dirt. "What is this place?" she whispered.

"It's your new home and where we're trained."

"What training?"

The man leading them turned and shushed them both.

They traversed a dark hallway and climbed a pair of spiral steps, then stopped at a large red wooden door.

"In there, you two. Hurry." He pushed them both into a well-lit room, with gray stone floors and white brick walls.

The boy released her hand and walked to the center of the room, fully visible now. Dust, grime, and wetness covered his black clothes. His shoulder-length hair was too dirty to tell whether it was brown or blond.

Alioson ran to catch up to him.

"No! Stay there. Don't come near me or else I may hurt you when I change."

She halted and watched his clothes rip as his flesh underneath pushed through.

He bent over, holding his stomach, then fell to his knees. A terrifying sound of bone snapping followed.

Someone grabbed her from behind and tucked her under their arm. They carried her out the room. The boy, down on all fours and screaming, was the last sight she caught before the door shut.

"Let me go!" She kicked and gripped at the arm around her waist.

They carried her down corridor after corridor, which were clean and well-lit compared to others.

"Where are you taking me?"

The person didn't answer and kept walking.

"Mommy!" Alioson's energy waned, her arms and legs hung.

"Good, you're finally quiet. All that screaming was really getting on my nerves. If I put you down, will you hold my hand like a good little girl?" The voice was feminine, but Alioson couldn't see her face. The woman's forearm tightened around her middle.

She nodded, not knowing what else to do.

"I can't hear you. You are to answer when asked a question here."

"Yes."

"Good." She lowered Alioson to the floor.

Her legs gave out from under her, and she fell.

Alioson didn't look until the woman said, "Look at me."

Hesitantly, she met the dark brown eyes of a long black-haired woman.

"I'm called Vadeina, and I will be your trainer." She stooped in front of Alioson to scrutinize her. "You're young, but that doesn't mean I'll take it easy on you. What's your name, and how old are you?"

Alioson didn't answer.

"I *said*, what's your name and age? Don't make me ask again."

"Alioson, Alioson Acharya."

"And how old are you?"

"I'm seven."

"Hmm …" She sucked her teeth. "I can't believe I'm stuck training a baby." She frowned, sighing heavily.

"I'm not a baby!"

"Yeah, sure." Vadeina shook her head, standing once again. "Okay, on your feet."

Alioson stood.

"I've got my work cut out for me." Sighing, she took Alioson's hand and led her to a smooth white door down the next corridor. "Alright, I want you to go into this room, wash yourself, and change into the clothes that fit you. I'll be back in thirty minutes. Be ready, got it?"

Alioson nodded, looking around.

Vadeina slid a keycard across the panel next to the door.

Alioson investigated the entrance of the dark room but made no move to go farther in.

"There's nowhere else for you to go." She shoved Alioson from behind, making lights shine from above. "Now get changed."

The door slid closed, leaving Alioson alone. Fear sat in. Alioson realized the white walls had no windows. She strode past a twin-sized bed and a dresser to open the only other two doors. One was a closet with containers and hangers. The other was a bathroom. Tears threatened to overflow. She knew no one was coming to save her.

Alioson did as the woman had instructed and bathed herself quickly with just a wet cloth. She found jeans and a t-shirt, along with a comb. She dressed, leaving her hair a knotted mess. She waited by the main door and noticed a wall mirror. The face that stared back at her was wide eyed, tear stained, and worrisome.

She recalled the man biting into her mother's neck. A deep scowl and clenched jaw replaced her previous appearance. Anger boiled to the surface. She picked up the nearest thing, a decorative silver bowl, and smashed it into the mirror, shattering it. The broken pieces reflected her haggard face staring back.

***

Caliostro flew in the direction he'd felt the hunters' energy. His eyes widened when he sensed Duncan's energy added to the group of at least three—and Duncan made four. He burst forward in his haste to reach the area faster.

Once within range, he heard battling and saw flashes of light from below.

Duncan wore his usual attire of dress pants, dress shirt, and vest in an array of dark gray tones. He flipped and dashed about, fighting the hunters.

Caliostro moved to descend but stopped.

"I can handle them, Milord."

Caliostro watched, suspended in the air, but ready to intervene if there was a need.

Duncan's short bangs lay against his sweat-covered brow, his silver hair glistening in the hazy moonlight. He leaped into the air and shot a ball of blue fire over the head of one hunter, whose bones snapped and changed, to burn the decomposed flesh of one creature. He focused on fighting the Lycrians who had transformed.

Both beasts rushed him.

He made quick work of the two, using magic to hold one encased in a fireball, and the other he kicked in the neck, knocking it to the ground. Before the beast could get to its feet, he snapped his fingers, burning it asunder.

Caliostro landed moments later next to Duncan, who stooped to investigate the remains of the first creature he had set ablaze. "A Dadrangrul slave?" Caliostro inquired.

"Yes, a pretty nasty one at that." Duncan saw in the leftover mess of sticky flesh that seven Dagaru Worms had inhabited the host's corpse. "I think we are seeing more attacks due to Miss Alioson's presence. Living humans don't reside here, so besides the Hunters Guild, we have random attacks now from those picking up her scent." He stood and spied Caliostro from the corner of his eye.

Caliostro ran one hand through the front of his hair to lift it back and up out of his face. He stared at the leftover corpses, knowing Duncan was correct. "So, it would seem. Yet there's not much I can do about that, since I have no obvious way of getting her through the veil."

Duncan nodded in agreement.

"Burn the rest, and I'll see you back at the manor," Caliostro said and took to the air.

Duncan set the remains on fire. Nothing was left when the flames died down.

**

Alioson's eyes fluttered open, and she sat upright. Tears streaked her face. *Are all my memories going to be like this?* She closed her eyes again and found herself in the center of the bed under a blanket. The room was dark; only the fireplace illuminated some of it. She glanced toward the bedroom door and felt the swift movement of expensive cotton sliding against skin that was not her own and the smell of sandalwood and citrus—Caliostro. *I couldn't figure out what the mixed scent was before, but now, somehow, it's familiar.*

A knock sounded.

"Come in," she answered. Her gaze froze on him. It was like seeing him for the first time.

A glow emanated from him. His long black hair hung loose, but it glistened with every move. His muscles contracted under his white long-sleeve shirt with every breath, and his eyes were like blue moons hovering over an illuminated sun.

How can he even be real? I know this isn't a dream, but I may have gone crazy.

Caliostro stopped in his approach. "Is something wrong?"

She forced herself to look away.

"Am I so captivating that you must look away?" He sat on the edge of the bed.

She looked back at him. "Are you reading my thoughts again?"

"Yes. Although a few thoughts slip through to me, even when I'm not trying." He smiled. "But most of those are only incoherent mumblings."

"I see." She rolled her eyes and glanced to the side.

"Are you angry?" he asked with a chuckle.

"Yes and no." She quickly rose from the bed and moved toward the bathroom.

Caliostro grabbed and hugged her from behind, not fully holding her but letting her rest against him. "Did any memories return to you while you slept?"

152

"Nothing I can understand yet, but when it all comes together, I will share." She felt him nod in agreement.

He turned her in his arms, smiled down with reassurance, then pulled her close again.

Did I ever have such a look directed at me before? she pondered, taking in his scent.

"How are you? That trancelike sleep took you again."

"I feel better now I'm awake."

His arms tightened around her an instant before moving away.

"Please don't," she pleaded.

He froze, then tightened his hold again, resting his chin atop her head. "As you wish."

"I'm okay. I recalled more, so we know it works."

"I've never withdrawn or exchanged with anyone to help them recover lost memories." He paused to glance at her. "This is new to me as well. I want to be careful and not hurt you." He inclined his chin. "Your energy feels different when it flows into me. I can only explain it as … something I have been missing returning to me."

She smiled at his words, feeling the truth in them.

"I want to claim you. I want to keep you. That's what screams inside my head. I haven't been afraid in a long time, but now …"

Alioson leaned her head back to get a better view of his face. She lifted her hand and traced his brow, down and around his jawline, ending with his lips. "I want to say don't be afraid, but I'm also afraid, not knowing fully who I am yet. Also, I don't understand half of what's happening around me. I'm in this fantasy, but it's also my reality—and a nightmare." She lowered her head and snuggled into his embrace.

He held her until her growling stomach broke the silence. "I think dinner is in order, yes?" He stepped backward and released her.

Alioson felt the immediate loss of him.

Caliostro's tone became very casual and light. "What would you like? I can have anything prepared for you. Just name it." He grabbed her hand and lead her toward the bedroom door.

Alioson pulled back. "Wait, I will not have dinner dressed like this." She laughed.

He looked confused. "Why not? It's only us, and that's what you were wearing earlier when you were to dine."

"This coming from the guy who is always decked out in a three-piece suit. No, I want to change. And I've been meaning to ask you about the full-on wardrobe." She pointed toward the bathroom.

"Ah, that." He placed both hands in his pocket.

She looked perplexed at his silence. "Is it an answer that requires thought?"

"Well, no. However, you may not like the answer."

"And why is that?" Her heart skipped a beat.

Caliostro took her hands in his.

She pulled them away and stepped backward.

"Our relationship is changing. You are important, and I want to be honest with you."

"Then please, be honest."

"This room and everything in it was waiting for someone else."

"Obviously. So, who is she?" Her heart sank.

"Someone I'll tell you about later." He scooped up his abandoned suit jacket. "See you downstairs." He left without another word.

Alioson stared at the closed door. *So, all this was for someone else? Of course, it was.* She went to the closet and found a one-sleeve, body-fitting, open-backed black dress that pooled at her feet. She hadn't looked through the shoes yet but found some black stilettos with silver-tipped ends.

She checked inside the shoe for its size—seven. The shoes she had worn so far had been flex style and could fit most feet within range. *Whoever this woman was, I guess we wear the same size.*

She wore her hair pinned up, leaving loose strands in the front. A touch of makeup came next, some dark eyeliner to enhance her eyes and lip gloss. *It feels good to dress up like this. I wonder if I enjoyed it in the past.* She stared at herself, turning left, then right in the mirror. *Time to find out who this woman was ... or is.*

UNLOCKED SECRETS

Caliostro waited in the dining hall, sipping a glass of red wine. He'd changed for dinner, into a relaxed styled two-piece black suit. Under it, he wore a white dress shirt opened at the collar. Eyelids fluttering closed, his thoughts wondered. *How do I tell her about Catherine? No matter how I explain it, she may distrust me. No one way sounds better than the other.*

Caliostro turned at the echo of Alioson's footsteps. When she rounded the corner, his heart stopped. "You look breathtaking." He set down his glass and approached her.

"Thank you, though I suppose I should also thank whoever this dress belongs to, yes?" she replied in an annoyed tone. She passed him, grabbing a glass of wine.

Caliostro sighed. "So, is there nothing you have to tell me? You said the exchange helped you recall more, but what more, you didn't say."

"There wasn't much. I would rather wait till I recall more of the puzzle. All I can say for now is it seems my mother is dead." She sipped the wine. "I saw her being killed when I was seven, from what I recall." Her tone was devoid of emotion, though he knew deep down the memory probably hurt.

"I'm so very sorry, Alioson."

"Thank you." She took small sips of wine.

"Let's move to the terrace. I thought dinner under the night sky would be nice. Or would you rather dine in here?"

"I'm not opposed to it." She headed straight for the foyer.

Duncan stood at the open terrace doors.

Caliostro noticed she hadn't greeted Duncan on her way out. He eyed Duncan as he passed him.

Duncan said nothing and closed the doors.

"Are you upset about the previous owner of the things in that room?"

She had her back to him, and he beheld the detailed muscles sculpted down her naked back. "Upset? No. What right do I have to be upset? Honestly, I'm a stranger here. I have no claim on you, no matter how things may seem in my head."

"Alioson, I …" His eyes looked all about before resettling on her.

She waited, not responding.

"I want to explain something to you, but I don't know how to say it."

"When you tell the truth, don't you just say it?"

He turned away and rubbed his hand through his hair. He placed both hands on his hips and pushed back his suit jacket at the waist.

They faced each other. The torch light danced all around them, casting shadows about the furniture. Duncan had set up a small table for two in the center of the terrace, which held the first course.

Caliostro approached her, but she stepped backward from his advance. He paused for a moment, then continued forward to lightly wrap one arm around her waist. His body heat encased her, but he did not pull her fully against him. The intense glow of his eyes stared into hers. "First, I have something to say. Never step away from me; I can't let you go. And I don't say that as a command. I say it as a plea."

Both their hearts raced.

"It sounded like a command." She looked away but didn't pull from his embrace.

"It's too late for me, so no matter what I tell you now, don't run away, because whether plea or command, I will chase you." He pulled her to him and cradled the back of her head against his shoulder.

At first, she didn't respond, then her arms wrapped around him.

A sigh escaped him. After a minute, he released her and sat on the couch next to the table where they were to dine. "Please?" He indicated she should sit across from him.

She sat and leaned back into the cushion.

Caliostro sat forward, tucking loose strands that had crawled from his hair tie behind his left ear. "Two centuries ago, I met a girl, a human girl inclined to magic, who later would become an enchantress. This girl grew into a woman who loved me—or, at least, what I was. I loved her in return, and that was her downfall."

"Two centuries ago? Then why do you still have a bedroom and everything set up for her?"

"You recall I have said, time and again, that I had only exchanged with two people in my long life."

She nodded.

"She was the other. Her name is Catherine, and she lives to this day."

Alioson's mouth fell open, then closed. She looked down and away, followed by a deep sigh. When she looked back at him, a slight frown had hardened her soft features.

"When I did a full exchange with her, she never woke again. To this day, she sleeps unchanged, in a comatose state." He paused, searching her face. "I am responsible for her. I watch over her, hoping one day she will awaken."

Alioson sat forward, studying her hands. She shook her head, then met his eyes. "Now I see why you have been so hesitant about doing an exchange with me. It all makes sense now. And what about Duncan?"

Caliostro looked confused. "What about him?"

"You two seem connected as well."

"That's because he is my watcher. There's a ritual behind that."

She nodded. "Is she here?"

"Not anymore."

"Not anymore? And when was the last time she was here?"

"I had her moved recently. I couldn't take a chance that the invading hunters would realize she was here, or that they were sent for her."

"I see …"

"What are you thinking? I would like it if you told me."

She got to her feet. "Well, I think we should eat."

Caliostro followed her, his brows drawing together in confusion. He pulled out Alioson's chair to seat her before he took his own. The first course was an almond pumpkin soup. Caliostro watched her from time to time, but she focused on her meal. The second course followed in the same fashion. He couldn't hold back and attempted to read her thoughts.

"I wish you wouldn't do that." She looked up from her plate and squinted at him, head cocked to the side. "I can feel the push of you entering my mind every time now. It wasn't like that before, but now it's obvious."

"I don't wish to, but your earlier response has me in the dark."

"Doesn't feel good, does it?"

"What?"

"Being in the dark." She finished her red wine.

"Humans don't always tell the truth."

She chortled. "And non-humans do?" She dropped her fork and stood.

Caliostro looked around, sensing Dalidah.

A force pulled Alioson into the air, her stiletto heels falling.

Caliostro flew after them.

Dalidah held Alioson by one arm and shot through the air.

"Let go!" Alioson swung through the air as wind ripped and pulled at her.

Laughing, Dalidah sped forward. "Are you sure about that? Not a problem." She released Alioson and flew off.

Caliostro caught her just before she could hit the ground. He set her down, turning to an approaching Duncan. "If you catch her, bring her to *me*!"

Duncan bowed his head and bolted in Dalidah's direction.

Caliostro inspected Alioson.

She was panting and looked angry. She recoiled from him, got to her feet, and headed toward the manor.

"Alioson, stop."

"I'm so done with this shit, being attacked, not knowing anything."

Caliostro grabbed her forearm.

She jerked away, continuing.

A hair-splitting howl broke through the night.

Alioson stopped and eyed Caliostro just as he scooped her up and launched toward the manor.

"It's a trap. I was too distracted to sense them sooner! I must get you back inside now!"

Alioson held on tight.

The manor was in sight when something hit him between the shoulder blades, knocking the wind from his lungs.

Alioson screamed and fell from his arms.

He recovered quickly, catching her. The velocity of his landing made the ground burst around them, filling the air with dirt.

"Caliostro!" she screamed as a wall of fire engulfed the ground.

Caliostro's wings shot out and covered them both, deflecting the attack. When the flames dissipated, he stood, blocking Alioson with his body. Duncan's voice fluttered into Caliostro's mind.

"I'm not far."

"It's too late, Duncan. They won't wait for you to arrive."

Alioson shook with fear, her eyes trained on the four massive beasts running at them.

Caliostro fixated on them. *A fifth hunter is hiding somewhere. These beasts did not make a wall of fire.* He placed his left hand over the opal necklace, his eyes aglow with fire, and he called his sword forth.

The first werewolf reached them. Caliostro spun around and sliced with an upper arc, then down, killing it instantly. He flipped and took the head of an Lycrian that reached for Alioson, then spun again. He grabbed the next werewolf by the neck and twisted midair, slicing the last one, before pushing the one he held a good twelve feet from him.

It rolled and tumbled but landed on its feet.

Caliostro jumped and landed behind the massive beast.

Growling, it swung behind its back.

Caliostro dodged and landed on the beast's outstretched arm.

The Lycrian snapped its ferocious jaws, giving him the opening he wanted.

He shoved his sword into its mouth and pulled upward, splitting its head. Blood and brain matter squirted. The four beasts' pieces lay scattered at his feet and around Alioson.

She had closed her eyes and was on the ground, holding her legs to her chest.

Duncan arrived.

"Find the sorcerer. They may have run off or are still nearby."

"I'm on it." Duncan disappeared in a blur.

Caliostro approached Alioson, only to stop and stare at his blade. It had turned the color of onyx. He held it up, trying to figure out what was happening. His eyes and wings also turned the same color.

Alioson looked up finally. "Caliostro?"

166

He was a bit of a distance away, but he trudged toward her, his wings now dark as night.

She scrambled up from the ground. "Caliostro? What's wrong?" she shouted while backing away from his advancement.

Lycrians' blood covered him. Drops and splatters dotted his face, and the onyx-fuming eyes made him look every bit a monster.

She saw his sword disappear from his hand, but he was no less threatening. With an unsteady stumble backward, she turned to run. She had moved only a few feet before he grabbed her waist and pulled her back against him.

His hand moved like lightning to rip off the sleeve side of her dress and expose both shoulders. Fangs protruded from his mouth.

She attempted to scream and push him away, but all her moving ceased when he bit her neck. He drank her blood so fast her eyes rolled into the back of her head.

"*Caliostro*!" Duncan screamed.

Caliostro's eyes returned to normal, and his wings followed. He came back to his senses as Alioson went limp in his arms.

167

BUSINESS OF THE UNNATURAL

The taste of her blood lingered on Caliostro's tongue. After regaining his senses, he acted fast, giving her inner force. His eyes bore into her still form as the wound closed. He gathered her close and returned to the manor.

Moments later, he laid her down. *What happened to me? How could I hurt her like that? How could I?* He repeated the condemning questions in his head.

Alioson mumbled, her head tossing side to side.

His eyes glassed over, and his heart caught in his throat. He left Alioson's room and went to the terrace.

Duncan stood behind him, silently watching.

"What happened to me, Duncan?"

He stepped closer. "I'm not sure. What do you recall?"

"I recall killing the Lycrians, then looking in Alioson's direction when I felt this cloak of darkness fall over me." He raised his hands and lowered them on either side of him for emphasis. "And then I only recall seeing her unconscious form, blood dripping down her neck." He shuddered.

"You may not want to answer this, but did you enjoy it?"

Caliostro glared at him. "Did you honestly ask me that?"

Duncan raised both brows high, looked down, and sighed. "You know what blood courses through your veins."

"Yes, however, in all my centuries, I have never desired blood. Even after my blood connection with Dalidah, never have I had bloodlust."

Duncan looked skyward, locking his hands behind his back. "I wish I had some knowledge to share of what runs through your veins and what that mixture has born. One cannot know those facts until one knows." Duncan placed one hand on his shoulder in comfort.

"How will she ever trust me again? How could I ever ask her to? Or face her, for that matter?" Caliostro hung his head, rubbing the back of his neck. "Duncan, I need you to keep her within the manor walls while I'm away, and I need you to protect her, as if she were me."

Duncan looked shocked. "Are you sure now's the time for you to leave?"

"I need time away from her, and I need to investigate a way to return her to her world, if possible. Can you make an inquiry with my grandfather's pack?"

"Yes."

"Don't go into details as to the reason behind the request. You know what—"

"I got it."

"I'm counting on you."

Duncan nodded, staring straight ahead.

Caliostro stood, watching the moon, lost and confused.

***

"Again? We do not have time for any more errors! Do you understand?"

"Yes, Vadeina, I understand." Alioson swung her sword again at her sparring partner, who was older by three years and taller than her.

He dodged her attack, sidestepping. "Come on, Ali, fight me for real. You should be able to at least take me, right?" He laughed, backflipping to avoid her kick.

I'll get you, Ashley. You won't see this next move coming. Alioson side kicked again, and Ashley backflipped. She moved in and swept her leg, but before he landed, he twisted and bounced over her, kicking her in the back. Alioson slammed into the stone wall, dropping her sword. She recovered fast, though blood ran from the corner of her mouth. She gritted her teeth, grabbed her sword, and charged at him.

"Alright, that's enough!"

Alioson froze and eyed Vadeina. "But why?"

"Don't speak. Those who are so easily defeated should stay silent and train harder, because, at the present time, you are worthless! You've been training for ten years, and you can't even beat a Lycrian?"

"But it's Ashley. He's not just some random—"

"Quiet! I'm done with your excuses." She left, slamming the door behind her.

"I fucking hate it here!" Alioson tossed her sword to the black-tiled floor.

"Don't worry about her, Ali. She has to be a hard ass to help you improve."

Alioson glared at him as he collected the shirt he had thrown off before they had sparred.

He probably hasn't even broken a sweat. They had been at it for hours. She pinched the fabric of her drenched tank top and pulled away its wetness.

Ashley moved toward her, his obliques undulating with every step. Dark brown hair fell to his mid back, the ends glistening.

Alioson ogled him. She'd never say it, but she had a huge crush. *Oh, so he was at least a little affected by the fight.*

His piercing lavender eyes locked on her, and his smirk turned into a full-blown smile.

"Fuck you, Ashley. You didn't have to hit me so hard!" She balled her fists.

Ashley pulled a black t-shirt over his head and lifted out his long hair once it was in place.

Alioson shrieked as Ashley pinned her against the back wall.

He moved his knee between her legs, while one of his hands held both her wrists above her head.

Once the initial surprise wore off, she scowled at him.

He leaned in, smelling her along the neckline, and both top lateral incisors grazed her collarbone. "Oh, Ali, I'd love to fuck you."

"Hmm, promises. You going to let me down?"

"In a second." He looked her in the eye. "You know you have so much potential, Ali. Something's hidden deep within you that's not quite human."

Alioson squirmed but stayed put.

"Your scent is human but with a hidden undertone." He leaned in again, taking another sniff. "Yet I'm unsure what you are. Do you even know yourself, little Ali?" He laughed, releasing her wrists, and backed away.

Alioson cast her eyes down, resting one hand over her pounding heart. She looked back up and jumped at him, wrapping both legs around his waist. She grabbed a fist full of his hair. "Yes, a fire's burning within me, but I'm still human!" Her mouth covered his as her hand fisted in his hair.

Ashley reciprocated, wrapping his arms around her.

The room darkened, warning lights flashed, and sirens blared. "All hunters report to the main gate," a male voice repeated over the intercom.

"What the hell?" Ashley leaned back from Alioson.

She slid down his body as the lights flashed. "What's happening? Are we under attack again?"

"Yeah, looks that way." He smiled at her. "But they have the worst timing."

Alioson blushed, looking away.

"How can you act all bashful when you just climbed me?" He laughed, adjusting his sweats.

"We better report to the gate," she said, moving past him.

He grabbed her hand and pulled her back. "And where do you think you're going, huh, trainee?" He held her firm when she tried to wriggle from his grip.

"Why can't I go?" she yelled, still pulling away.

"The call said hunters, and you haven't graduated yet, so you stay here, and I'll be back." He released her and ran for the door.

"Come on, Ashley! That's not fair!" she said, but he had already run out. "I bet it's those fucking vampires again." She pulled herself together, sheathing her sword, and followed despite his words. Her heart raced with excitement as she ran through corridor after corridor. She reached the gate but hid to eavesdrop when she saw Ashley standing with a group of elite hunters.

"Yeah, it's them again. After Cordaglen killed their maker, they have been attacking us nonstop," a hunter, with coal-black hair tipped in white, said.

"I don't know why we didn't just finish them all off," another hunter chimed in.

She placed her hand on her sword's hilt and waited.

A young female vampire scaled the gate and charged the nearest hunter. Her head rolled upon the ground almost immediately.

"Yup, untrained," Alioson whispered, still waiting in the shadows. She scanned the hunters waiting for the next attack and noticed Ashley was missing. Before she could react, two large hands closed around her wrists and locked them behind her back.

"Who's untrained? 'Cause, unless you're talking about yourself, it's irrelevant." Ashley shoved her away before she could retaliate and stepped toward her. "Didn't I tell you to stay put and wait for me?"

She glared at him over her shoulder. "You said stay put but nothing about waiting for you, so ..." She folded her arms and watched the hunters fighting back more vampires. "I'll do what I want."

"You need to follow orders, Alioson." His voice turned serious, making her face him when he used her full name and not the nickname he had coined.

"I want to fight, and I'm ready!"

"You say that, but your actions say otherwise." He glanced at the other hunters. "I have to get back. You head inside."

"I don't want to!"

"Ashley," Vadeina said, joining them, "let her fight. That's the only way she'll learn."

Alioson stepped around Ashley and locked her gaze with Vadeina's. "I can do it." She ran toward the group of vampires, flipped into the center of them, and smiled. "Let's go!" She swung her sword at the nearest assailant.

***

Alioson's eyes fluttered open. Once they focused, she discerned the ceiling of her bedroom at Caliostro's manor. The smell of sandalwood and citrus surrounded her. *Caliostro?* Alioson felt overcome with lethargy but pushed herself to a sitting position. She surveyed the empty room, sighing.

A sharp pain shot through her head, making her clamp a hand on either side. The memory of black eyes and Caliostro biting her neck jumped to the forefront of her mind. Her hand shook as it rested where the wound would have been.

"Alioson," Caliostro said, entering and closing the door.

Alioson regarded him, then glanced away. "What happened to you? I thought you didn't drink blood. But you …" She squeezed her eyes shut.

"Alioson, I don't know what happened. I honestly cannot explain it. And no, I don't drink blood. I have never drank it. All I can conclude is my Lycrian side must have manifested beyond my control." He took a few steps toward the bed. "I never meant to hurt you."

She furrowed her brows, and her mouth opened and closed.

Caliostro moved to take hold of her hands, but she jerked away before he made contact. He backed away, staring at her. "I'm not surprised you're afraid of me now, nor can I blame you."

"I'm not. I just feel tired, and I want a shower."

"Alioson, I can sense what you're feeling, so be honest with me."

She said nothing as she got up from the other side of the bed.

"If I frighten you, I want to make it right."

"How would you do that, even if it were the case? If I'm afraid of you, how do you think you can just change it back?"

Caliostro's gaze darted around, his frustration apparent.

"Like I said, I'm not afraid. Confused, yes. But I think that's *normal*!"

"No, normal would be you running out of here, getting as far away from me as possible. Aren't you disgusted with me? I could have killed you."

"Do you want me to be afraid of you? I would think you'd be glad I'm willing to understand."

He looked away. "Willing to understand and not being afraid of me are two completely different things."

"Caliostro, I understand you weren't in control of yourself, because if you were, I believe you would have never done such a thing."

"But it still doesn't—"

She held up her hand to silence him. "No matter what you say, I'm okay now, and I won't run away, not that I could go anywhere really. And didn't you say you'd chase after me?" She smiled, though it didn't reach her eyes. "I'm going to take a long, hot shower, get out of these clothes, and rest a bit more. I still feel tired."

He looked unsure but obliged. "I will send Duncan up with something for you to eat." He turned to leave.

"Will you bring it? I would like to see you after my shower."

"I can't. I must leave on urgent business."

"How long will you be gone this time?"

"However long it takes. I have put things in place, so you will be protected." He left before she could ask more.

Alioson closed the bathroom door behind her and slid to the floor as tears streaked her face, but she quickly dashed them away. "No, you will not do that," she chastised herself, getting up.

She removed the ruined gown and threw it to the floor. Her feet dragged, the energy within her body returning. At the sink, she inspected herself in the mirror. *Was I a hunter? If I am …* Staring at her reflection didn't give her any new answers, but Caliostro had unlocked memories hidden within her. *I was right; his inner force is freeing my memories.*

She leaned her neck to the side, seeing nothing but smooth skin. *Being afraid will not get my memories back. I won't run.*

"What would Caliostro think of me now, if he knew I was a hunter?"

Alioson stepped into the shower, letting the hot water rush over her.

***

Two Weeks Later

"Look, Colette, I don't date, nor do I have any interest in what you're offering on that front. You said you have the information I need, and I said we could do this collaboration." Caliostro lifted the file in front of him that read, *Free-Water Hotel Collaboration*. He slammed it down and spun his office chair to face the massive twelve-foot-pane glass windows.

Caliostro grabbed the bridge of his nose and sighed into the receiver. His gaze rested on the white marble floors, then he glanced up, the glaring sunlight making him squint. He twirled his chair back around.

"You don't need to sound so put out, Caliostro. I simply asked you to be my date at the dinner party tonight. What's the big deal?" Colette said in her usual sultry voice.

"I agreed to attend the dinner party so we can discuss the collaboration and you can give me the information you seem set on doing in person."

"Fine. I'll see you tonight, then." She hung up.

He hated to ask her for help. Caliostro had known Colette for a century, and she still sang the same tune. Now an ex-Magic Guild sorceress, he trusted her a little more. He had called on everyone he knew in the last couple of weeks since his return to mortal society. His search had led him to items related to bypassing the workings of the veil. Those in the Magic Guild had the most recorded knowledge since some of them were of human descent.

Caliostro signed all the required documents; he had been away too long as of late. His hotel chain was doing very well, even in his absence. The financial reports spoke for themselves. Business was good.

A knock at his door drew his attention from the reports for a second. "Enter."

A tall woman wearing a two-piece skirt suit and red hair pulled into a neat bun walked in. She reached into the hallway and rolled in a rack displaying different suits, then closed the door behind her. She approached his desk and waited for him to look up from the papers.

He smiled at her. Victoria Drake had been his assistant for the last ten years and had learned his habits well. He was happy to have her. "Miss Drake."

"The company car will be ready at the front in two hours. Also, I had your tailor prepare a line of suits for you to choose from for this evening."

"Thank you, Miss Drake."

She inclined her head before turning to leave.

Caliostro watched her exit, the rack of suits catching his eye as the door clicked behind her. His gaze fell on the papers in front of him as he battled his mind to focus on work and not on Alioson.

***

Caliostro sat in the back of a black sedan that his international hotel chain owned. Classical music played softly from the radio as the driver moved through the streets of Drawdtic city. Caliostro loosened the button on his three-piece suit's frock coat and readjusted himself in the seat. He really hated dinner parties, but they were unavoidable in his industry. The upside was he could get what info Colette pertained to possess on getting a human through the veil. He recalled his earlier conversation and hoped she wouldn't be too annoying.

The car pulled up to the Avalanche Hotel. Caliostro lowered the window to see the name in bright blue and illuminating the side of the hotel. The building was twenty-three floors; Colette owned the chain, and it was this location's grand opening.

The driver opened the door, stepping backward to prompt Caliostro to exit. "Sir?"

He entered the glamorous hotel, filled with Victorian artistry and furniture. The colors throughout were snow white and ice blue. He moved across the white and blue floral Victorian woven carpets toward the main desk.

Before he could reach his destination, the feel of an ominous presence engulfed him. He halted and glanced at people bustling about—some carried luggage, couples sat in the lobby chairs, while others checked in. He turned to his left and caught sight of an old lady moving through the crowd. Caliostro could only see her back, but he knew she was old.

Her hair was exceptionally long and silver, and she was short and slim with a slight claudication in her step. She wore variations of grays and whites, her attire like rags. She stopped at the exit and peered over her shoulder at him. Her eyes were coal black and held an emptiness. Wrinkled skin hung pale and loose. She had a nose shaped like a snout. A smirk creeped to life, crinkling one corner of her decrepit mouth, then a full-on smile covered her face, showing darkened sharp teeth.

He stepped toward her, but she was gone. He stared for a moment before putting the old woman out of his mind. Shrugging off the chilly feeling of death she had left, he moved to the front desk, where they directed him to the hotel's largest ballroom. He entered the room and immediately regretted agreeing to attend.

Hundreds of humans, with a mixture of supernatural beings, covered the massive room. Crystal chandeliers lit the room and made a beautiful setting. The carpets and walls matched the rest of the hotel. Circle-shaped tables lined the room near the walls for dining. Servers moved about with trays of wine and hors d'oeuvres.

Caliostro approached the center of the room, and all those near gazed in his direction. He kept his eyes straight ahead, but it was hard to ignore the open minds. Thoughts from every direction floated at him, making his insides clench in annoyance.

"I wonder if he's still single."

"He thinks he's a big deal."

He spotted Colette and beelined for her.

She still looked every bit of twenty-five; her mahogany brown hair hung to her narrow waist, the ends settling at her wide hips draped in a black gown. She laughed at something the person standing in front of her had said, brushing back her hair. Her gray eyes focused on him, ignoring the person she had been chatting with.

"Colette," he said, greeting her.

"Caliostro." She smiled from ear to ear. "Shall we?" She led him to one of many dining tables on the left side of the room. Each table setup alternated, five seats, then two. Colette chose the latter.

Caliostro pulled out a seat for her. Once she was sitting, he took the chair across from her and reached out. "The information, if you would."

Colette laughed. "Aren't we in a rush."

Caliostro cleared his throat and waited.

She waved a server down and grabbed two glasses of red wine from the tray they carried. She placed one in front of him, while she sipped the other.

"No, thank you," he said.

"Oh, so you don't like red wine now?"

"I like it just fine. However, I'm not in the mood."

She looked away, sipping more wine, toward a pianist playing soft music from the other side of the room. "Aren't you even a little happy to see me, Caliostro?" She turned back to him.

"Sure, just about as happy as I am to see any human."

"Wow, you ask for my help, then you throw insults after only moments of being here?" She chuckled, sipping more wine.

"You know why I agreed to meet you. If you please, let us get down to business."

She set down the glass, squared her shoulders, locked gazes with him, and said nothing.

Oh, a battle of wills? I shall oblige.

The minutes ticked away, neither of them blinking. Bystanders whispered and stared, though they both paid no attention. Caliostro could see her getting annoyed the longer the staring contest went on. The crystal chandeliers flickered with her silent anger.

"Are you quite done with the games? If you plan to withhold the information, I'll take my leave." He rose.

Colette grabbed his wrist, stopping him. "Okay, relax. How about we discuss the collaboration first, then we can go somewhere more private for our other chat?"

Caliostro gently reclaimed his wrist and sat again. "Did you bring the papers I sent to you?" He took his first sip of wine.

Colette glanced across the room and beckoned someone.

A man in a black suit and tie approached with a blue folder. He handed it to Colette, then stood by the far wall and waited.

"I agree with the terms you laid out in the contract. The percentages all seem fair," she said, flipping through the contract.

Caliostro watched her. He knew she was wasting time again. "I'm sure you have looked through it enough if you are aware of that information. Since you agree with the terms, let's get on with it."

Colette looked up at him and smirked before turning to the last page. She waved the same man over again. "Pen." She outstretched her hand toward him, pumping her fingers up and down in haste.

The man retrieved a pen from his suit jacket and handed it to her.

She signed, then slid the contracts around and handed Caliostro the pen.

He flipped through the pages to confirm it was all the same, before returning to the endorsement sheet. He signed his name on the line above hers that read, *Colette Summers*, on both copies. He folded a copy and slid it into the inner pocket of his suit jacket. With a twirl of his fingers, he returned the pen, then slid the folder with the remaining copy to her. He sipped his wine again and waited.

The man in the black suit took the folder and headed into the crowd.

"Well, that's that. Shall we?"

Caliostro stood and pulled out her chair. They headed to the main lobby, Colette leading the way.

"The hotel came together nicely, and it's already busy," she boasted.

"Yes, very well done."

They stopped in front of the lobby's elevators, and she pressed the ascend button.

"Where are we going?"

"Isn't it obvious?" She smiled at him from over her shoulder.

Caliostro sighed and looked down, sliding one hand into his left pocket and raising one brow in frustration. He knew where this would lead but said nothing.

The elevator dinged, and they entered. Colette removed an elevator key from inside her bra. She flipped open a small panel below the elevator numbers, inserted the key and turned it. "My penthouse." She stepped backward as the elevator traveled to the top floor.

The doors opened to a lengthy hallway. Gold trim adorned the pure white walls, unlike the white and blue setting throughout the rest of the hotel. At the end of the hallway was a golden door.

Caliostro followed the black train of her evening gown in silence. Once inside, he waited at the door.

Colette continued into the pitch blackness of the space. "Lights on." She peered over her shoulder at him as the room illuminated. She smirked, then disappeared behind a white column to the right of the room.

Caliostro entered the space. It contained a cream-colored sofa and loveseat. Large floor-to-ceiling windows stood in front of him, a magnificent view of the city and night sky greeting his sight. Off to either side of the room were long white tables, and in the center sat a large matching marble table with an onyx statue of a Lycrian howling. Caliostro walked to the windows and waited. He heard her return to the room after a moment.

She had shed the black lanky evening gown for a red negligee. Her hair draped over one shoulder, and she eyed him mischievously as she approached. "Like what you see?" She paused her advancement.

Caliostro cleared his throat. "Colette, please stop with the games and give me the information you said you had."

Colette rolled her eyes, huffed the biggest sigh she could muster, and left the room. She returned a moment later with a wooden carved trinket box. She passed it to him and sat on the loveseat, crossing her legs.

"What is this?" He turned the box this way and that.

"Open it."

He opened it to find a large black onyx stone that emanated black smoke. The omniums feeling he had felt earlier from the old woman filled his senses. He glanced around, expecting to see her smiling at him again, but she was nowhere to be seen. Caliostro refocused on the stone. The feeling was coming from it. He quickly shut the box. "Where'd you get this, and what is it?"

"It doesn't matter where it came from, only that it could help with your issue." She swung the foot on her crossed leg.

"It matters." He set the box on the marble table and sat on the edge of the sofa across from her.

"Do you want the info I have, or do you want the history of the thing that will help you achieve your goal?" She leaned toward him.

Caliostro stared at her with raised brows and lips set in a hard line.

She chuckled. "Fine. First, the only way a human can pass through the veil from either side is to be dead—or, at least, so near death one would think they're dead. That's when the stone comes in. Let's say you don't want to take the chance and kill the human, you know, a little too much." She laughed. "Then you would take that stone and

191

lay it against their chest while they pass through. Now, I will warn you, if they keep the stone against them for too long, well, let's say the outcome will not be to their liking."

Caliostro eyed the box that held the stone. He wasn't sure he trusted this. "Where'd it come from?"

"Someone I know knew someone who was nice enough to trade for it."

Caliostro didn't even want to know what she had traded for the stone.

"Aren't I so very nice to you?"

"I can wire you the cost of the trade," he said, glaring at her.

"Honey, you would never have paid for what I traded. So, just say you owe me one." She walked toward an archway to the left side of the main room. "Lights on. Would you like something to drink?" she yelled from the other room.

"No, thank you."

She returned with a glass of wine and sat again. "So, you need to get a human through the veil alive?" She took a healthy sip.

"Does it matter?" Caliostro stood, retrieving the box from the table.

"Oh, one more thing. You shouldn't keep that here in the human world for long, and you should also get rid of it completely once the task is done."

"I'll make sure."

Caliostro left, calling for his car before entering the elevator. Once outside, he looked at the night sky and wondered how Alioson fared.

NEVER TO WAKE

On the way back to the company, his cellphone rang. "Yes?" Caliostro answered.

"They found us," Daloren said, panting. "I couldn't stop them. They took her."

Caliostro sighed, frustration apparent in his voice. "How long ago did they take her?"

"Maybe fifteen minutes. But, Cali, you shouldn't go it alone." Caliostro heard shuffling over the phone. "They held me off while the others grabbed her. There were dozens of them." After a few moments of silence, Daloren yelled, "Cali, you still there?"

"I will take care of it. Are you injured?"

"I'm healing, so I'm good. Should I call the pack?"

"No, I'd rather they stay out of this. We don't want to draw that kind of attention. Hold on a second." He pressed the button to his right, lowering the window between himself and the driver. "Kevin, we're not going to the hotel."

"Where to, sir?" The driver regarded Caliostro in the rearview mirror.

"Drop me off when you can pull over."

"Yes, sir."

Caliostro raised the window. "Daloren, track them as best you can."

"I'm already on it!"

"The closer I get, I'll be able to locate her." He hung up.

The car rolled to a stop. Caliostro got out. Once the car pulled away from the curb, he strode through the chilly night crammed with mortals. He turned down an alleyway to his right. It smelled of rotten food and stale urine. Caliostro scrunched his nose and marched along the cemented ground. He stopped midway and glanced about, ensuring no one saw him.

His wings appeared, and he launched into the air. The tops of the surrounding buildings zoomed by as he rose high above the clouds until the air was still. Caliostro paused, his wings pumping. He closed his eyes and turned eastward for Pardus.

***

At the Manor

"Argh! I'll never sleep with all this stuff on my mind," Alioson said to the empty room. Sighing deeply, she rose from the bed, made it, then straightened things on the vanity top. Caliostro had been gone for a while now, and she was wondering if he would return.

She left the room and headed to the first floor. *It feels empty without him here for this long.*

The lights in the foyer were dimmed, and she noticed that if someone were to drop a pen, she would hear it throughout the manor. Alioson entered the dining hall. The wall lights here were also low but glowed enough for her to see. She went through the far door and padded to Caliostro's office.

The room was dark with only the hazy moonlight streaming in from the window behind Caliostro's desk.

She closed the door behind her and moved to the window. The light from it revealed a small lamp to the right side of his desk. She turned it on, lighting up part of the room in a warm glow. To her left were shelves of books. She rubbed one hand across a few volumes, then glanced at her palm. *No dust. He's either well read or clean, or both.* She smiled to herself. At the far side of the room was a large window, much like the one behind the desk that was draped with long black curtains. She tiptoed farther into the room.

Alioson had reached the center of the room when she heard creaking outside the office door. She turned, expecting to see Duncan coming through any second. After several moments, no one came, and her heartrate normalized. She walked around the large desk, running her hand over the surface. The office still carried Caliostro's scent. It covered every inch.

Above her, the ceiling creaked, making her twitch. *Why am I so jumpy?*

She sat in Caliostro's chair and swiveled herself around, lifting her feet like a small child. A smile crossed her face as she came back around, facing the desk again. The surface had nothing on it but the lamp. She noticed four drawers. She tried each, but all four were locked. *What am I doing? If Duncan came in right now, I'd die of shame.*

Leaving the desk, she searched the books on shelves nearest to her and found a book titled, *Beyond the Myth*. Alioson slowly used her fingertips to pull the book from its space. The red cover, adorned with gold-colored lettering, was made of soft, crushed fabric. She ran her right hand over the title before opening the book. After flipping a few pages, her eyes fell on an inscribed note.

You should find this an interesting read, my sweet brother.

Your beautiful sister, D.

She frowned at the words, knowing Dalidah had given him the book and making her want to return it to the shelf. Once she pushed her annoyance aside and refocused on the book, she found age had yellowed and weakened the pages. With great ease, she turned the first titled page. After turning a few more, she came to one titled, "Vampire's Blood." The first line caught her eye.

Vampire's blood has a healing agent. If used correctly, a vampire's blood can heal serious wounds, and many know of this in our guild.

She raised her eyebrows when she read the word, 'guild.'

Vampires have more of a connection to spiders than bats. With many years of research, we now understand this connection. These studies have shown us the similarities, such as how bats can fly and drain the life from their prey, but spiders drain the life from their prey by trapping, and then injecting a paralyzing agent or venom. They also could petrify their prey, much like vampires. These creatures of the night are damned and are a great threat to humanity, as they see us as prey. They show themselves to us as beautiful creatures, but they are after our life force and cannot exist without it.

We have also found out through study that they can produce offspring no matter the corresponding being; this news came as a shock to our community. We previously believed they were indeed more dead than alive. Our leaders have concluded it must be dark magic within them that gives the ability to reproduce.

Who wrote this book? Is it some kind of cult? The book went on and on about the effects of vampiric abilities. Ink drawings of what vampires looked like under the guise of beauty followed. Some photos showed very graphic images of them, with faces twisted in rage, draining women and men alike, tearing at their necks and shredding their bodies.

Alioson closed the book when she heard another creak from the hallway. *I better get back to my room before Duncan catches me.*

She opened the door to find him standing there. Alioson gasped. "Duncan, you scared me." She chuckled nervously, hiding the book behind her.

Duncan stared at her with cold silver eyes. "Was there something you needed, Miss Alioson?" He looked past her into the room behind.

Alioson stared at him, noticing the details of his features for the first time.

Duncan wore no sweater nor vest over his button-down shirt like usual, and he wore his silver hair pushed back away from his face. Though it wasn't long, it rested just above his shoulders, and he sported a light stubble across his chin and cheeks. He regarded her, as she had yet to answer him.

"Oh … ah … no. That is … I just couldn't sleep, and so I came to … to walk around."

Duncan's brow raised, and his eyes became hooded.

"Have you heard from Caliostro recently?"

"No. However, I'm sure he will return soon."

"Please let me know if he contacts you."

"I will be sure to do so." He stepped aside.

Alioson took that as her cue to leave and headed for the stairs, pulling the book in front of her. She didn't look but felt his eyes boring into her back. Once in her room, she put the book on the end table by the bed. Her gaze settled on the crackling flames of the fireplace as she sat in front of the hearth. *What would Caliostro think if he knew about my latest memories?*

The kiss she'd shared with the other hunter replayed in her head. *What was his name again?* "Oh right, Ashley." She blushed, recalling how she had jumped on him.

Sadness filled her. *My memories have been sad and dark so far. Though I still want to remember, no matter how terrible and frightening they may be.*

Alioson patted either side of her face, sighed, and retrieved the book she'd set down. Reseated, she opened the book again. "Where was I? Oh yes, vampires." She turned the page.

These creatures are not so easy to destroy, as they have faked most of their own weaknesses, such as holy water, crosses, and sunlight. Sunlight doesn't affect them in the way many have thought; it only weakens them slightly. Most of these weaknesses should be obvious, but we will state them here.

1. Falseness of the sun's infliction. They put this into place so they could feed by day, while humans would think to hunt them during that time, setting more traps for feeding.

2. Holy water is just water, no effect.

3. The Cross also has no effect on them in most cases. Sometimes, one's faith could work on a vampire, but they would have to be more like a Nosferatu. (Look under 'Nosferatu' for other types of vampires).

They have some weaknesses, however. With great difficulty, we found them, and with significant loss of our guild members.

1. Rain is one of their weaknesses. It dulls their vampiric senses when falling. This is based on elements and weather, so this weakness is only helpful at certain times.

2. Wood and silver weakens Lycrians, but they also work on vampires, though both only stun them for a brief period. The most effective thing against a creature such as them would be a well-trained hunter.

Alioson screamed and dropped the book as a numbing pain hit her chest, followed by a sharp pain through her shoulder. "What ... was ... that?" She grabbed at her chest, her breaths shortening. Afraid to move, she waited. With great ease, she bent to retrieve the fallen book, only to have a stronger pain strike her in the center of her back.

She wailed, her knuckles forming fists on the floor in front of her. This pain was so severe her vision faded to dark, and she knew nothing more.

***

Caliostro sped through the night, his wings spread wide. Varying thoughts raced through his mind, ones of Alioson and others of Catherine. As he drew closer to the location, he could feel her. Whoever the Magic Guild members were, they would not give her up with ease.

Caliostro gritted his teeth in silent rage. He and the Magic Guild never were harmonious. They had never liked the relationship between himself and Catherine, and once the incident had occurred, they requested her body, and he'd refused. Over the past two centuries, while Catherine slept, Caliostro had hidden her. Knowing this was a trap fueled his pursuit that much faster. His speed was unearthly, causing sudden bursts of wind and trimmers. If any human eye were to glimpse him, they would only see a flash of light speeding across the night sky. When he came close to buildings, he tucked his wings against his body, shielding his form in a beautiful blue and white light, giving him the look of a shooting star.

Caliostro could tell she was nearby. He had closed in on them. *Why does her inner force feel so faint? Are they somehow blocking our connection? Possibly weakening it?* He landed two buildings away from where he could feel her and carefully surveyed his surroundings. *I don't care for this.*

Tight buildings lined the streets of Pardus. He would be hard pressed to ensure they hurt no mortals doing the altercation. The darkness of night would help a bit, though humans lit the streets here and there. Pardus was beautiful during the day, but night was its mistress.

Catherine's scent wafted to him from the street below. He spotted a black SUV pulling up to the curb, two buildings down from the one he perched on. Caliostro scanned the empty streets again. After standing erect, he loosened the button on his suit jacket and jumped to the street below. He landed with no pause in his step until he was twenty feet away.

Two males emerged from the vehicle, one with waist-length, coal-black hair and the other sporting a bald head. They carried a long, enclosed gray case, the size of a casket. Catherine's scent and heartbeat came from within.

Before they could enter the building, Caliostro stood in the entryway. "What do you have there, gentlemen?"

The two men looked at each other, then at him.

"It looks rather heavy. Shall I give you a hand?" Caliostro flipped and landed next to the casket, sword in hand.

The two men charged him. One summoned a fire spear, thrusting it forward. The other transformed both arms into blades of ice.

Caliostro dodged the spear by twisting around the assailant and deflecting the tip with his sword. An ice blade caught him in the shoulder, burning through his suit jacket. He jumped back, slashing across the magic user's neck, taking his head. Caliostro felt a stab of fire pierce the center of his back. Gritting his teeth, he expelled his wings and propelled himself forward, away from the attack. He turned, flew at the spear wielder, and stabbed his blade through the man's crotch. Blood sprayed from the assailant's mouth as Caliostro arched his sword upward, splitting him in two. He looked around, sensing no more danger, and dispersed his blade.

His wings faded as he quickly opened the casket, only to find it empty with a note and a glowing vile of blood. *Oh, aren't they clever? I haven't seen that magic trick in centuries.* Caliostro reached for a folded piece of paper that lay next to the vile of blood. *It will not be that easy.*

We weren't sure that old trick would work on you. Look harder. Don't worry, we are waiting for you this time.

His brow lowered in frustration as he glared at the vile of blood. He scooped it up, the heartbeat fading with his touch. A waft of smoke escaped, the magic dying as he sniffed it, proving it was indeed Catherine's. *They're holding her in the city. Things just became more complicated.*

He crumpled the note in his fist, crushing the vile along with it. "They will pay."

Caliostro took flight and soon picked up her trail. *No matter what they have planned, I will get you back, Catherine.* With his silent conviction, he headed toward whatever waited.

***

The moon was high, and mist settled around her booted feet. Alioson traversed the dark alleyway as fast as her feet would carry her. She reached a large parking lot with an overpass. The silence was deafening as drops of leftover rain ricocheted off nearby puddles. A loud screeching and hissing came from above, making her peer up. A spotlight beamed down, blinding her. With a deep resolve, she readied her sword.

207

Footsteps thundered from all sides, surrounding her.

Her eyes took count of the enemies—eight. She spread her legs and braced for the attack. It was dark sans the light shining from above. She heard snarling and heavy breathing, knowing they outnumbered her. She closed her eyes and listened, waiting.

Two charged her.

She ducked the first assailant on the right, taking their arm. Blood sizzled on her imbued blade as the creature grabbed at the wound.

Another attack came from the left, making her stagger backward. Someone jumped on her, making her lurch forward.

Pain shot through her shoulder as she screamed, blood running down her arm.

A force ripped away the vampire who had bitten her, and Ashley stood at her back. "You okay?"

"Yeah, it's just another bite." She wiped at the blood and charged the next creature.

***

Alioson jackknifed into a sitting position on the floor. Sweat beaded her forehead, and her shoulder and back still throbbed. Using the chair for leverage, she sat and retrieved the fallen book as tears escaped the corners of her eyes. "What's happening to me?"

***

Caliostro tracked Catherine's smell to an abandoned building devoid of lighting. The structure stood alone and away from any other buildings for miles. *Oh yes, it's a trap.* Caliostro landed on the rooftop of the building across from where her force radiated from. *She's here.*

The windows in the building were all broken out, making his entrance simple. He jumped through the closest one, crunching broken glass beneath his dress boots. It was pitch black, but he felt the energy levels of over twenty different beings farther inside. Caliostro moved along the right side of the window he had come through and crouch-walked along the first hallway.

A male in black and gray clothing stalked just beyond the doorway.

Caliostro sniffed, the scent of a Lycrian filling his nostrils. *Seems the Magic Guild is recruiting outside help these days.* He moved through a nearby doorway, avoiding the confrontation. The damp and rotting building held a musky scent that stung Caliostro's nostrils. Green moss-covered sections of the floors throughout made the ground slippery. He stayed in a crouching posture until he reached a large foyer. Catherine's scent and force strengthened. *She's close.*

He stood when a large black misty barrier covered every window and doorway. Lights shone brightly from every corner. Caliostro materialized his blade and focused.

A burly male with green catlike eyes barged through the black smoke, shifting into a were-tiger. Fangs and fur replaced teeth and hair. The beast charged him.

He dodged and ducked to the side, swinging his blade up in a high arc, and cut his assailant in two, from armpit to opposite shoulder.

The beast's remains fell to the floor as they charged Caliostro from all sides. The black misty barriers faded to allow hunters and magic users to attack.

Caliostro's wings appeared, and he slashed and twisted through the sea of attackers. His momentum carried him up the wide flight of stairs. He heard the ones he hadn't cut down charging from behind. Bolts of lightning struck all around, and fireballs assailed him. Once he reached the second floor, he half ran, half flew down corridor after corridor. He fought hunters and sorcerers around each dark corner and in the multiple rooms he navigated through.

The place was like a maze, with doors on both the left and right, some missing and some hanging off at the hinges. Caliostro stopped when he entered a second large foyer. A split spiral staircase ascended to yet another level. The hunters were mere seconds behind him. It was here he would fight them, then he would find Catherine and escape.

***

Alioson sighed in defeat at the realization that sleep would be a stranger again that night. She went into the bathroom, wet a cloth, and wiped the sweat upon her brow. "Funny, I hadn't broken a sweat in my recent memories." As she patted herself dry, her thoughts turned to Caliostro. *Where are you?*

With one last look in the mirror, she turned off the sink and returned to the bedroom. "The bed or the balcony?"

In bed, I'll stare off, and it's not safe outside.

She ended up in the training room on the first floor. Her eyes closed as she stood in the center, listening to her own heartbeat. She tuck-rolled and came up in a kneeling position, followed by a straight punch. A glint from one of the blades on the weapons rack caught her eye, calling for her to take it in hand. Her fingers wrapped around the hilt and squeeze before swinging it. Muscle memory took over. She felt something burning deep down, crawling to life within her, and she liked it.

***

Caliostro fought his way through all the hunters on the second floor. Blood poured from an open wound on his left shoulder. *My healing has slowed.* He flew up the right side of the spiral stairs, sword in hand, and prepared to take on more. *I must get this done. My blade won't last much longer.* Caliostro's sword flicked, fading, then reappeared.

Two Lycrians in full transformation lunged from the left, knocking him through the wall to his right.

He took the force of the attack by landing in a half roll, which brought him to his feet.

The beasts were right on him, mouths opened and claws at the ready.

Caliostro ducked under one claw and blocked the attacking bite of the other with his sword. He swung his blade, decapitating one. His sword came around and under

212

the other Lycrian's thigh, severing it at the hip. Caliostro stabbed his blade down into the creature's neck, while it thrashed about on the floor.

The wound on his shoulder closed, healing. His suit was torn in many places and stained. He removed the tattered and bloodied jacket and threw it to the floor.

Caliostro opened his senses even more to his surroundings, giving him Catherine's exact location. He placed his hand against the wall at his left, forcing a burst of energy through it and several others. Propelling himself through the openings brought him to a room with plain white walls and a bed that held Catherine's sleeping form. His wings dissipated as he rushed over, then stopped short of the bed. He raised his blade, pointing it at her neck. "Get up! I won't fall for such witchery!" The blue in his eyes intensified in anger.

The woman who looked like Catherine laughed. Her eyes opened. As she sat upright, her white hair faded into black, and her eyes became an inhuman teal color. She hovered over the bed, fixating on him.

Caliostro stepped backward but kept his sword trained on her.

"What they say is true. Magic doesn't really work on you." She hovered closer and studied him. "I can see why Catherine wanted you, even though it didn't work out as she planned."

"I know she's in this room. Release her from your chains."

The woman raised her eyebrows. "Oh, so you know a bit about magic, I see."

Caliostro lifted the tip of his blade closer under her chin. The light that emanated from it singed her skin, making her flinch. "If you don't release her now, I will kill you slowly instead of quickly."

"I don't think you'll be able to threaten anyone for much longer." She laughed.

His sword flickered, then solidified.

She twirled the finger on her right hand that was down at her side.

Caliostro caught the movement and slashed his sword in a Z-shape at her.

She phased in and out, then hovered to the other side of the bed, making him miss her.

Caliostro stiffened when he heard snarling and rustling from behind him. But his worry quickly turned

214

into relief at the smell of his cousin and as those of his father's clan filled the space.

Lycrians barreled through what remained of the walls and seized the room.

The sorceress, seeing they outnumbered her, tried to flee.

Caliostro intercepted her, his hand gripping her neck, and lifted her higher in the air. "Release Catherine, now!"

The Lycrians watched in silence as Daloren stepped through the crowd. "I got it, Cali." He raised a stone in front of him, and the room flickered in a purple hue.

Catherine's sleeping form appeared, suspended above the bed.

Daloren moved under her, and the magical chains that held her wrists and ankles disappeared.

She fell into his waiting arms.

Caliostro refocused on his captive.

Her eyes went wide with shock that someone could break through her magic with such ease. She struggled against his hold with one hand and kept waving the other in Daloren's direction. "How?" she asked, her voice barely a whisper.

Caliostro's eyes glowed stronger. "My touch nullifies magic."

Blue fire engulfed the hand that held her. She screamed in agony as her eyes bulged and skin melted, her head disintegrating. The remains fell to the floor with a resounding thud.

Caliostro retrieved Catherine from Daloren's arms. "What took you so long?" he asked, going back the way he had come.

"Well, we tracked her scent to the first location, only to find the empty casket and remains of the magic users you obviously killed. Then we tracked you here."

"So, you brought the pack, even though I told you I didn't want them involved."

"Since when have I ever really listened to you?" Daloren smiled while following Caliostro out.

The Lycrians who waited silently returned to their normal states; the sounds of bone and flesh phasing into place followed Caliostro and Daloren out.

Once Caliostro reached the second landing again, he spotted French doors to the side. His eyes widened, and the doors blew open for him. Through them was a half-moon-shaped balcony. He launched himself onto the railing and stopped. "I'll contact you in a few days. And thank you for having my back."

He took flight and held Catherine close to his body as he sped through the night sky.

MAKE ME WHOLE
AGAIN

After a much-needed shower, Alioson wrapped herself in a white bathrobe and stared out the balcony's double glass doors. *I think it's safe to have the doors open at least.* Alioson let the night air drift over her. The hazy moon and dull stars filled her vision. In the distance, she spotted a light approaching. A moment later, like lightning striking a metal post, she came to attention and knew it was Caliostro.

He slowed his speed. The velocity behind him whipped her hair back, along with the fabric of her robe, making her clutch it. Her eyes went wide, and their gazes locked. He held someone in his arms, but he continued onward, making it hard to see.

"Caliostro," she said, looking in the direction he had flown. She closed the doors and sat in front of the hearth, waiting. She wasn't sure how much time had passed, but her patience was short. Her fingers tapped on the robe over her upper thigh. The feeling of restlessness settled in, making her retrieve a hairbrush from the vanity. She detangled her damp hair, placed it in a ponytail, and sat at the vanity.

A knock sounded at the bedroom door, yet she made no move to answer. A second knock followed. "Alioson?" Caliostro's voice called from the other side of the door.

She crossed the room and opened it. Her heart raced at the mere sight of him.

"May I come in?" he asked when she made no move to give him entry.

"Sure." She stepped aside, letting him pass. "So … umm, how was your trip?"

"Well, it was busy." He moved farther into the room.

"So, I see you flew home."

"Yes, it's the fastest way besides teleportation."

"Of course, that makes sense." She chuckled before looking away. *That makes little sense at all, but then again, in this world, it sounds about right.* "Do you also do that?"

He faced her. "Do what?"

She blinked at him, arms folded over her midsection.

"Oh, teleportation, yes, but it's tricky, and I haven't perfected it while traveling with someone."

"And that someone that you were carrying, are they hurt?"

He stared at her.

"Of course, you don't have to tell me. I mean, only if you want to."

Caliostro searched her face. "It's Catherine. I had to bring her back with me. There was some danger."

Her mouth formed the shape of an *O*. "I see. So, will she be okay?"

"Yes," he answered in a clipped tone.

"Well, I'm glad to hear that, and I'm happy you returned safely."

He nodded. "It's very late, and I'm sure you need your rest." He passed her and opened the door.

Alioson blocked his way, closing the door, and kept her back to him. "Is that all you wish to say to me?"

"For now, yes."

Tears sprang to her eyes, impossible to hide. "Why did you run away?" She stepped up to him.

"I did not run. I've been away, and you know why." He reached around her for the doorknob.

Alioson put both arms around his neck, making her stand on tiptoes.

He didn't move, his hand still on the knob.

"Please, you know I need you ..."

He took her into his arms, and she sank into them, as if she were a stone and he was the ocean.

"You know I have no hope of recalling my memories without you."

Caliostro stiffened, making Alioson glance up at him. "Alioson, I don't want to hurt you again."

Her lids shut at the tender sound of his voice. Unshed tears soaked into the fabric of his collared shirt as she hid her face in the crook of his neck.

"Have any more memories returned to you?" He pulled back to search her eyes, but she would not meet them; instead, she hunched her shoulders and shrunk from him. "I would like for you to tell me. I do my best to not read your mind, but when you respond like that, I want to."

"No, no, not much, just … umm, small flashes of this and that, nothing that makes any sense to me right now." She stepped back from him, putting her back against the door.

Caliostro gave no quarter and shadowed her steps. He slowly rubbed the pad of his thumb along her jawline, which made her gasp. "You mustn't fear sharing your memories and thoughts with me, Alioson." Their eyes bore into one another. Caliostro's blazed anew with fire, then became a melting pot of heat in one blink. He leaned in, trapping her against the door. His mouth lightly grazed hers, then gently suckled and pulled on her lips.

She opened her mouth to him as they tasted each other. Her right hand fisted in the silk black hair at the nape of his neck, making him growl. She changed the angle of her head to better accommodate the force of the kiss.

Caliostro's hands moved to her waist and held her in place. He turned them, then stopped abruptly and pushed her from him.

Alioson opened her eyes. A gasp escaped her, and she stumbled backward. His eyes were those same black orbs with smokey fumes crawling from the rim that she'd seen before when he'd bitten her.

Caliostro lowered his head into the palm of his hand, then looked at her. His eyes had returned to normal.

She stepped toward him, then stopped when he lifted his open palm between them, his lids fluttering shut again. "Caliostro …" she said, pleading in her tone.

He glanced at her, opened the door, and left.

Alioson placed her hand on the door and rested her forehead against it. She inhaled his scent that filled the space, sliding to the floor in defeated frustration. After several minutes keeping her head resting on her gathered knees, she crawled into bed and closed her eyes. Within moments, a deep sleep claimed her.

***

"Do it now!"

Alioson flipped off the roof and impaled the vampire on her landing.

The foul creature now lay immobile upon her sword.

She withdrew her blade, blood misting across her face. The sound of steel sliding against leather emanated as she sheathed her sword and produced a curved knife. She dismembered the creature and peered over her shoulder at a man with black hair, who wore a dark gray suit.

"Very good. You are improving." He walked past her and got into the black limo waiting for him at the end of the alley.

Alioson watched the car leave, rolling her eyes. "That's fine. I'll just walk back!"

Her gaze returned to the remains of the creature at her feet. She spat on it, pulled out a matchbook and set both the head and body on fire.

"Disgusting creatures," she said, sneering at the burning piles. She pulled a cloth from her back pocket and wiped her blade free of the blood.

Alioson felt uneasiness settle around her. "Who's there?" She turned every which way, searching the dark.

A mist swirled around her black leather boots, followed by the stench of rotting flesh.

She readied her sword, eyes shifting left to right. "Whatever you are, I'm not in the mood for games, so let's get on with it!"

No one answered. Just as quickly as the mist and stench had arrived, it dissipated.

"Yeah, fucking monsters. Cowards, the lot of you!" Alioson boasted to no one, yet she felt someone or something had been there with her, and the evidence was now the missing vampire remains. "What the hell?" She looked around her feet, as if the fires would reappear. All that remained were bloodstains. "Okay, then." Alioson kept her weapon in hand as she ran into the night to report back.

***

"Seriously, Ashley. One minute the leftovers of the vamp were there, then they were gone!" Alioson reenacted the fight and what had happened after Master Cordaglen had driven off. "Oh, and Dad ... I mean, Master Cordaglen just left me there in the dark, so uncool, I might add."

Ashley laughed.

"I know he always does that, since it's a part of the training, but I guess at least he stayed for the fight," she said, walking ahead of him.

"Did you report back yet?" Ashley asked as they entered the training corridor.

"No, I wanted to shower first. Do you not see all the blood on me, or did you think this was a fashion statement?"

He just looked at her sideways as they walked. "You know, you're very sexy when you get all sassy like that." He grabbed her hand and locked fingers with her.

"Sure, if you say so." She snatched her hand away.

"Well, up to you, but reporting on arrival is the rule. Never mind your … attire." He gave her a once-over.

"Yeah, sure, but I think I'll do it my way."

Before Ashley could further instruct her on what would happen if she broke the rules, she ran ahead of him to the showers, leaving him to shake his head in her wake.

Alioson reached the locker room and slowed her pace. Lockers inscribed with every trainee's name lined the left side, and floor-length mirrors lined the other side. She turned to see her reflection upon entering. *Dammit, fucking vamps.*

She hurriedly undressed, clenching her teeth at the sucking sound her clothes made as she removed them piece by piece. The blood had soaked through to her skin, making her stomach turn. She always undressed facing away from the mirrors—the sight of blood on her

226

rehashed old memories she'd rather forget. "No, Alioson, don't even go there."

Once her clothes were off, she threw them in the large black trashcan next to her locker. She grabbed a bar of soap and a towel, then entered the first stall she reached. The steaming hot water rushed over her dirty form, blood pooling around and under her feet. She washed and washed, as if she could wash away her hate of vampires and the last memory of her mother.

She finished and wrapped herself in a thick white towel, letting her hair drip wet down her back. Barefoot, she walked to her locker to grab the change of clothing she'd always left in there.

Annoyed to find they weren't there, she returned to her room, passing a few trainees on the way who looked her up and down. At her door, she used the keycard and her code—2567—to enter.

"Please stand still for an eye scan," the voice from the intercom to the left of her door said.

Alioson leaned in. A light moved down, then up over her right eye. Once inside, she dropped her towel, got dressed, and pulled her hair into a high ponytail. She glanced in the mirror, then left to make her mission report.

***

Alioson stepped off the elevator on the top floor and spotted the auburn-haired woman sitting behind the white marble table at the far end of the hallway. She looked away from her and instead focused on the large double cream-trimmed French doors. *Oh, yay it's the snitch.*

"Hi, Ali," the woman said in greeting.

"Don't fucking call me Ali. We're not friends, okay?" Alioson could feel the woman's eyes on her as she approached the doors but kept her gaze straight ahead, ignoring her. She lifted her hand to knock.

"He's waiting for you, so you can just go in."

Alioson froze, then knocked anyway and pushed the door open to enter. She shut the door and moved farther into the massive office.

"You're late making your report," the deep voice boomed from behind the enormous desk.

Alioson came to attention. *Why does the mere sound of his voice do that to me?* "Yes, forgive my lateness. I was—"

"Covered in blood. Yes, I figured as much. I know that bothers you. No need to explain. Please go on with your report."

"Yes, umm, I finished the vampire off with minor issue, as you know. I burned the remains, but ..."

"But?"

"After you left, Dad ... I mean, sir, I felt a presence to be sure." *Shit, almost called him Dad. I don't want to be reprimanded again for that.* She bit her lower lip.

"Alioson? You felt a presence ... *and*?"

"Well, a dark feeling surrounded me. I'm not really sure, but I didn't care for it."

"And ...?"

"And then the vampire's remains were gone, without a trace. I do not know how they could have disappeared." She locked one hand around her wrist behind her back. She stood within four feet of his desk, staring at his high-backed chair. He had yet to face her. "Sir?"

"Yes?"

"Will that be all?" She was in a hurry to be away. The presence she had felt earlier settled over her yet again.

"Yes, that will be all. Have a good rest. Tomorrow will bring even harder training. Be ready."

"Yes, sir." With one last glance at the back of his chair and his desk that only held a cup of ballpoint pens and a nameplate that read, JERRICK CORDAGLEN, she turned and left. Her eyes darted about the space, searching for the dark presence surrounding her.

The woman behind the desk looked up, but Alioson paid her no attention as she headed for the elevator. The doors opened, but before she could enter, an explosion from behind blasted her into the elevator, knocking her out.

***

Caliostro paced in the foyer. *What's happening to me? What is this darkness I feel looming?* For the next hour, Caliostro practiced with every weapon in the training room. He flipped and dodged invisible enemies. He removed his jacket and shirt as he danced a battle against himself. His mind replayed the dark feeling he'd felt when last with Alioson.

Panting, he stopped his practice and went to his bedroom. He took a shower and changed into another suit without donning the jacket. Upon entering the main hallway, he felt Alioson's distress.

"Alioson?" He knocked on her door, listening closely. He heard the thrashing of sheets and rustling coming from the other side of her door. Caliostro rushed in.

She lay tangled under the covers, her head thrashing back and forward.

"Alioson," he said gently, approaching the bed. He laid his hand on her forehead, closing his eyes. A flash of Alioson fighting a vampire, killing it, then reporting to the leader of the Hunters Guild played through his mind. Caliostro stepped backward, his eyes going cold as he stared at her.

Alioson slowly opened her eyes and sat upright in the center of the bed to find him standing over her. "Caliostro?" She rubbed the back of her hand over her eyes.

He was silent, both hands fisting at his sides.

Alioson glanced toward the balcony. "It's still dark out? I guess I didn't sleep long." She pushed away the covers and rose.

Still, he said nothing.

Alioson stopped in front of him, reaching for his face.

He caught her wrist and moved backward. His mouth drew a hardline, and he turned and approached the hearth, staring into the fireplace. "Do you have something to tell me?" He could hear her heartrate rise. It beat so loudly he was sure it would burst from her very chest. "You have something to tell me, right? Something about your past?" he rephrased, moving closer.

She opened her mouth, then closed it. Her widened eyes dropped to stare at her wringing hands. "What do you mean? You know about as much as I do. You know I don't recall my past enough to share more yet."

His brow lowered, and the base of his ears pulsed. A muscle in his jaw jumped in frustration.

"I'm trying to remember, you know that!"

"Alioson, look at me."

She partially looked up, her head still lowered.

"Look me in the eye."

"What do you want me to say, Caliostro? What?" she pleaded, finally looking at him.

"I came to check on you, because I felt your distress. I attempted to calm your thrashing by resting a hand on you when I saw ... a memory of yours."

Her eyes spread wide in shock.

"Please stop lying to me. It will do you no good. Do you not understand the fact that I'm trying to help you?"

"I'm not lying. I don't know who I really am. Even with the unlocked memories I have now, everything about me is still a blur."

"Not everything. You are a *hunter*. And that's a fact. You learned that, and yet, here you are, keeping it from me!"

"Yes, but it's not what you think. I was afraid to tell you, afraid you would hate me. You know I don't know how I got here. I don't know who I really am. I don't!"

They stared at each other in silence.

"Say something, Caliostro. *Please*."

His eyes tightened, hurt clear within them, but they turned cold. "I need you to stay in this room." He headed toward the door.

"Am I to be a prisoner now?" Anger filled her tone.

He stopped, his hand hovering over the doorknob. "Just stay. "With that, he left. "Lock," he said, once in the hallway. Blue light emanated around the door, then disappeared. The feeling of betrayal rested upon his shoulders as he retreated to his office below.

WE ARE...

Caliostro entered his office. *She showed up out of nowhere. How could I be so blind?*

"Duncan, I need you in my office now."

A knock sounded on his door moments later.

"Come in."

Duncan stepped in and closed the door behind him. "You called, Lord Masterson?"

"Yes. I need you to move Catherine to the lower keep, into the secret tunnels. We haven't used them in some time, so I need it set up for her and security measures put in place for the entire manor. You understand?"

"Yes, right away," he replied, leaving.

Caliostro replayed his and Alioson's first meeting in his head. *Was she alone? Was she a plant by the Hunters Guild? If so, how did they get her through the veil while still alive? Maybe they had an item like the stone Colette gave me.* Caliostro glanced at the box that held the mysterious stone before focusing on the forest line in the distance through his office window. *What does she have planned? Does it matter? In the end, I'll have to decide.*

He opened his senses, feeling for Alioson.

***

Alioson rested her hand on the knob, though she did not turn it. Tears soaked into her bathrobe, her hand falling to her side. "Fuck this!" She wiped at her damp cheeks. "If you don't believe me, I'll make you believe me."

She hastily dressed in black jeans and a white t-shirt. "This will do." She inspected herself in the vanity and returned to the door to try the knob. A deep frown creased her brow. *So, you won't talk to me, and you locked me in?*

Alioson closed her eyes, breathing deeply, then placed her palm against the solid wood, focusing on the door. "Unlock."

Blue light flickered around it.

She stepped backward, waited, then tried the knob again.

***

Caliostro stood over Catherine's sleeping form. "Somehow, I will save you from this accursed fate I have damned you to. It seems the past shall repeat." He sighed and left.

As the door shut behind him, a single tear stained Catherine's face.

Caliostro returned to his office, just as Duncan did.

Alioson's scent and inner force emanated from within his office. She sat in the chair behind his desk, their eyes locking when he entered.

Duncan moved toward her, but Caliostro's glare stayed his advancement.

"Duncan, leave us."

Duncan exited and closing the door behind him.

"So, I'm the enemy now?" She smiled, though it didn't reach her eyes.

"Why are you—"

"I refuse to be a prisoner. I've done nothing wrong. That I was a hunter isn't something I can help right now."

"*Was*? Hmm, it seems you still are."

"I don't know that, and neither do you."

"I asked you to stay in your room."

"Yeah, you did, but I don't see how that helps. Seems pointless to ask me to stay there while you lead your own conclusions."

Hmm, sassy, why do I like it? "Well, we have an issue, then, since I need you to stay in your room, and you appear unwilling to do so?"

"Like I said, I will not be a prisoner, Caliostro. If I am no longer welcomed here, then I wish to leave."

"I never said you were not welcomed, but lying to me does not make me trust you."

"Well, if you don't trust me, then I think it would be best if I go."

Caliostro stepped toward her. "You will stay until--"

"No. I will not!" She rose to her feet.

"You will. There is no other option until I—"

"Until what? Until you decide you want to make me disappear?"

His mouth drew a hardline, and he looked away. His hands fisted at his sides, then flexed as he regarded her. "How could you think that of me, after I have shown you nothing but kindness since you have arrived? Do you not understand our connection? And ..."

"Yes, you have shown me kindness, but now it's different, right?" Tears brimmed, stinging her eyes, but she suppressed them.

"Alioson, just do as I ask." He moved past her, to his desk.

She glared at his back. "Why should I? Obviously, I mean nothing to you, despite your words, if you can just dismiss me so easily."

"So easily? Is that what you think?" He stared intently at her. "And I'm not dismissing you. Have you forgotten our conversation from the terrace?"

A blush filled her cheeks. She glanced away, not answering. When she looked back, he stood a breaths' length away, surprising her. Alioson's eyes widened, tongue darting out to moisten her lower lip in nervousness.

Caliostro reached for her cheek, his eyes glued to her mouth. He leaned in, and her eyes closed, but he froze, moving away.

Alioson's eyes popped open to find him back where he had been.

238

"I saw your memories. I saw you hunting, working for the same guild who has hunted me!"

Alioson stared at him with scrutiny. "You say that as if I tricked you. I just wasn't ready to share what I did recall!"

"You say you don't recall who you really are, yet I saw those memories, and you expect me to believe you were drowning in the lake outside on my very property, by chance?" Caliostro's eyes blazed with barely contained anger.

"I can't answer that, I—"

"I'm not done! Despite the implication of your being here, I saved you from that lake. Why? Because your heart called to me, and I was drawn to you. So, no, I don't dismiss you easily. If I didn't care for you, do you think you would be alive right now?" His eyes flared brighter.

"Caliostro, I can't change who I was, or am— whoever that is. I can only be me now."

"And who is that, exactly?"

"A woman who will fight for the love I feel for the man standing in front of me." Her heart raced at the declaration.

"Even if there is truth in that statement, I still need you to return to your room. Now."

Alioson's eyes rolled. "I'll leave your office, but I will not be a prisoner," she informed him, storming out.

Caliostro repressed his desire to follow her and called Duncan to meet him in the lower tunnels.

***

"Lord Masterson, what are we going to do about Alioson?" Duncan asked, walking ahead of him.

"That's for me to manage. You are to stay out of it," Caliostro said, leaving no room for more questions.

They traversed the long stone corridor and stopped at a red wooden door. The room they entered held twelve wall-mounted candleholders, four on each one. Red and cream-colored antique paper covered the entire room. A four-poster canopy bed covered with cream-colored silk sat in the center of the space. Next to the bed on the left side was a high-backed antique chair and a matching end table with a gas lamp.

"Is everything to your liking?" Duncan asked.

"Yes. Please bring her below."

Caliostro sat next to the bed and waited. The minutes ticked by, his mind wandering to the past.

***

Mortal World 1821

"How much longer before we get there?" Catherine asked.

Caliostro led the way. Dewy trees lined the wooded trail into the deep forest. He smiled at her question. "You asked that only moments ago. Do you honestly expect it has changed since then?" He glanced at her over his shoulder. "Also, it's a surprise, and you love those, do you not?"

"Well, I suppose I do. Though I would like to know this one time, please?" She jumped in front of him to block his path.

He smiled and passed her, maintaining his pace. "This time I can't give you what you want because you will love this surprise. It's something you have wanted for some time now." Caliostro turned to see why he no longer heard her footfalls on the damp leaves and found her standing still and watching him. "What are you about? Come along," he said, but she didn't move.

The sun broke through the treetops, casting light on her eyes and making the shadows bounce off the left side of her face. Her beauty frozen him in place, making him

241

realize he would never concede to her demands of becoming like him.

Catherine noticed Caliostro was staring at her and returned his gaze with the same intensity. "Is it a new house that has its own lake?"

Caliostro rolled his eyes at her lavish guess and marched through the forest as rain drizzled. "Still not telling!"

He passed between two trees that reached for each other and stopped at a large moss-covered bolder. Someone's scent came across his path, then a few more. He hadn't sensed them sooner because of the rain. "Keep up, I want to reach the veil line by sundown."

"Wouldn't it be faster to fly?"

"You know I only do that for emergencies when in the mortal world." He glanced back at her.

Their eyes met as an arrow slammed into Catherine's chest.

Caliostro caught her before she could hit the ground. "Catherine! No! No!"

Her eyes fluttered close.

He lifted her into his arms, ready to move.

"Cali …" she whispered.

He glanced down at her, then scanned the area. "Don't speak." Whoever had shot the arrow was retreating, but he had no time to pursue them. Within minutes, he broke from the wood line and onto a dirt road. *Should I fly? No, someone might see.*

Caliostro knew his only chance at saving her was a giving of his energy. He ran across the dirt road and through another line of trees. The veil line was just ahead, along with the new manor he had built on the other side of the veil. Sprinting, he broke through the veil with Catherine in his arms. His wings emanated, illuminating the surrounding space in a blue glow. He took flight. Minutes later, he landed on his bedroom's balcony.

Caliostro kicked open the doors and moved her inside. He kneeled, holding her into a seated position on the floor. He broke off the arrow at her back and cradled her to him. His lips covered her mouth, pushing his energy into her. The remaining part of the arrow still protruded from her abdomen. After a moment, he pulled back, watching her. "Catherine?"

Her eyes eased open but closed again.

"Don't move. I have not removed the rest of the arrow. Are you ready?"

She nodded.

Caliostro took hold and pulled while placing his other hand on her lower belly.

Blood burst from her mouth, a cough chasing it.

Caliostro hovered his mouth over hers. His inner force poured into her, the wound healing within seconds.

Catherine touched his lips with hers, then kissed him. Her arms locked around his neck and pulled him down and over her.

He returned the kiss with deep-seated passion.

Catherine pressed her body into his, and he lifted her into his arms.

They kissed feverishly as he walked to the bed. He laid down with her under him.

She moaned deep in her throat, making him moan in reply.

In the heat of passion, he fed on her soul energy. Several moments passed before he pulled back, but Catherine held tight to him. "We have to stop," he said after forcefully breaking the kiss.

Catherine smiled at him and attempted to pull his lips back to hers.

"No. You need to rest."

"Caliostro? Please. Why not change me?"

Caliostro moved from the bed to the fireplace and built a fire.

"We have had this talk many times now." He stacked logs and tinder in the fireplace.

Catherine approached him. She folded her arms, and a frown crinkled her features. "Yes, we have, but can't you now see that if I were like you, I would not be in such danger?"

Caliostro stopped building the fire and faced her. "Did you have something to do with the attack in the woods? Tell me you did not do something that foolish!" He listened closely.

Her heart rate galloped, and she could not meet his eyes. "What's foolish about wanting to be with you forever?" She stomped her feet in protest.

He said nothing and resumed building the fire.

Catherine walked up behind him. "Why are you doing that the human way? You can just make fire appear, so why bother?" She laughed, resting her head against his back and wrapping her arms around his waist.

Caliostro sighed. "Because you need to remember you aren't like me and that sometimes you must live as a human, even if you are of magic."

"Well, I'm not truly human, else I couldn't walk through the veil. So, again, why bother?" She walked around to stand in front of him. "Just kiss me again. I want you to. I know you want to, as you know I want more."

Caliostro turned away, but she grabbed his wrist. He looked back at her, frozen in her gaze.

Their lips met, and their hands tore at each other's clothes like a tidal wave raging against a thunderstorm. Caliostro's wayward coat flew one direction, and her green mid-length dress flew another. Catherine ripped at his shirt buttons, baring his chest, as he pulled her undergarment over her head. A battle of passion and want ensued on the rug before the fire.

Catherine pulled back. "I want to be with you for eternity. I beg you to turn me."

Their lovemaking became feverish and rough. Caliostro, in the throes of passion, performed a soul exchange. They soon melted into each other's arms, panting—sated yet drained.

"Caliostro, you know what I want. I think it's time we discussed it."

Caliostro's arms that held her tight a moment ago laxed.

"Why do you do this? Why? I want to be with you for all eternity. Don't you want me?"

Caliostro released her and got to his feet, pulling on his pants in one movement. "What just transpired has connected us. I can't offer you anything more than that." He pulled on his shirt and boots. "Why must we keep rehashing this? And now you have gone to such lengths to have your way." He turned from her in disgust.

Catherine came up behind him and put her hand on his forearm. "Why must I beg you?"

"You don't even know what you are asking for. Even I do not know. There is no evidence to support the claim the Magic Guild gave you. You believe I hold this power to change you!" He lifted his hands on either side of him, shrugging off her hold.

"But we won't know unless we try!"

"No, I won't do it. You could die; you more than likely will. Listen to yourself!" His eyes blazed. "You want me to drain your energy to the brink of death, then replace yours with mine?"

"It could work."

"Their theory is based on vampirism, which I am not," he stated, pulling on his coat.

"Then what's the harm in trying?"

He glared down at her. "If you don't give a care for your own life, I will."

"Who asked you to decide for me? Who?" she yelled, gathering her clothing. She dressed in a hurry, then headed for the bedroom door.

"You can't go," he said, grabbing her arm. "You don't even know where we are."

She yanked her arm from his grasp. "I'll do what I want."

Catherine stormed out, slamming the door behind her.

***

Duncan returned, carrying the sleeping Catherine, and jolted Caliostro from his memories.

He lifted her into his arms and laid her on the bed. Seated again, he took her hand.

Duncan stood by the exit, waiting.

"You may go. I wish to be alone with her."

"As you say," he said, and the door clicked upon his exit.

"You're still a beauty, completely unchanged," he whispered, as if his voice would disturb her. "I wish I could go back to that day and change what happened, change my decision, but it's too late."

SECRETS AND LIES

Caliostro readjusted the sheet on Catherine's shoulders. "I will free you," he said, leaving. *Anyone foolish enough to enter here will pay with their lives.* He placed his open palm on the center of the door. "Seal." he said, and the door disappeared.

His thoughts wandered to Alioson and how best to proceed. Leaving the lower area, he picked up her scent. It led him to the terrace.

There she stood, her back to the doorway.

"Can't you do as I ask for more than an hour?" He passed her and stopped at the edge of the terrace.

"I only agreed to leave your office."

Caliostro's hands slid into his pants pockets. He inhaled loudly, breathing in the night air, his head leaning back. "I must ask this, though I am in speculation of the truth. At what point did your memories return?"

"To be honest, it started with the first exchange. I have my reasons for not telling you. From your reaction, I wasn't wrong."

"How do I know you're not a plant by the Hunters Guild?"

"Look. I'm not your enemy."

"Correction, you are, based on the current situation." He headed inside.

"No, you stay. I'll go. After all, I'm the prisoner."

Before she reached the first step to the upper level, he grabbed her arm, forcing her around to face him.

Alioson twisted away, pulling. "Let me go!"

"Stop," he said, barely above a whisper.

Her eyes cut like daggers as she glared at him, her hair and clothing disheveled. The neat bun atop her head had released strands all around her shoulders. Her shirt was twisted and in disarray.

"Don't pull away from me."

She scoffed. "You really need to cut the commanding tone. What if I said, only if you beg?"

Caliostro pulled her in tight, staring at her lips.

Alioson averted her gaze. "No. Don't kiss me. Neither of us can think in that state. I'm a hunter, or was, and that's a fact you can't seem to ignore."

Caliostro released her arm and watched her ascend the stairs and turn the corner. He returned to the terrace, lost in his new feelings for Alioson and his old feelings for Catherine. The day she had become comatose echoed in his subconsciousness.

***

The Manor, 1821

Caliostro and Catherine sat facing each other, both glaring.

"I've been over this with you. How many times? I will not change my mind. Any ideas you may have of hoping to force me need to stop!"

Catherine's frown deepened. Both eyes closed, a sigh escaping her. "You should want to turn me. Do you want me to be an old hag and you to look forever as you do? Is that why you keep saying no?"

252

Caliostro scowled, saying nothing.

Catherine's hair hovered, and little sparks of lightning shot from her upper arms and neck, nostrils flaring.

"You need to calm down." He casually crossed his legs. "You know your magic is uncontrollable in an angered state."

Her fists tightened on the chair's armrests. The temperature in the room rose, and the lights flicked in protest.

"Catherine, control it."

Her fingers flexed and relaxed; both eyes shut as she took deep breaths. The temperature normalized, as did her hair.

"If you study and grow your abilities as a magic user, you can slow or stop the aging process."

Her glare returned. "Don't you understand, Caliostro? Can't you see my side of things? I want to be with you forever, as your life mate."

"You could die. You are asking me to do something I haven't done before and wouldn't do under normal circumstances." He sat forward in his seat. "Your life shouldn't be thought of as if it's not important."

"I don't care how dangerous it is! You either love me or don't!" She shrugged.

"I don't want to argue about this any longer. I have given my reasons."

"I understand your concerns, I really do, but I won't change my mind."

Caliostro opened the balcony doors and flew into the night. He returned hours later, back across the veil. His senses felt the change in their ethereal connection; she was fading. His heart pounded in his own ears as he sped toward home.

Something had destroyed the balcony doors, and singed markings adorned what remained of the frame.

"Catherine!" he yelled, running inside. The smell of her blood filled the space. He scanned the area to see the bedroom destroyed. Furniture lay in pieces here and there. Holes dotted many of the walls, and burn marks covered the wooden floors. Running to the open door of the bedroom, he saw smeared blood, and in the middle of the hall lay Catherine.

"Catherine!" In an instant, he held her unresponsive form. "Please, please. No."

Blood covered her emerald-colored dress, torn at the waist and revealing singed flesh.

He transferred his soul energy into her through mouth contact. He pulled back to check her wounds.

She wasn't healing, and her heart had stopped.

"No! Catherine!" He performed an exchange, desperate to save her. His energy flowed between their lips, the last of her inner force filling him.

Her eyes shot open, matching the blue glow of his own.

He stared at her in shock.

Her eyes drifted closed, and she was still.

"Catherine!" He checked her body but found no wounds.

Her breathing was even, and the sound of her heartbeat was no longer the same. She was changed.

***

Caliostro stared into the darkness that filled the night sky. "Never again." He returned to his office.

Not long after sitting behind the desk, Duncan knocked at the door.

"You may enter," he said, swiveling his chair to face him.

"I know you won't like my advice."

Caliostro cocked his head to the side, pinched the bridge of his nose, and sighed. "If you know I won't like it, then why bother me?" He eyed him over his interlocked fingers, elbows resting on the desk. "It's not out of character for you to give unwanted advice, now, is it?"

"Lord Masterson, I feel you underestimate Miss Alioson. You still know very little of her. and how she came to be here. It's suspicious, to be honest."

"I understand your concerns, Duncan. Believe me, I have had them myself. However, as I don't fully have all the evidence at hand, I will not throw her out," he said, keeping direct eye contact.

"Milord, I did not mean for you to … simply throw her out. I think the problem at hand would need a much more direct approach to secure the safety of this manor and your holdings."

Caliostro stood quickly in response to Duncan's words and stepped around the desk. "Let me state this for you. Anyone who's present will never harm her; is that clear?"

They both stood within a few inches of each other. Caliostro's eyes glowed, resting his head back, looking down his nose at Duncan.

Standing his ground, Duncan emanated an orange glow around his frame, not breaking eye contact with Caliostro. "Even so, I will watch out for you, even if you don't want me to." Duncan backed away, turned on his heel, and left.

Caliostro rolled his head in a full circle, pulling his collar. He loosened the two buttons at his throat and glanced at his desk, thinking of the black stone. *I must make a move.*

***

Caliostro stood in front of Alioson's door the next morning. Closing his eyes, he listened to fabric rustling and a drawer opening, then closing. He waited a moment, then knocked twice.

There was no answer.

"Alioson?"

Still no reply.

"We need to talk." He paused, hearing a door close. "Alioson, I'm coming in." he opened the door and entered slowly. She wasn't in the main room, but he heard the shower running. He looked around, waiting for her to finish. Everything was neat and in place. Her smell filled the room as usual. He had yet to compare the scent and fully analyze it, but now he took the time to do so. The strength of cedar enveloped him, while the comforting blend of jasmine, vanilla and magnolia soothed his senses. A smile spread across his face, his head falling back. He drew in the aroma.

Minutes later, the bathroom door opened, and steam flooded out. Alioson exited amid it. Her hair was wrapped in a towel atop her head. She wore an all-white dress that fell to the floor, covering the tops of her feet. "Oh, I'm allowed visitors, am I?" Her eyes rolled as she walked to the vanity and sat.

Caliostro cleared his throat, his eyes following her every move. "I knocked and called out to you."

"Why would you need to ask a prisoner like myself?" She watched him through the mirror, grabbing for a brush and comb.

Her bare neck caught his attention as her hands worked to unwrap her hair. He stepped toward her but stopped himself.

Alioson saw his movement. Her hands froze, and their gazes caressed one another.

Focus. You've been alive long enough to focus. He rubbed the back of his neck with his left hand.

After a drawn-out moment, she broke their stare to dry her hair.

"You're not a prisoner."

"Sure, if you say so." She looked away, a heavy swallow caressing her throat.

Caliostro reached his mind to hers, searching, but he heard nothing.

The towel stilled in her hand. Resting it on the vanity top, she looked at his reflection in the mirror. "I asked you not to do that. I told you I can feel you sliding along my mind, and I don't want you there right now." She ran the brush repeatedly through her hair.

"You've changed."

"I don't think you know me well enough to make that statement. You have clarified that we're strangers. Possibly enemies."

"I'm not sure what we are, but I see the change in you. You are a hunter, after all."

"I haven't changed. I'm remembering who I am," she said, rummaging through one of the vanity drawers.

"What do you remember?"

"Not much. The most important thing is me being a hunter."

"I need to know what you remember," he said, taking a seat.

"What good will that do?"

"I would trust you more if I didn't believe you're keeping things from me."

She sighed, turned toward him, and recounted what she recalled.

"Is that everything?"

"Everything important."

"You want me to trust you, then all details are important."

"Where are you going with this?"

"I hadn't said before, but I think either magic or some other type of power is involved with you being here."

"Great, so you're saying I'm some part of a bigger plan? And what? Was I sent here?"

"That, I don't know. The Hunters Guild has never left me alone. The only reason they don't bother me more is because I kill every hunter they send. Maybe you are their new tactic."

"I see. So, you're convinced I'm a plant?"

"More than likely, that's the case."

"But what sense does that make? I mean, you have killed so many of their hunters. What could I accomplish alone? And what about my memories?"

"Your memories seem to be only locked away but all still readily there."

"You sure are assuming a lot. Couldn't I just have hit my head or something?"

"Under the circumstances, no, and that would have nothing to do with how you came through the veil. The facts are, only humans who have died pass naturally through here. Somehow, you're here."

"How do you know I was here for you? Maybe I had another mission, or an accident occurred."

"Yes, but how did you come to be in my lake? Why were you on my land? Also, that you're a member of the Hunters Guild makes me suspicious." Caliostro felt the same darkness in the foyer surrounding him. He looked over his shoulder. Nothing was there, but a chill creeped up his spine.

"Caliostro, do not covet what is not yours," an inauspicious voice whispered through his mind.

He approached the balcony doors to check the seal. It was in place. He listened, waiting for the voice to speak again. Silence.

"Are you listening to me?" Alioson arched one brow at him.

"I assume you didn't hear that?"

"Hear what? Anyway, it boils down to me remembering who I am. If not, I'm stuck here, and you're left wondering."

He didn't answer, the whispers still distracting him.

"You know the only way to make me remember."

He faced her, his mouth drawing a hardline.

She walked over to him, and their gazes bore into one another.

"Exchanging any further could be dangerous. I don't want to hurt you. I won't hurt you." His hands became fists at his sides.

"How do you know it won't be me hurting you?" She stood on tiptoe, wrapping her arms around his neck, bringing her eyes level with his.

A bitter chuckle escaped him. "One minute, you're angry with me and saying not to kiss you. Now you wrap your arms around me. Are we both going to ignore the facts of the situation?"

"If that's what it takes."

"Let's not do this." He pulled her arms from around his neck and stepped backward.

She frowned. "It's the only way I can remember; you know that. Every time we've exchanged, I've recalled some part of my memory."

"There are too many secrets between us, too many unanswered questions." He walked around her and left.

TRUTH AND CHANGES

Caliostro's black dress boots dug into the soft ground beneath his feet. He paced under the canopy of the trees. The woods were silent, and the sun was high. His right hand ran roughly through his loose hair. *She must be a plant. I know I should kill her, but I can't.* Caliostro stopped his pacing when Duncan walked up.

"Lord Masterson?"

"What is it?"

"Have you decided what you will do?"

"I'm not discussing this with you. You are to stay out of it." Caliostro turned away, staring into the woods.

Duncan's scrutinizing scowl bore into his back.

"Why are you still here?" He glanced over his shoulder. "Leave me."

Duncan headed toward the manor.

Caliostro walked deeper into the woods, lost in thought.

***

The next day, Alioson practiced in the training room. For hours on end, she let her body recall what her mind could remember. She felt she still had many holes to fill, but she kept practicing.

Covered in sweat, with a towel wrapped around her neck, she sat on the padded section of the floor when Caliostro entered. He wore his usual dress pants, but he had no vest or jacket over his button-down shirt. Black was his color of the day. His sleeves were rolled to the elbow, showing the fine detail of his muscular forearm. He stopped in front of her, staring down.

Alioson did not acknowledge him past her ogling and jogged around the room. She could feel his eyes following her but kept jogging.

Caliostro suddenly appeared in front of her, making her halt.

Alioson rolled her eyes and jogged around him.

"Alioson!"

She stopped but didn't turn to face him.

"If I feel your life is in danger, I will not continue," he said next to her ear.

She met his gaze. The energy in the room heated. Their lips met, and the desire they felt for each other took over. Caliostro led the kiss, changing angles multiple times. The light from the exchange streamed between their locked lips. He pulled back, breaking contact.

"Don't," she commanded, her right hand fisting in his hair.

Their kiss reignited. The exchange of inner force pulled and exploded within them.

Alioson as a little girl playing with her mother, going to school, and more flashed through both their minds. Then she was training, fighting. Flashes of blood and death spread around them as he absorbed her inner force, and she, his. Alioson's grip lessened in his hair.

A growl escaped Caliostro's lips, and he pulled away.

Alioson opened her eyes to find the black smokey-eyed Caliostro leering at her. She had no time to react as his incisors lengthened and sank into her neck. The sound of sucking and gulping filled the room. Alioson couldn't scream or move. Her head fell back and to the side. "Cal … Caliostro," she whispered, her body going limp.

He returned to his senses to find the unconscious Alioson at his feet. "Alioson!" Blood dripped from the corner of his mouth. Realization hit him. "No, no, no! Not again!" Kneeling, he gathered her to him.

Her heart wasn't beating, but he was determined. His lips covered hers. Inner force pumped into her as he took the last drops of hers into him. The wound on her neck closed, her heart beat again, and warmth returned to her skin. He pulled away, looking down. She didn't move.

"Alioson?"

Still, she did not stir.

"What have I done? Please don't end up like Catherine." He cradled her to him and headed for the upper level.

Hours passed as he paced in front of her bed.

Duncan knocked on the door.

"Come in."

"What has happened?" Duncan glanced from Alioson to Caliostro.

"She'll wake up. She will."

Duncan said nothing but looked unsure.

"Leave us. I don't want to hear your negative thoughts right now."

Duncan left, shutting the door behind him.

***

A force pulled Alioson deep into the darkness of her mind. There was no sound, only the dark. "Where is this? Hello!"

A bright blue light shined in the distance. She walked toward it, but it moved farther each time she closed in. Alioson burst into a run. Multiple voices echoed around her. She came to a stop, the room filling with light. A familiar scene played out in front of her.

"Do you honestly think you can hide her from me, Ayina?" The man chuckled. "You still don't understand what I am? Do you?"

Alioson stood behind him, but he was a blur. Her mother's face was clear to her sight. The fear in her mother's eyes brought tears to her own. She glanced at the upper level to see her younger self ducked, watching.

Her mother clawed at the hand gripping her throat.

Alioson tried to lift her feet but couldn't. She was locked in place. "*Mom!*" adult Alioson screamed, but her words went unheard.

"Please, just leave her be," Ayina begged.

"My dear, that is not how it will happen. I will have her. It is what we agreed."

Alioson's feet moved. She glanced down, then back to the man holding her mother.

Ayina gurgled as he tightened his grip.

Alioson put one foot forward, but an invisible force pushed her backward, and she stumbled. "Let her go!" She spotted a lamp atop the long wooden table behind him. Alioson scooped it up and threw it at the back of his head.

"Really?" He laughed, throwing his head back.

Alioson balled her fist and screamed as she charged at him, the invisible force no longer present. She swung but stopped.

Long black hair pulled into a ponytail assailed her vision. The scent of sandalwood and citrus hung in the air.

She stood frozen, not believing what her mind was telling her.

"Why would such a thing work? Your little witchy powers will do you no good here."

He bit Ayina's neck. Blood sprayed. Her flesh ripping away.

Young Alioson screamed, making the man face her with bright blue glowing eyes.

Alioson gasped, her hands covering her mouth.

Caliostro regarded her younger self with a blood-covered mouth and chin, droplets staining his white shirt under his long black coat.

***

Caliostro stood over Alioson's sleeping form. Days had passed, and he considered she would share the same fate as Catherine. He heard a change in her heartbeat, then her eyes opened, and they were as blue as his and glowing. "Alioson ..." He reached for her.

She jumped from the bed and landed on the vanity. Her posture was that of a person ready to attack—feet shoulder width apart and crotched. Her brow deepened, fixating on him.

"Alioson, it's okay. You're awake now."

She glanced around, her eyes radiating.

Catherine had been right all along. He stepped toward her. "I don't know why, but I lost control again, and I hurt you. I was afraid I couldn't save you."

Alioson's hand went to where the bite had been, her eyes following. She frowned at him. "Stay away from me."

"Alioson, please. I don't know what happened. Something … felt as if it took me over."

She stepped backward, bringing the underside of her thighs in contact with the vanity. She jumped and turned.

Blue glowing eyes stared at her. "Alioson?" He hesitantly approached her.

"What have you done to me?" She turned, toppling the vanity chair.

Something I wish I hadn't.

"What do you mean? What did you *do*?" Her eyes intensified.

"Can you hear my thoughts?" He took another step. *Alioson, can you hear me?*

Her eyes widened.

"You can hear me. No one has ever been able to without my consent."

"It was you, Caliostro. How could it be you?" Her scowl deepened.

"What have you remembered?"

"Stay back! Tell me what you've done! *How could you? How could you hurt her?*"

"I don't know what you have remembered, but just … "

"I said stay back!"

Caliostro grabbed her upper arms and took her mouth with his.

Her inner force filled him. She pushed at his chest but fell into the exchange. Her hands fisted in his shirt and tears spilled down her cheeks. Her memories flooded into him, fully awakening in her.

***

"He's the one, the creature who took your mother's life. If you pull off this job, we will avenge your mother." Cordaglen spun his chair to face Alioson.

She spied the photos on his desk. It was him. She remembered his hair and those eyes. Alioson grabbed one photo to see Caliostro standing outside a black car in front of a hotel. Her top lip twitched as she slammed the photo onto the desk. "I'll do anything to kill him."

Cordaglen smiled. "Good. You must do as I tell you with no questions. Once you are at his location, you are on your own."

"I won't fail." Alioson's eyes hardened.

"If you fail, there's no coming back. Do you understand?"

"Yes."

***

Caliostro and Alioson jolted apart as the memory faded.

"You were, as I feared, a plant."

Alioson backed toward the balcony doors.

"Alioson, don't."

She regarded him in disgust. A glimpse of sadness settled behind her eyes. She shook her head, the blue glow of her eyes returning. She bolted for the doors, but he was there, blocking her way.

"Don't do this."

"Move!"

"I won't let you leave."

She threw a right hook.

He caught it, clutching tightly. "Alioson, please. I don't want to fight you." He released her fist.

"Then you should have let me pass." Alioson jumped, grabbed a chair, and threw it at him.

He lifted one arm to block it and broke it into pieces.

273

She side kicked him, but he caught her foot and twisted it, throwing her off balance. Alioson rotated her body midair, back-flipped, then charged at him. The force of her weight and speed knocked them both through the glass door at his back. Alioson leaped onto the balcony rail.

"Alioson! Stop. Listen to me!" He crept toward her. "You can't wander around on this side of the veil. You don't understand life here."

She flipped off the railing and took off at a mad dash.

He took to the sky, following her across his land and through the woods. She was fast, but he kept her within his sights. *"Alioson! Come back. You have it all wrong!"*

"Stay out of my head!"

Caliostro followed her to the nearest city. Her scent had changed, but with it, their connection had grown. Tracking her was easy. The town they entered looked like Drawdtic city. The nightlife here was busy and bright; clubs lined the streets. He smelled Lycrians, vampires, the rotting dead, and more.

Alioson ran inside a building marked with a red neon sign that read, KLEYS.

Great. She means to mingle with the locals. Once inside, he spotted her leaning on the bar with her back to it. Their eyes locked and held as he approached her. He leaned in and whispered in her ear, "Let's not do this here."

Her eyes blazed to life. Smiling up at him, she moved to the dance floor and swayed to the up tempo of the hard-bumping music with the nearest stranger. Vampires, Lycrians, shifters, and many other beings danced. She passed one partner for the next without taking her eyes off Caliostro.

He grabbed her arm and pulled her to a dark corner. His body trapped her against the wall.

A guy with lavender glowing eyes glanced in their direction.

Caliostro caught the smell of him—Lycrian and from his grandfather's pack. "Avert your eyes," Caliostro said to the Lycrian.

He obeyed and moved into the crowd.

Caliostro narrowed his eyes at Alioson. "Have you had your fun?"

She glared back. "No. And you don't get to decide anything for me, okay?" She pushed him away and ducked under his arm, only to have him pull her back.

"Don't make me chase you. We need to talk about your memories."

"I don't need or want to do anything with you." She sped away.

He followed her through dark alley after dark alley. *"Alioson!"*

She stopped and peered over her shoulder.

"You think you know things, but you don't!" He stalked toward her. "I'm not who you seem to think I am!"

"I know all I need to know, now that my memories are intact."

"You should think more about that." He advanced closer. "What you recall of me and your mother is not true."

She glared at him, then took off running.

***

Alioson doubled back and stopped at the location where he'd first shown her the veil. She stood in the clearing, waiting.

Caliostro landed, his wings dissipating. "I know you think I killed your mother, but you are mistaken."

She faced him. "I saw it happen. Anything you say now will mean nothing."

Caliostro observed the glow of her eyes deepening. "Alioson …" He eased closer. "They have tricked you, and someone has tampered with your memories. Come back to the manor and we can—"

"We can, what? You couldn't possibly trust me. And I want you dead!" She charged him.

Caliostro dodged to the side, deflecting her punch. "Stop, Alioson! I won't fight you!" Caliostro moved backward out of her range.

Alioson gritted her teeth. "I remember your face. I remember how you ripped into her throat, like you did to me!"

"They have twisted your memory. You are placing my face on your mother's killer. I know I've never harmed anyone in such a way."

"Only me twice, right?" she asked in a mocking tone.

"Listen to me! They're using you! We can't trust the Hunters Guild!"

Before she could reply, a large magical explosion burst where they stood, knocking them apart. Caliostro flipped midair. Dirt and dust impeded his vision. He charged through the cloud but halted.

A massive Lycrian stood at the veil line. Under its arm was an unconscious Alioson. Over fifty Lycrians marched through the veil, revealing themselves. In the center of the pack stood one man in mortal form.

Even from the distance where Caliostro stood, he discerned the silver-colored eyes. Caliostro's hands flexed and un-flexed at his sides. "Duncan."

"Your grandfather has requested to see you, Lord Masterson."

"No thanks, and a nice trick using the veil to hide the pack. I'll need you to return Alioson to me at once." He stepped forward.

"It would be best if you comply with your grandfather's request." Duncan straightened his black vest.

Caliostro smirked, looking off to the side. He sighed, settled one hand in his left pants pocket, and meandered to Duncan with glowing eyes. "Is this your way of staying out of it?" His wings appeared, illuminating the grassy field with blue light.

"Lord, it was for the best that I intervened when I did. Let's make this easy."

Caliostro called his sword forth. The opal handle appeared in his free hand, bright blue energy shooting from its base. "You are the one who decided to not heed my words. Why should I make it easy?"

"Your father would be very disappointed in the choices you have made as of late." Duncan cleared his throat and creaked his neck from side to side. He removed his vest, then glared at Caliostro.

Caliostro charged Duncan and the Lycrians, no fear in his eyes.

To be continued...

Winterwolf
Tale of the Watcher

MY FUTURE

Drops of sweat dripped from the silver ends of medium-length hair as eyes of matching color scanned into the woods ahead. Multiple branches snapped to the left, drawing the attention of the silver-haired male. Before he could turn in that direction, four large Dagaru worms emerged from among the trees.

"Shit!" he said, through clench teeth.

With a quick backflip, he landed on the large branch above his head. He made six leaps in rapid succession before checking behind him. Now there were five of them clambering over each other to get to him.

"Disgusting creatures." He spat.

As he moved to jump, a force knocked him off his feet. Slime and a sooty substance covered his black-clad legs and knee-high boots. A soul-shattering screech pierced the night, and five rows of razor-sharp teeth made themselves known.

Silver eyes glowed in the night, and an orange light emanated from the frame of the man the Dagaru had by the legs. The worm-like creature's massive, six-foot form flew back and away, while four others made their way toward him from all sides. He found himself surrounded and noticed two others quickly approaching the circle.

The creatures snarled and stood at their six-foot height. Their mouths were nothing but voids of teeth and nothingness.

"You won't best a Winterwolf that easily, no matter how hungry you are."

He closed his eyes and focused. They—now seven— all leaped. At that moment, a light blast from his frame knocked all but one creature into pieces. Blood covered the trees. One Dagaru escaped the blast and sank its teeth into Winterwolf's back, knocking him to the ground.

Sucking and slurping sounds echoed through the dark woods as the Dagaru attempted to devour him.

"Ahhhrrrgggg!" grunted Winterwolf as pain shot through his body and poison filled him.

With all the strength he could muster, he wrestled one more energy blast from his body, disintegrating the last Dagaru.

Already lying in the dirt and grime of the forest floor, he made no move to stand and took a deep breath, followed by another. After a few minutes had passed, he heard booted steps approaching him.

"You had best improve, Duncan, or you will become the largest disappointment to the Winterwolf clan," boomed the commanding voice.

Duncan didn't move or speak as he listened to the retreating steps of his father. With a deep grunt of frustration, he got to his feet in one move and dusted his pants off.

He gripped his left shoulder and could feel the wound on his back leaking fresh blood down and into the waistline of his pants. He easily tore the right sleeve of what remained of his long tunic. Now bare-chested, he made his way through the dark woods.

The last leg of the journey was exhausting as his magic drained and his wound festered.

Duncan came to a stop once his family's castle was in sight.

"Damn Dagaru worms." He groaned, reaching over his left shoulder to grip the torn flesh at the top of his back. The Dagaru had left a few teeth in the wound and he could feel dizziness setting in.

His boots picked up mud from the wet forest floor as his feet became heavier and heavier. After clearing the trees, he had miles to go before he would be at his family's gates. Screeching from above caught his attention. A darkling windrone circled above his head, calling out to others like it nearby. He watched it land on a patch of stones far to his left. Its ten eyes, which had red pupils, were watchful as he kept on his way. He looked all around him and knew that if he passed out in his current location, that windrone and its friends would surely make certain he never woke again. They would tear his flesh apart with their large, gaping mouths full of razor-sharp teeth, feathers flapping gleefully over his remains.

Silence lay heavily around him, and the poison within him flooded his body, making each additional step nearly impossible. The windrone stalked him, and now two others followed.

"You may be hungry but you will not have me!" Duncan yelled over his shoulder.

The creatures screeched in unison at his defiance.

With one final step, his knees gave out, the poison claiming his mobility. He braced his hands on the soil and glanced to the right when a bright light flashed past him and melted the head of the windrone that was closing in. The other two followed the fate of the first one. Their bodies hit the ground, each with a resounding thud.

Duncan looked all around him and saw no one.

"Who's there?!"

No one answered.

He got to his feet; his legs worked once more.

His eyebrows raised in shock as he wiggled his right foot in front of him.

He took one last glance around before he moved with renewed speed toward his family's castle walls.

***

The Winterwolf castle stretched for miles in an octagonal shape. Its high, dark walls loomed and gave off a stoic allusion to the centuries-old family's history.

Duncan made his way down the torch-lit stone path that led to the front gates of the stronghold. As he neared, the gates lifted, answering to the blood pumping within his veins.

"Lord Winterwolf! What has happened?!"

Duncan turned toward the screeching voice of young Onnisha, daughter of the Lycrian general. She came to visit often for magic training, but Duncan had heard the rumors that she came mostly to see him.

She ran over to him, dropping whatever books she had been carrying. With blood covering him from head to toe and his clothing torn up, he was sure he made an unseemly sight.

He held his hand up to stop her from grabbing onto him.

"I'll be fine once I restore my magic. Currently, the Dagaru poison in my body is blocking my magic."

Onnisha watched him walk away, her hands becoming fists at her sides.

Duncan made his way to the left side of the castle toward the Mage Infirmary. Blue and yellow lights engulfed his frame as he entered the portal at the end of the short corridor. In a blink, pure, white cloth surrounded him. Draped walls and white stone floors filled his sight. His booted feet clicked loudly across the floor as he made his way to the bright red door at the end of the long hall.

A bout of dizziness stopped him from advancing midway down the hall. His fingers gripped one of the pristine drapes at his side, giving him the leverage to stay upright.

His mind wandered back to the windrone attack, and how someone had dispatched them. He knew whoever that had been, also healed him enough so that he could make it back.

"Who was it? Father?" he said, perplexed.

After a few more moments, he made his way to the infirmary. The Mage Infirmary was a haven of peace and healing in the castle. As he stepped into the space, he felt light, and a feeling of calmness filled him. Green plant life grew everywhere in the partitioned yet massive space, except for one corner that was filled with dark vines. The ceiling comprised different forms of magical energy. Levitating beds lined the treatment area, surrounded by beautiful, draped fabric. Students of magic and seasoned magic users moved about with their prospective tasks and duties.

"Lord Winterwolf, what has happened to you?" asked a feminine voice to his right.

Duncan turned to find that a tall, slim female with long, black hair and fingers like spider legs was walking toward him. Her solid-black pupils stood out against her cloud-colored skin, marred with thin black veins from her neck to her lower jawline.

"Lieselotte? When did you return?" Duncan asked, before another bout of dizziness hit him.

"Dagaru poisoning? Come, let's get you treated."

She led him to the healing room. Once he was relaxed on a bed, she hovered her hands over his body, humming softly. Duncan closed his eyes and focused on her humming. Lieselotte was of the Spidral kind. They looked as though shrouded in darkness, but were natural healers.

Several minutes passed before her humming ceased and he could no longer feel the poison pushing its way through his body.

"It's all done, Lord Winterwolf. How did you get tied up with a disgusting Dagaru?" she asked, stepping back as he swung his feet over the edge of the bed.

"Part of my training, but I did not expect seven of them. One got the upper hand."

Lieselotte moved around to inspect his back.

"Yes, this wound is where the poison set in."

Duncan hopped down. Even with his six-foot height, stepping down was a bit much.

"Thank you for the help, Lieselotte," he said, turning to find her rummaging through a nearby cabinet.

"Here, change into this."

She tossed him a tan-colored robe.

"Thanks."

"Is your training complete, or is there more?" she asked, eyeing him with curiosity.

"There is always more," he replied, shuffling into the robe. "Heading to report in now."

"Good luck."

With a quick nod, Duncan left the infirmary and headed to his father's meeting room, where he spent most of his time.

Magic fully restored and pulsating in his blood again, he quickened his pace to see his father and get the reporting done.

He came to the fifteen-foot double doors that were lined with green gems in the white stone. Before he could announce himself, his father's voice thundered from the other side of the doors.

"You may enter."

Duncan pushed through the heavy doors and slid in, closing them behind him.

"Father," he said, inclining his head before walking further into the room that looked like an old library. A large, white marble desk was in the center of an overly large window.

"I'm here to report, father."

"Go on."

"As you know, I was overwhelmed by the swarm of Dagaru worms, but I overcame them in the end."

"You call that 'besting' them, do you?" he scoffed.

Duncan's jaw tightened, but he did not speak.

"Well, you survived. Though with embarrassment," his father continued, not looking up from the book in front of him on the desk.

Duncan stared at the top of his father's head. He looked much like him. The same silvery white hair covered his head and olive skin. When he looked up, his silver eyes mirrored Duncan's perfectly in color.

"Your training in connection with the Winterwolf family has ended."

Duncan raised his eyebrows, glanced down, then looked back at his father in bewilderment.

"You mean . . . what exactly?"

His father closed the book and stood, walking around his desk, never taking his eyes from Duncan's.

"Your fate has called, and you will be the next Winterwolf to enter the Watcher Academy and become a Watcher for the Mastersons."

"Wait, I'm the oldest of your sons. Am I not to lead the clan?"

"No, that will fall to whomever I choose when the time is right. Out of your four brothers, one of them will take the lead. You will fulfill your duty to this family by entering the Academy, as I have said."

He went back to his seat, reopening the book he had been reading before.

"I have no desire to do this. No, I will not do this. I am the eldest. What sense does it make that I would be called to be a Watcher?" His voice rose in pitch on the last few words.

"You will do as you are told. We all must follow the calling of our world, and this is your fate. Fighting against it will only lead to your demise and show a weakness of this clan," he said, looking back at the book once more.

"Are you implying I am that weakness?!"

An orange aura emanated from Duncan as he continued to stare at his father.

"You had better rein that magic of yours in before I do it for you. Leave me and prepare to depart when I give word," he said, without an upward glance.

Duncan took a step toward his father when the doors at his back swung open.

A female with teal colored hair that almost touched the ground, skin blessed by generations of sunlight, and caramel-colored eyes floated into the room. Though she was only five-foot two, magical power breathed from every pore on her frame that was delicately covered by white robes of lace.

Duncan faced her, then glanced once more in his father's direction before his eyes returned to hers.

"Mother," he said, inclining his head before he moved past her, shutting the doors behind him.

"Darwin, why do you insist on being like that with him?" she asked, coming to stand next to him.

"Riella, my love, it is for his own good. He is old enough to understand. But it is out of my control that he was fated to be chosen. You know this."

She wrapped her arms about his shoulders from behind and leaned in close to his left ear.

"I know, my love, but Duncan has a strong and independent will."

Darwin became quiescent, then turned, pulled her onto his lap and hugged her close.

"Yes, and that will not serve him well now that he will become a Watcher for the Mastersons. It is how it must be."

There was worry on both their faces as they sat and cuddled.

REBELLION

Duncan closed his eyes as hot water from the shower ran over his thin, toned frame. His body, fully healed, showed no signs of the Dagaru worm's attack. He stayed under the water's current until it got cold. His eyes roamed over his reflection on the mirrored wall along the shower. The magic that coursed through his veins differed from his siblings'. His magic was not only elemental. He had the ability to control the unknown spirits; a connection with the dead, healing, and control of energies. Even after existing for as long as he had, he'd still be young for one of his clan.

He exited the shower, donned a soft robe, and stepped out onto his balcony, into the night air .

"I will not be ruled over," he said, a light breeze rustling his hair.

Once back inside, he packed a light bag and threw it over his shoulder, and left for the closest town. With the connections he had curated over the last few centuries, there were friends who ran some of the local shops and taverns there that could help him get settled.

Duncan went back to the infirmary and activated one portal that he had used in the past to travel to the nearby towns. He stepped through after one last look to make sure he was alone. The magic of the portal transported him to a dark alleyway. He could hear people chatting from a window just above his head. The alley was dark and dank and smelled of rotting flesh.

He hiked his bag higher on his back and walked out of the alley, making his way down the cobblestone walk path. Businesses and homes alike lined the street. Different species, male and female, moved about, going here and there. Noise and music came from one particular building, so he headed straight for it.

A bright red painted sign reading "Nowhere Man" hung above the doorframe. Inside the tavern, everything was constructed of old wood, and darkness enveloped the space. In the far-left corner, there was a makeshift stage where a male with large horns, dressed all in black and red, played a violin. Duncan took a seat at the bar and waited for the barkeep to get to him.

"What are you having, stranger?" asked the burly, pointed-ear male behind the bar.

"What's popular?" Duncan asked, setting his bag on the stool next to him.

"Well, most newbies like our Ghoul Gin." he said, with a smirk.

"I'll try it."

Duncan pulled up his sleeve and took out a small onyx blade, slicing open his index finger on his left hand. A few drops fell on the octagonal sigil in front of him at the bar. It lit up, then fizzled out, the blood absorbed.

The barkeep's eyes widened when the name Winterwolf appeared on his side of the sigil with a sign of an allowed spending limit—which was unlimited.

"Whatever you want, Mister Winterwolf, is yours."

Duncan glanced around, making sure no one heard the barkeep, then ordered the Ghoul Gin. After finishing his drink, he went to visit his one friend who owned many of the local businesses.

The large house at the tail end of town belonged to his friend. He knocked on the bright white door minutes later. The door swung open to reveal a male of five-nine with a muscular build. His black hair hung to his waist and his differently colored eyes—one jade and one yellow—stared at Duncan in shock.

"Wolf?! Wow, I'm surprised to see you. What's new?"

"It's been some time, Victor. I need a place to stay for a bit; a place not of the mainstream options."

"Hey, yeah, not a problem in the least. Let me grab a shirt and I'll be right out."

He stepped back inside, leaving the door ajar. Duncan could hear a woman's voice inside asking him where he was going.

Victor emerged not long after, a light frown on his face.

"Did I interrupt anything?" Duncan asked, stepping back so he could precede him.

"Not at all. Let's head over to my blacksmith shop and have a talk."

***

Duncan followed Victor through the winding streets of the town. The glow of the streetlights cast long shadows across the cobblestones. The night air was alive with the sounds of laughter, music, and the occasional shout from revelers spilling out of taverns.

As they approached Victor's blacksmith shop, Duncan couldn't help but feel a sense of nostalgia wash over him. The familiar scent of hot metal and burning coal filled his nostrils, bringing back memories of a time long past. He stepped through the doorway behind Victor, the warmth of the forge enveloping him like an old friend.

They settled into a corner of the shop, away from prying eyes and ears. Duncan took a seat on a sturdy wooden stool while Victor leaned against a workbench, his arms crossed over his chest.

"So, what brings you to my neck of the woods, Wolf?" Victor asked, his voice tinged with curiosity.

Duncan sighed, running a hand through his damp hair.

"I need to lie low for a while. Things have gotten . . . complicated back home."

Victor raised an eyebrow, his mismatched eyes studying Duncan intently.

"Complicated how?"

Duncan hesitated, unsure of how much to reveal.

"Let's just say there's been a change in future leadership plans, and I'm not exactly behind the decisions being made. So, I took off unannounced."

Victor's expression darkened.

"I see. And you think they'll come looking for you here?"

Duncan nodded grimly.

"It's a possibility. I can't afford to take any chances."

Victor let out a low whistle.

"Sounds like you're in quite the predicament, my friend."

"That's one way to put it," Duncan muttered, rubbing the back of his neck.

There was a moment of silence between them, broken only by the crackling of the forge. Duncan could sense the weight of unspoken words hanging in the air, heavy and suffocating.

Finally, Victor spoke, his voice soft but resolute. "Well, you're welcome to stay here for as long as you need. Consider my home your sanctuary."

Duncan felt a surge of gratitude wash over him, accompanied by a pang of guilt. He hated burdening his friends with his problems, especially when they had their own lives to worry about.

"Thank you, Victor," he said quietly, meeting his friend's gaze. "I owe you one."

Victor waved off his gratitude with a dismissive gesture. "Nonsense. We look out for each other, remember? That's what friends do."

Duncan was about to say more when a soft, melodic voice drifted through the air, cutting through the silence of the blacksmith's shop like a silver blade. He turned, his attention drawn to the source of the sound, and his heart skipped a beat.

Standing in the doorway was a woman unlike any he had ever seen before. Her presence filled the room, exuding an aura of magic that sent shivers down Duncan's spine. She was tall, curvy, and graceful. Her skin was ash brown, with an undertone of sienna. Flowing locks of midnight-black hair cascaded over her shoulders like a silken waterfall. Her monolid, light caramel eyes sparkled with an otherworldly light, captivating and hypnotic.

Duncan found himself unable to tear his gaze away from her, his senses overwhelmed by her enchanting beauty. It was as if she held some mysterious power over him, beckoning him closer with each graceful movement.

Victor glanced up to see what Duncan was staring at. An expression of mild surprise crossed his face.

"Ah, Vandrah," he said, a hint of warmth creeping into his voice. "What brings you here at this hour?"

The woman—Vandrah—smiled, her lips curving into a knowing smirk, eyes locked on Duncan. "The usual. New steel for my guards, Victor," she replied, her voice like honeyed velvet. "But tell me. Who is your friend?" she said, her stare boring into Duncan's face.

Victor chuckled softly, shaking his head in amusement. "This is Duncan," he said, gesturing in his direction. "He's . . . passing through town and needed a place to lie low for a while. And Duncan, this is Vandrah, as you heard me greet her. Though you may know of her. She is the Guardian of the Veil."

Neither Duncan nor Vandrah made a move and only stared at one another with heated gazes.

Victor looked back and forth between the two. "Okay, then. I'll see about your steel order," he said, before walking away, shaking his head slowly.

There was something about Vandrah that set Duncan's instincts on edge, a primal instinct warning him of danger.

Vandrah's lips curved into a knowing smile, as if she could see right through Duncan's carefully constructed facade. "Ah, so," she murmured, taking a step closer to him. "A traveler in need of refuge. How . . . intriguing."

Duncan felt a shiver run down his spine as Vandrah approached, her presence enveloping him like a warm embrace. He could feel the magic crackling in the surrounding air, a potent force that seemed to pulse with every beat of his heart.

"What truly brings you to this humble town, Duncan?" Vandrah asked, her voice low and hypnotic.

Duncan swallowed hard, suddenly feeling as though his tongue had turned to lead. "I . . . I'm just passing through," he stammered, struggling to find his voice. "Trying to stay out of trouble, you know?"

Vandrah's smile widened, revealing a flash of pearly white teeth. "Trouble seems to have a way of finding us, no matter how hard we try to avoid it," she said cryptically.

Before Duncan could respond, the sound of heavy footsteps echoed through the shop, followed by the creaking of the door as it swung open. In the doorway stood a group of mages that Duncan recognized. All three had the signature Winterwolf silver-white hair. The shadows cast by the flickering torchlight outside obscured their faces.

Victor's expression hardened and his hand instinctively reached for one of his blacksmithing tools. "Can I help you, gentlemen?" he asked, his voice tight with tension.

The leader of the group stepped forward, features twisted into a sneer of disdain. "We're looking for someone," he said, his voice dripping with malice. "Duncan Winterwolf. We know you know him. Have you seen him?"

Duncan stood up, but Vandrah grabbed his forearm and pulled him to a door in the far corner near where their table was. Once through the door, he saw a burgundy, wheeled, enclosed carriage tied to four fierce-looking wolf beasts.

"Come with me."

Duncan hesitated a moment. He weighed his options. Go with Vandrah or go back with the mages his family clearly sent to find him. Doubling down on his determination to be free, he entered the carriage beside Vandrah without another word. The door closed behind them with a soft thud. The interior was dimly lit; the flickering torches cast dancing shadows across the walls.

"Where are we going?" Duncan asked, his voice barely above a whisper, his nerves on edge.

Vandrah's expression was unreadable as she settled into the seat opposite him, her gaze fixed on the window as the carriage lurched into motion. "To safety," she replied, her tone tinged with a bit of urgency.

"Where we are going, no one would dare come claim you by force," she promised, her voice soft but resolute. "Trust me."

Duncan nodded, a flicker of doubt crossing his mind before he pushed it aside.

As the carriage rolled on, Duncan found himself lost in thought, his mind swirling with questions and uncertainties. He knew nothing of Vandrah personally. The little he had learned was based on rumors he had overheard among the travelers and students who came to the Winterwolf castle.

"Deep in thought . . . aren't we?" she asked, glancing in his direction.

They rode into the night, leaving behind the familiar streets of the town and venturing into the unknown. And as the miles stretched out before them, Duncan couldn't shake the feeling that his destiny was hurtling toward an inevitable collision with fate.

***

Darkness enveloped the carriage as it rocked on. Duncan adjusted his overcoat and glanced at Vandrah from the corner of his eye.

"You have something to say, Winterwolf?" she asked, turning to face him.

Their shoulders brushed, and a shock of current went through his body. He closed his eyes for a moment and did his best not to react. After a minute, he opened his eyes to find her staring at him.

"Why did you help me if you know that I'm a Winterwolf?"

She chuckled. "Your surname means nothing to me; I simply overheard the men in the shop use it and wanted to see what it sounded like on my tongue."

Duncan faced forward once more, unsure what to make of her statement.

"Surely you know who the Winterwolf clan is," he said.

"I know of the clan and have met others in the past, but the name still means nothing to me. But . . ." She paused, leaning toward him. "However, I am interested in you, Duncan."

Her breath, so close to his ear, sent a small chill up his spine. She returned to her upright position, and soon they arrived at their destination.

After the carriage came to a stop and her guards opened the doors for them to exit, Duncan's eyes swept across the massive walls of the fortress before him.

Vandrah proceeded him, the train of her lavish black gown trailing behind her.

"Coming? Or do you plan to stand there and gawk?" she asked, a smirk lifting one corner of her full lips.

Duncan ran his hands through his hair, then took the wide staircase to the large double doors ahead.

The corridors of Vandrah's fortress twisted and turned like a labyrinth as they made their way through. Each shadowy hallway led deeper into the heart of the ancient structure. Duncan followed closely behind her; his senses were heightened by the eerie atmosphere that permeated the air. Torches flickered along the walls, casting dancing shadows that whispered secrets of ages long past.

Vandrah moved with purpose; her steps echoed faintly against the stone floor as they navigated the dimly lit passages. Duncan couldn't help but marvel at her grace, the way she seemed to glide effortlessly through the darkness. There was a magnetism about her, a dangerous allure that stirred something primal within him. He found himself drawn to her, unable to resist the pull of her enigmatic aura.

They came to a dark corridor that had many doors on either side. Vandrah stopped in front of the one at the end of the hall. The door swung open with no help, revealing a lush and fancy bedroom. Black silk, black leather and chains hung, covering different surfaces and draped on walls and over windows.

"This is where you can sleep as long as you are here."

"This is a rather grand room for an unknown guest," Duncan said, looking around the space without fully entering the room.

"Well, it would be, since it is my room."

Without another word, she turned and headed back the way they had come. He closed the door and followed her. The implications of her statement played over and over in his head, as they moved once more through the fortress that stretched on endlessly.

Duncan wondered what mysteries lay waiting to be discovered, what dark truths lurked in the shadows of such a structure or that of its owner. And yet, despite the foreboding atmosphere, he couldn't shake the feeling of excitement that coursed through his veins.

"This room is my sanctuary," Vandrah said, before the aqua-colored, giant double doors opened before them.

A vast chamber was bathed in an ethereal blue light. In the center of the room stood a grand indoor pool, its surface shimmering like liquid sapphire. The air hummed with power, the echoes of ancient magic vibrating through the very walls of the fortress.

Vandrah turned to face Duncan, her eyes gleaming in the dim light. There was a spark of mischief in her gaze, a hint of something wild and untamed. Duncan felt his breath catch in his throat as she approached him, her movements fluid and graceful.

"Welcome, Duncan," she murmured, her voice low and husky. "Here is the place I take daily refuge. Will you join me?"

Her words made him swallow, the promise of lust and danger intertwining in the air between them. He hesitated for a moment, the weight of their shared attraction hanging heavy in the air.

But then, with a sense of recklessness he couldn't quite explain, Duncan nodded. "I'll join you."

Vandrah smiled, a wicked grin that sent his pulse racing. Without another word, she shed her robes, the fabric falling away to reveal the smooth curves of her body. Duncan couldn't tear his gaze away; his heart pounded in his chest as he watched her step gracefully into the pool.

The water rippled around her, the surface breaking into a thousand shimmering waves. And then, with a daring glance in Duncan's direction, Vandrah disappeared beneath the surface, leaving him standing alone on the edge of the pool.

For a moment, he hesitated. But then, spurred on by an irresistible urge; after removing his clothes, he followed her into the depths, the water closing over his head with a soft splash.

She reemerged a few moments later, and Duncan followed. He pushed his wet hair back and out of his eyes just as she moved in close, pushing, hard, her naked form flush against his own.

"I would like it very much if you stayed here as long," her gaze left his eyes and landed on his lips, "as you would like," she said, as her hand slid over his glistening shoulder and into the hairs at the nape of his neck.

Duncan stared for a moment, lost in her words. Then slowly he leaned in, but he stopped just before his lips claimed hers. Their eyes locked and their breath echoed in the space.

Vandrah closed the distance and Duncan took control. With arms locked around her frame, he pushed her against the pool's edge, bracing his hand behind her as their kiss intensified.

Skin to skin and limbs entwined in the cool embrace of the pool, they surrendered to the currents of passion and desire long into the night. Hours later, Duncan held a slumbering Vandrah in his arms within the black silk sheets of her bedchamber. For the moment, he had found a place that wanted him.

YOU WERE CHOSEN

As the days blurred into nights, the intoxicating allure of the sorceress's desire dulled his senses. In all the centuries he had lived, she was the only woman that filled his mind constantly.

This is where I belong . . .

He thought as they once again found themselves in her pool. The room swirled with unspent magic, and Duncan never wanted to leave Vandrah's side.

But fate called in that moment.

Knock, knock.

Vandrah pulled back from their kiss. "What is it?!"

"There is a Riella Winterwolf here to see Duncan Winterwolf. She said she will not leave until he speaks with her," the guard said through the closed door.

"Tell her I will be there in a moment," Duncan said as he got out of the pool.

Vandrah grabbed his arm, stopping him. "Do what you must, but I would like nothing more than for you to return."

Duncan turned his hand over, gripped her wrist, and pulled her up out of the water into his arms.

"I will always return to you. Though our time together has been short, I plan this thing between us to go on to infinity."

He cupped either side of her face, kissing her until they were both gasping for air.

"I will be back soon."

He donned a black silk robe and pulled his pants on before heading to the front entrance of the fortress.

When he rounded the corner, his mother paced by the front door as if she could not wait to be away. Her eyes met his as he approached.

"Duncan," she began, her tone grave and filled with a weight that threatened to crush him, "how could you leave like that?"

"Mother, I refuse to be forced."

"You are a chosen one, ordained by powers far beyond your understanding."

Duncan's heart pounded in his chest as he struggled to comprehend her words. "Chosen?" he echoed, his voice barely above a whisper. "By whom? Father? The Mastersons?"

"It's not that simple, but yes, you're the one who must bear the responsibility, and it goes beyond the Mastersons," his mother confirmed, her gaze piercing through his soul. "Fate has chosen you to be a Watcher since before your birth," she continued as she stepped closer. "It is not something you can fight against."

A sense of dread coiled in Duncan's stomach as he listened to his mother's revelation. He had heard stories of the Watchers, of their solemn duty and the sacrifices they made to protect whomever they watched over. But he had never imagined that he would be one of them.

"And what if I continue to defy this fate? Will death be my outcome?" Duncan asked, his voice trembling with slight anger.

His mother's expression darkened; her features etched with sorrow. "Death is the least of your worries, Duncan," she warned, her words echoing with the weight of centuries of wisdom. "There are fates far worse than death, fates that twist and corrupt the very essence of your being."

Duncan's breath caught in his throat as he contemplated the magnitude of his mother's words. He imagined giving in and going. But then he feared he would never see Vandrah again, nor have his freedom.

"So, if I do not become a Watcher, I will no longer . . . what? Be me?"

Unshed tears threatened to spill as she took him by the shoulders. "You must not test fate, Duncan. A Winterwolf in the past also defied his fate to become a Watcher. He bled out, but not his own blood, and soon he was no longer himself. He became some other creature."

She looked at him but did not see him. "Mother, how do we know that the Mastersons are not the ones who decided his fate?"

She blinked and came back to the present, tears spilling over. "What does it matter? If they hold such power, what could we hope to do against them? There are things, even in this realm, that go beyond us. It is in the very air we breathe."

Duncan stepped back from her. "I have existed long enough to decide my fate. The demands of others will not rule me."

His mother's eyes softened with compassion, but her resolve remained unyielding. "You must choose wisely, Duncan," she urged, her voice a gentle yet firm reminder of the path she wished for him to take. "What you want cannot always come first. Fate is the defector in this case," she said, her voice gentle yet firm. "To ignore it is to invite destruction upon yourself and possibly the Winterwolf legacy."

Riella hugged him, pulled her hood up, and left. Duncan stood there several minutes after she had gone.

His resolve to not become a Watcher now had a crack in it. But Duncan felt an odd connection with Vandrah, and he had no desire to leave her.

With his mother's warnings and cryptic message echoing in the back of his mind, weeks passed.

One day, while he and Vandrah were riding near the fortress, he came to a sudden stop.

"Is something amiss?" Vandrah asked, as she pulled her wolf beast up next to his.

After blinking a few times and shaking a thick fog from his mind, he faced her. "Nothing, just my vision went blurry for a moment."

"Maybe we should head back?"

"No, I'm fine. Let's keep going."

As they continued their ride, Duncan felt the weight of his mother's words pressing down on him like a physical burden. Each trot of his beast seemed to echo with the reminder of his looming fate. His insides felt like they were on fire. He tried to ignore the feeling, focusing instead on the rhythmic thud of clawed paws against the ground and the wind whipping through his hair.

But the sickness was insidious, creeping through his veins like a shadowy serpent, coiling tighter with every passing moment. Duncan clenched his teeth against the rising waves of nausea, willing himself to ignore the mounting pain that threatened to consume him.

"What she said was true?" he asked aloud.

With his fist clenching the front of his shirt, he tightened his hold on the reins with his other hand.

Vandrah rode beside him, her presence a balm to his troubled soul. Her midnight mane cascaded behind her like a river of melted obsidian, her eyes bright with concern as she glanced over at him. "Duncan," she said, reaching out her hand to touch his arm, "you don't look well. Perhaps we should really turn back."

He shook his head stubbornly, his grip on the reins reaffirming. "No," he insisted, his voice strained with effort. "I want to enjoy this ride with you now."

But even as he spoke, Duncan could feel his strength ebbing away like sand slipping through his fingers. His vision swam before him, the world blurring into a hazy kaleidoscope of colors and shapes. With a desperate gasp, he swayed in the saddle, his muscles trembling with the effort to stay upright.

Vandrah's eyes widened in alarm as she reached out to steady him. "Duncan, you're burning with fever," she exclaimed, her voice tinged with panic. "We are going back. Now!"

But Duncan could only shake his head weakly, his breath coming in ragged gasps. "No," he choked out. "I can't . . . I won't . . . give into this . . . ."

And then, with a final, shuddering gasp, he slumped forward, his body betraying him as he tumbled from the saddle and crashed to the ground below. Vandrah cried out in horror, leaping from her own wolf to kneel beside him, her hands trembling as she brushed the sweat-soaked hair from his forehead.

***

The next evening, he felt wetness on his cheeks and liquid draining from his ears. When he looked at the fingertips he'd dabbed at it. A blue substance covered them.

Over the next week, he became weaker, and his magic abilities withdrew. Soon he was spitting up the blue liquid. Vandrah, at a loss for what to do, had him rest in the center of her bed while she called on her magic and attempted to heal him.

She placed a knee on either side of his legs, straddling him. Her eyes skyward, she hummed aloud and with purpose. Her eyes were closed as she hummed and hummed an unfamiliar tune.

Duncan faded in and out, listening to her throaty melody. When next her eyes opened, they emanated dark blue smoke. The essence crawled down her face and covered her and Duncan. Soon, the smoke filled the room.

"Vandrah," Duncan whispered her name.

No answer came. Lost in the magic, her head fell forward, then arched back violently. She repeated these movements over and over until she became still. Vandrah's mouth opened wide, and a bright blue light shined from within her.

Duncan's eyes came open as she lowered her mouth over his. But just when her lips were an inch from his, she experienced a powerful force, far beyond her comprehension, that repelled her back and slammed her into the far wall. In that moment of defeat, she realized the extent of the danger he faced. A power beyond that of the veil.

Vandrah recovered. Standing over his unconscious form, she was at a loss for what to do.

"This is beyond my power," she said, gently covering his body with the black silk sheet. "I must take you to your family and hope that they can help you."

***

Nightmares gripped Duncan, dragging him into a well of darkness. He faintly heard Vandrah's voice fading. He could only see darkness. No light penetrated the space where he stood.

"Where am I? What is this place?" he asked, turning in a full circle.

He closed his eyes and tried to focus on his magic. Nothing. He felt nothing move within him. His magic was gone. The power that coursed through his veins since birth had fled him.

"This is not real!" he yelled.

Whispers echoed throughout the dark space around him, and then in the far distance he could make out a light. He moved toward it. The whispers became louder the closer he got to the light. As he reached out his hand toward what looked to be an open doorway, he came awake.

He was in the back of Vandrah's carriage. The rocking came to a halt as his vision focused.

"Where?"

"You are home, Duncan," Vandrah replied.

He blinked a few more times before he looked out the carriage window to see his family's castle.

Before Vandrah or Duncan could exit the carriage, a hooded mage knocked on the door.

"A message for Winterwolf," said the deep voice of the hooded figure.

He pushed a folded paper into Vandrah's hand.

Wait!" Duncan called out, a surge of apprehension coursing through him, but the figure paid no heed, vanishing beyond the castle gates.

With a heavy sigh, Vandrah unfurled the parchment, eyes scanning its contents with a furrowed brow before she handed it over to Duncan.

The note read,

You must be feeling the effects of fighting against the pull of fate, my son. Your father and I need you to go to the Mastersons' Tree on the Moors. All we can give you for your journey is your wolf mount. Ride fast and ride steady, my son.

Your Mother~

As Duncan's eyes met Vandrah's, a silent understanding passed between them. There was no escaping fate, no matter how fervently he might wish otherwise.

Resigned to his fate, Duncan steeled himself for the trials that lay ahead. With the castle looming ominously in the distance, he kissed Vandrah once more before climbing onto his wolf mount. With a fresh bout of the sickness washing over him, he did not look back but focused on staying upright.

COUNCIL WITH THE KING

The desolate Moors stretched out before Duncan, a barren expanse of twisted heather and overgrowth of bush. Yet the closer he got to his destination, the greener and flatter it became. The ground was dewy and soft. Grass grew stronger, and the trees showed more life where the Mastersons' Lycrian tree stood. Its gnarled branches reached skyward like the bony fingers of some ancient sentinel.

The wind howled mournfully across the Moors, pushing at his damp back. He almost slipped from the saddle, but his wolf popped its front left leg up, which bounced him back into place. The wind continued its howling, carrying with it the whispers of forgotten souls and lost dreams.

As he approached the towering Lycrian tree, Duncan felt a sense of annoyance that he must give into the demands of those he did not know. With renewed strength, he dismounted. With every step between the twisted limbs of the tree, the color in his skin returned and the fullness of his hair was back once more. He lay his right hand on one of the thick, dark roots of the massive trunk, and within moments, he could feel himself become whole again.

They hold such power over my fate . . . .

Anger shot through him; his knuckles turned pale against the dark wood. A bluish-white light shaped like a door beamed into his line of sight from the center of the tree.

With one last look around, he entered. After crossing the threshold, he opened his eyes he'd shut to the blinding light out of instinct. Two males dressed in brown leather and who stood nearly seven feet tall with long dark hair, blocked him from going any further.

"Come with us. King Kalius is awaiting you," the male on the right said.

He followed them down one dimly lit hall after another until they came to a stop in front of a large door with odd symbols shaped like crescent moons twisted all about each other.

As Duncan stepped into the chamber, the heavy oak door creaked shut behind him, echoing through the vaulted halls of the castle. King Kalius sat upon his throne, an aura of power and authority emanating from his regal figure. Duncan could not fully see him, as shadows covered his form.

"First, you ran. Now, you have come to your rightful place, Duncan Winterwolf," the king's voice boomed, filling the chamber with its commanding presence. "But understand: you still have a long road ahead before you prove you are worthy in my eyes."

Duncan inclined his head respectfully, his gaze steady as he stared toward the king's voice. "I had no other option, as I'm sure you know," he replied firmly, his voice filled with loathing.

The king moved to the edge of his seat, which brought more of his form into the light. He was easily over eight feet tall, muscular, and had eyes that shined bright blue in the dark. A small chuckle filled the chamber. "Nothing is by your choosing in my world, only what I command, as you will later find out once you become a Watcher," he said, his tone grave yet tinged with a hint of pride.

"Why was I chosen? Why must it be me, or the Winterwolf clan?" Duncan demanded, his voice edged with suspicion.

"It is not the why that is important, nor will it change your fate for the knowing. But I will say that it is the very essence of light and dark that runs in the Winterwolf line that has fated you to being a Watcher."

King Kalius relaxed back on his throne once more.

"There are many in this realm with magic stronger than my own."

"Enough. You are not being asked. And I have humored your questions. You will begin your training immediately as the birth of your charge is underway."

The king lifted his hand, and two large stones to Duncan's left moved to reveal a door.

"Guards, show him to his living space. Your training will begin at dusk."

***

After his audience with King Kalius, the guards led Duncan to what would be his private quarters. Once he and the guards stepped through the door, the path veered away from the bustling heart of the kingdom, winding through a labyrinth of magical portals that transported them to a secluded location. Each portal took him and the two guards through one shimmering gateway after another. The air crackled with arcane energy as they traversed the ethereal pathways.

Finally, after having taken many portals, and having walked through winding corridors and twisting passages, they emerged into a secluded enclave hidden amid the verdant embrace of an ancient forest. There, whispering trees swayed, purely by magic—for there was no wind because of the purplish magical force-field that enclosed the area. The hazy sunlight from above made everything look even hazier.

"What is this place?" Duncan asked one guard.

"Your designated living quarters, obviously."

There were three small, white dome structures, and the guards led him to the one in the center.

Ancient runes adorned the walls of his private space, their intricate patterns pulsating with latent power.

Shelves lined with tomes of knowledge stretched from floor to ceiling, their leather-bound spines promised untold secrets and forbidden truths. A crackling fireplace cast a warm glow across the room, providing solace amid the uncertainty of his confinement.

Duncan looked around the space and found a separate room within that held a midsize bed, an end table, and one wall completely made of glass that looked out into the green enclosure outside.

"You are to stay here until the first lap of your training ends," said one guard before they left him alone.

"First lap?" Duncan said.

He flipped through the different tomes and scrolls. All were on the studies of magic, energy essence and the force within those who carried such gifts.

"Why would I need to know this? I am like the very ones within these pages," he said, tossing the tome aside.

After looking around the place fully, he found a bathing room and wardrobe filled with pants, tunics, and boots. He stifled a yawn and decided after changing his clothes to sleep until dusk. But at dusk, no one returned.

Days stretched into weeks, and weeks into months, the passage of time marked only by the shifting patterns of sunlight filtering through the canopy above. The walls of his prison became his sanctuary also, suffocating him with their constant embrace.

Every day, his meals appeared at the portal entrance. He tried waiting for whomever was bringing his food, but no matter how long he waited, he saw no one. Only the meals would appear. His magic energy shots and blasts did nothing to the sealed portal, and his magic that connected him to the dead was useless in such a place.

Honing his magical skills was his focus; that, and reading all the tomes and scrolls he came across. A year in isolation had passed. One day, while jogging around the enclosure, the portal door finally opened. A sliver of light that beckoned him to exit poured onto the grassy area in front of the oval opening.

With a mixture of trepidation and anticipation, Duncan stepped through the portal, which led him to a long, twisting hall. He recalled the different portals he and the guards had originally taken to get to their destination. With a steady breath, he shut his eyes.

Remember the way . . . .

A few moments later, he retraced the steps he had taken long ago. The halls were twisty and long. The wrong turn would take him to the wrong portal. Once he reached the seventh portal, he moved down the last hall that led back to the room he'd met the King in. Duncan braced himself and entered.

***

"So, you have returned, Winterwolf," the king said, his voice emanating from the shadows. "I can feel you have grown stronger from that brief stay through the portals of ever. Now it is time for your second round of training."

Duncan ran his hand through his now shoulder length hair, pushing it back and away from his face as beads of sweat dried on his forehead. The time that had passed toned his thin physique. When he had finished reading all the books, he had physically trained his body, which differed from the way it had been during his past, relaxed life at Winterwolf castle.

"I will now send you to a location where you must use your magic and natural skills to refine your abilities," the king said, moving out of the embrace of the shadows. "Even though you are a Winterwolf, the training of a Watcher requires . . . more."

Duncan's eyes widened when the large, over eight foot tall hulk of a man-beast stepped forward into the torchlight. The king looked to be a Lycrian in mid transformation. His dark hair hung in waves beneath his wide shoulders. His eyes were almond-shaped and glowed a bright blue. He wore dark brown and black leather pants and a laced-up tunic. His hands were large, with black claw-like nails, and his booted feet were just as large.

Duncan stared as he stalked toward him, but held his ground.

King Kalius regarded him, his piercing gaze seeming to penetrate to the very core of Duncan's being. "Your next wave of training begins here."

Duncan looked around at the dark chamber of the throne room, a cathedral of shadows and whispers—but it was nearly empty.

"Here?" Duncan asked, with a look of confusion.

"I will be the window to your next leg of training, Winterwolf. Ready yourself."

The king stood in the center of the chamber. His presence was a palpable force, muscles rippling under his leather-covered physique, eyes glowing with an eerie light. Duncan knew this would be his greatest challenge yet.

The air crackled with tension as the two stared at each other, neither making a sound. Duncan's long silver-white hair glinted in the dim light, his silver eyes gleaming with determination. He was ready, his body humming with charged energy.

Kalius lunged forward, his massive size belying his speed. Duncan sidestepped, narrowly avoiding a crushing blow of razor-sharp claws. He retaliated with a blast of fire from his palm, the flames roaring to life in the dark chamber. Kalius growled, leaping back, but the fur on his exposed forearms smoldered and singed.

Duncan pressed his advantage, launching a series of quick, precise spin kicks, his movements fluid and deadly. He combined his physical attacks with bursts of magic. Each punch landed, accompanied by an explosion of fire or a crackle of lightning. The air was filled with the scent of ozone and burned hair as the two combatants clashed.

Kalius roared, his powerful arms swinging in wide arcs. Duncan dodged and weaved, but the king's sheer strength was overwhelming. A glancing blow sent Duncan skidding across the stone floor, pain radiating through his ribs. He pushed himself up, summoning a surge of energy. Lightning arced from his fingertips, striking Kalius square in the chest. The Lycrian king grunted but merely shook off the attack, his eyes narrowing.

"You have spirit," Kalius growled, his voice like gravel, "but spirit alone is not enough."

He charged again, faster than before. Duncan raised his arms, and a shield of fire sprang to life. Kalius plowed through it— flames licked at his fur but failed to stop him. Duncan barely had time to react before a massive hand closed around his throat, lifting him off the ground. He struggled, legs kicking, hands clawing at the iron grip.

"Impressive," Kalius rumbled with hot and fetid breath, "but too slow."

Duncan's vision blurred, darkness creeping in at the edges. Summoning the last of his strength, he unleashed a desperate blast of energy, a blinding explosion of light and force. Kalius staggered back, momentarily releasing his grip. Duncan dropped to the ground, gasping for air.

Before he could recover, Kalius was upon him again. This time, the king's strikes were merciless. Duncan blocked and parried as best he could, but each blow felt like a hammer, driving him to the edge of his endurance.

Finally, with a bone-rattling impact, Kalius knocked Duncan to the floor, pinning him down with a massive foot.

Duncan looked up, breathing hard, his body bruised and battered. Kalius loomed over him, a giant in the flickering darkness. For a moment, silence reigned in the chamber, broken only by Duncan's ragged breaths.

"You fight well," Kalius said, his voice softer now, almost respectful. He reached down, lifting Duncan by the throat once more, but his grip was gentler this time. "You have the heart of a warrior. You will make a fine Watcher."

With that, he released Duncan, letting him collapse to the floor. There he lay, exhausted but alive, the king's words echoing in his mind. He had lost the battle, but he had earned the respect of the Lycrian king. As he slowly rose to his feet, he knew whatever was next would be harder.

The king sat back on his throne, covered once more by the shadows.

"You are to journey to the Field of Beasts," the king said, then fell silent.

"What is this 'Field of Beasts?'" Duncan asked, straightening his clothes.

"It is a place to hone your survival skills. An untamed mirror of truth, yet twisted all the same. You will travel there through one of our portals."

"Portals again," Duncan said under his breath. "And just how long will I need to be there?"

"That will be based on your will. As well as when I feel you are worthy and trained enough to my satisfaction in offense and defense in combat, you will return here."

Duncan looked toward the floor and palmed his face, dragging it from his forehead to his chin.

"When do I leave?"

"Now. And there will be no amenities; those you will need to find on your own to survive. I'm sure you can handle those sorts of basics . . . yes?"

"Would it matter if I could not?"

"Not really. If you cannot, you are . . . ."

"Not worthy, understood."

The doors to the throne room opened, and one guard he had met before stepped in.

"Lead Winterwolf to the Field of Beasts portal."

"Yes, my king."

The guard glanced in Duncan's direction, then turned and left, leaving the door open for him to follow.

Duncan left without one more word with the king and shut the door behind him. He followed the guard through two corridors before they stopped in front of a glass wall with a matching glass door. Through the glass, he could see a large, black, oval portal in the center of the white room. Dark smoke seeped from its edges into the space.

"This is where you will enter. Once you step through the door, the portal will pull you in." The guard said, putting his hand on the handle of the door.

"One moment. Can I have a message sent to someone?"

The guard let his hand drop from the door and looked at him pointedly. "I suppose that would be fine. The king did not forbid outside contact."

"Send a message to Vandrah, The Guardian of the Veil. Let her know I am well, and once I am done with my training, I will seek her out—and say it's from Winterwolf."

The guard dipped his head, then lifted his hand toward the door once more. "Are you ready?"

Duncan nodded and stepped over the threshold when the door swung open. The door shut behind him with an echoing click.

The dark void of the ominous portal suddenly pulled him in before he could take one more step toward it.

ON THE OFFENSE

Duncan landed in a tuck roll; he heard the sound of the crunching leaves that were enmeshed in his hair as he came to his knees. It was pitch black before his eyes, but he could smell the spearmint-like scent of the trees. He cast his eyes above his head, but even then, there was nothing to be seen. As he stood erect, he could hear heavy breathing only a few feet away. There was something with him in the dark.

An open flame came alive in the palm of his hand, casting a dim light into the darkness. Yellow, glowing eyes lit up all around him, followed by a screech. Small, silver wings zipped by him at high speed, giving him tiny cuts on his arms and cheeks.

"Damn, it's dark-wood Pixies," he said, before ducking back down.

Hundreds zoomed over his head as he closed his hand, putting the flame out and putting himself back into the dark. With a wave of his hand, a blue line of light trailed across the ground, shooting straight through the woods he found himself in. While still in a half-crouched position, he followed the light and made his way out of the woods without another interaction with the Pixies.

Back on his feet, he dusted the last of the leaves from his hair. The moon that he could now see was blood red. A howling wind from the east pushed at his clothes, making him turn in its direction. There in the distance he could see the fortress of the Sorceress. His heartbeat loudly in his chest.

"Vandrah."

He moved unconsciously toward the fortress with her name dancing on his tongue. His magic at its peak gave him heightened speed, and he ate up the distance in no time across the Moors. Once at the gates of the fortress, a magical wall of resistance greeted him.

"Vandrah!" he yelled.

At the foot of the stairs leading to the entrance was a line of seven Lycrian guards, in full silver armor. Though they had their eyes trained on him, none made a move in his direction.

After several minutes of him calling her name, the double doors at the top of the stairs opened wide, and then Vandrah stepped out.

"Winterwolf, why have you darkened my gates? You are not welcome!" she said, her tone laced with anger.

Duncan's brow furrowed in confusion. "I know the time has been long, but surely you do not mean that?"

She glided down the staircase, her dark hair flowing behind her as she came to a stop right before him.

"Vandrah, I . . . ."

Duncan's words died on his tongue as he took in her swelled belly.

"After what you tried to do, you dare return here? You will never wield the power of the veil."

He couldn't take his eyes off her enlarged belly.

"Vandrah, I don't know what you're speaking of. Open the gate. Let me speak to you. I don't understand what is happening!"

"If you return here again, all you will find is death! That, I promise!"

And with those parting words, she glided back up the stairs.

"Vandrah! Vandrah!"

The doors shut once more. Duncan stepped back, not sure what to think. But with deep determination to find out what she was accusing him of, he blasted the wall of magic with his essence of energy. The light hit the wall with a light tremor. Then he did it again and again. This prompted the guards to move toward the gate. It swung open and Duncan flipped back. The Lycrians charged through and surrounded him.

"I must speak with Vandrah! Take me to her or I will go on my own!"

Snarls and growls greeted his demands.

"She has no desire to speak with you. If you do not leave, we must make quick work of you, Mystrelk."

Duncan faced the Lycrian that spoke.

This one knows of my family line, what we are. I will not run.

Duncan's eyes lit with fire as he readied his magic. With a deep breath, he summoned his power. Fire blazed in his hands. He hurled a fireball at the Lycrian who had spoken. The beast dodged, but the fire licked its fur. The other six spread out, forming a large circle around him.

One of the Lycrians lunged, claws extended. Duncan dodged to the side, shooting a streak of lightning at it. The bolt struck the beast, piercing a hole straight through its left arm. A howling yelp followed as another Lycrian closed in. Its large maw snapped at Duncan's right shoulder, but missed its mark by half an inch, when he ducked and landed an uppercut with a flaming fist. He followed up with a sidekick, knocking it into another that was charging him. Duncan spun, using an energy blast to knock the other two that closed in.

Two more of the Lycrians attacked at once. Duncan created a wall of fire. They hesitated a moment, but charged through the raging flames, their silver armor glowing red-hot. Duncan kneeled, placing both hands on the ground, and closed his eyes. Just as the two beasts drew near him, a gigantic spectral wolf emerged, taking one of the Lycrians down by lunging into its lower abdomen. A loud howl filled the space as the spectral wolf tore open the Lycrian's stomach.

The corner of Duncan's mouth curled up at the sight of the wolf's successful attack.

It worked . . . .

Before he could celebrate his new magic, the other Lycrian was on top of him. He flipped over as its massive weight bowled into him. With a push of his left leg, he propelled himself back and away from his attacker.

The Lycrian guard swung its massive claw at him, but he deflected the strike with an energy shield.

Meanwhile, the summoned spectral wolf took down another Lycrian that broke through the flame wall, its ethereal fangs tearing into the beast's armor.

The Lycrian leader who had spoken before busted through the fire, flanked by the other Lycrian guards. Duncan found himself surrounded once more.

He took in his predicament as the Lycrian he'd been guarding against beat against his dome shield.

There were now five of them. The summoned wolf had taken out two.

I have to end this soon; I can't keep up this fight with magic alone.

His shield blinked in silent agreement. The fire wall dissipated, followed by the summoned spectral wolf. He was alone with his five assailants now.

Duncan cast a glance toward the front entrance of the fortress. He knew he would not make it inside. With one last blast of energy, his shield dropped and knocked the Lycrians surrounding him yards back. He sprinted for the forest line. The five guards recovered and were in hot pursuit.

***

As he pushed through the forest branches, everything went dark. He stopped dead in his tracks and did a one hundred eighty–degree turn, then he fell. The ground under him gave way and as he looked down, he could make out firelight until the largest Dagaru worm he had ever come across opened its huge gapping mouth, with its six rows of sharp teeth waiting to devour him.

"Fuck!!" he screamed.

There was no escape. He fell into its awaiting abyss and was devoured whole.

"Fuck!!"

Duncan's arms and legs clawed at the ground around him as he screamed. Then he went silent as the realization that he was still alive got his attention.

He sat up and looked around him. With a wave of his hand, a ball of light hovered in front of him. He was in the woods and above his head Pixies zipped past.

I'm back where I started? How? What the hell?

His brows raised as the truth dawned on him.

Loop magic . . . .

One of the Pixies spotted him and alerted the hundreds of others and swooped down, breaking him out of his musings.

He felt his energy surge within, and he and the forest lit up. The bright orange light disintegrated everything within three miles. He knew his energy magic would drain him, but it took care of all the Pixies. Now low on power, he made his way back to the forest's edge. The same blood red, hazy moon set in the sky. And there in the distance was the Guardian's fortress, though this time he only made it halfway to the fortress when he encountered shadow harpies. They flew in circles above him.

A laugh escaped him. "What is this?"

"You are to journey to the Field of Beasts."

"It is a place to hone your survival skills. An untamed mirror of truth, yet twisted all the same."

"When I feel you are worthy and trained enough to my satisfaction in offense and defense in combat, you will return here."

The words of King Kalius played over and over in his mind.

The harpies sank their claws into his body. Then he awoke once more in the dark woods.

Sitting up, Duncan sighed aloud in annoyance, attracting the unwanted attention of a Pixi that had been near him.

"I'm already tired of this!"

Duncan fought his way through the horde of Pixies. The realization that he would be stuck in the portal of loop magic, fighting for his life, was daunting.

***

Through blood and will, the days turned into weeks, and weeks into months, then years and finally centuries had passed. But within the Field of Beasts, there was truly no time. Duncan became attuned to the play of the magic field. His spirit intertwined with the very essence of the realm within himself. In the timeless expanse, he

347

discovered a truth about himself and the false world around him. He realized he possessed greater strength than he had ever imagined and that the world he'd stepped into merely served as another glimpse into his own realm. After the centuries of fighting and surviving, he unlocked the secrets of magic that had eluded him for so long.

He had just won another battle with the Lycrian guards at the fortress when a black portal opened in front of him. Black smoke bled from it, beckoning him to enter. With more composure than he felt, he stepped through. The same glass walls and door he had used to enter the portal greeted his sight.

A Lycrian waited for him on the other side. "The king wishes to see you."

Duncan followed the Lycrian back to the throne room and there sat the king in his usual resting place. Though the chamber was much brighter than before, the king somehow still hid in the shadows.

King Kalius inhaled deeply. "You smell of the dead and brimming magic. A perfect mix for a Watcher."

Duncan said nothing and only stared.

The king stood and walked over to Duncan, studying him.

"You look to need a bath and a haircut," he said, lifting Duncan's silver strands of hair that rested in the middle of his back.

"There weren't many amenities to be found in such a place. And since I only had time to fight, sleep with one eye open, or eat what I killed," Duncan patted his hands over the hides he had fashioned into clothes out of some of those kills before continuing, "worrying over hair length was the least of my thoughts."

The king burst into laughter, throwing his head back, before returning to his seat. "Well, you have proven yourself fit to be a Watcher. So, do bathe and rest, then we will move on to the last leg of your training before you take your place as the Watcher of my grandson."

Duncan's ears perked and his eyes widened at the announcement that he would be a Watcher for a direct descended of the Mastersons'.

"Take Winterwolf to his new quarters," King Kalius said to the Lycrian standing guard near the door. "And Winterwolf, return here in three days' time. I give you leave to do what you want for that time. Things will be ready for you, so do not be late. I dislike to be kept waiting."

Duncan left then, following the guard to his new living space.

IN LOVE OF HER ESSENCE

Duncan wasted no time leaving the Lycrian homestead. After bathing and cutting his silver mane to his usual short style and dressing in a dark blue short tunic and black leather pants and boots, he called for his wolf mount and headed to the Guardians' fortress.

Some time later, he stopped in front of the gates of the fortress. The scene of Vandrah from the Field of Beasts played through his mind. The gates opened when he walked up to the wrought iron, granting him immediate entry. He jogged up the steps as the double doors opened, and there stood Vandrah.

Her stare was nothing like the other Vandrah's. She looked at him with passion and care. His gaze left her eyes and fell to her midsection.

Not with child . . . .

His eyes found hers once more, then she was floating into his arms the next moment. Their embrace was that of lovers who had been apart for too long. While holding her tightly, he leaned his head back and gazed down at her, saying nothing. His fingers inched up and moved a stray hair from her cheek. Then he claimed the kiss he had dreamed of for however long he had been gone.

Minutes passed, their kiss and embrace a show for the night sky. Both eased back, still holding onto one another.

"You were gone far too long, Duncan. I have been patiently waiting since you sent that brief message."

"How long is too long?"

"Centuries, by mortal time. Not nearly as long here, but even here it was too long."

"I can only be with you for a short time. My training is yet complete."

She stepped back. "You have grown accustomed to their demands, I see."

"As you know, I had no choice. I have gone through a lot. Fighting to exist, dying, and coming back, at least in a sense. I am much more than I was, the last you saw me," he said, shadowing her movement and taking hold of her hand.

His eyes rested on her belly once more. "Would you keep secrets from me?" he asked, pulling her back into his embrace.

She fell silent, then a smile curved her cherry-colored lips. "We all have secrets and mine are mine to keep. Don't worry, it will be nothing that will affect you."

"Let's go inside. I have to leave in two days' time. Let us not waste it," he said, shutting the doors behind them.

***

Duncan returned to the king two days later for the last part of his training.

"It is time, Winterwolf. You are to become a temporary Watcher to Onnisha. She is the daughter of my general. If you do well as a Watcher for her, then you will become the marked Watcher of my grandson."

"I see. When do I start?"

"Tomorrow, you will leave for the Guardian's fortress. Your charge will train under the Sorceress Vandrah. While she is there, you will stay with her as her Watcher."

Duncan hid the shock at finding out his destination was at the fortress and that his charge was Onnisha. "Understood, king."

He did not sleep and was ready the next day to start his new position as Watcher. When he arrived at the fortress on his wolf mount, he noticed a black drageer pawed at the ground. It had a saddle on and was drinking water. He ascended the stairs and let himself inside. No one was in the foyer, so he went to the room he knew Vandrah would be in, only it was someone else in the center of the warm pool when he entered.

"I have a guest, my dear Winterwolf. So, you will need to recall knocking before entering while she's here. And what brings you back to me so soon?"

Duncan averted his line of sight as Onnisha stepped naked from the water. Shuffling was the only sound in the room while he waited. Once he was sure she had covered herself, he slowly gazed back in her direction.

"Onnisha."

She was as he recalled. Around five-seven, with a muscular build, Golden cream-colored eyes that glowed, marking her strong Lycrian heritage. She was the daughter of the Lycrian general, and it showed. Not just in the way she stalked toward him, then around him. No, her bone structure was that of her father's, pronounced and sharp.

"Duncan Winterwolf. It has been a while."

"Yes, it has, Onnisha. I am to be your watcher."

The glow in her eyes intensified as she continued to stare at Duncan. She stepped in close. He did not step back.

"Oh, I think I will enjoy having a Watcher for once in my life."

Duncan glanced at Vandrah, who had not said a thing since the entire encounter started. She had moved over to a little jewel-shaped table, looking through its contents.

He turned his attention back to Onnisha, who still beamed up at him. Duncan cleared his throat, but she did not take the hint and grabbed his arm.

"It seems you have been here before, Winterwolf. Could you give me the tour instead of the Sorceress Vandrah, as she looks to be busy at the moment?" Onnisha said, throwing a fast look over her shoulder in Vandrah's direction.

"That's a fine idea. Duncan, show her the place. I need to gather her lessons."

Vandrah waved them off and continued rummaging through the table drawer. Duncan let Onnisha lead him from the room, but pulled his arm free from her grip once they were in the hall.

"Onnisha, before I show you around, there are a few things you need to know."

"Oh, please tell," she said, heavily batting her long lashes.

"As your Watcher, we should keep some distance. I am here to advise you and guide you. I am skilled in magic and fighting as you know. So, if you ever find yourself in trouble while I am your Watcher, I will make sure things go smoothly."

"How much distance must I keep? I don't think I like the sound of that. Maybe I don't want a watcher after all," she said, with a pout.

Duncan cleared his throat one more time. "You will figure it out. And it's not a matter of 'like' or not. I am your Watcher, whether you want one or not. We all have a role to play for fate."

She stepped very close to him, eyes all big, and locked her fingers together as if she would pray or beg. He was unsure of which.

"You think we're fated?"

"This way, please," he said, ignoring her last question.

Duncan led the way down one corridor after the other. He showed her the many rooms the fortress had on the west wings side. Soon, they came to a stop in front of Vandrah's bedroom.

"There is no need for me to show you this one. This is Vandrah's private bedroom."

"Why not? I want to see," she said, reaching round him for the doorknob.

"I assume you know where your room is?"

She nodded.

"Then you should head there while I have a chat with Vandrah."

Duncan left her in the hall. When he rounded the corner, he heard the faint sound of a doorknob jiggling.

He chuckled, then made his way back to the natatorium. Vandrah had undressed and was floating in the center of the water when he entered and locked the door.

"I thought you were gathering her lessons."

Vandrah rolled her eyes and waved her hand dismissively. "Come to play, have you, Winterwolf? Or would you much rather play with your charge?"

Duncan stood at the water's edge. He watched her glide in a circle before him, breasts bobbing just beneath the surface.

"I caught her intention. I mean, who could not?" She giggled before swimming farther away.

Duncan undressed, taking one step at a time as he entered the pool. He watched her, and she took in the full sight of his body.

He swam in her direction, and she swam away and around him. "Is there something that you want? Something that you seek, my wolf?"

Duncan turned and dove, swimming so fast she had no time to get away as he took hold of her legs, lifting her up and out of the water. She yelped and braced her hands on his shoulders. Their eyes locked when he lowered her, meshing her mouth with his as her body reentered the water. Vandrah moaned when he teased her tongue with his. Then leisurely single lip kissed her until he'd pushed her back against the pool wall.

Vandrah broke the kiss when a knock came at the door. "One—"

Duncan pulled her mouth back to his, cutting her reply to the knock off. He reached his free hand between them, but stopped just before he touched her between her legs.

"You asked me what I seek? It's always you," he said, the whisper of his words tickling her ear.

They ignored the knocking as they swam to the back of the pool, disregarding anyone who would dare interrupt them.

DAUGHTER OF THE LYCRIAN

The days sailed by as Duncan watched over his charge with a slight emotional distance while staying physically close. Vandrah trained the young Lycrian in basic spell magic one night in the gardens of the fortress.

Duncan escorted Onnisha to her lesson, and she talked his ear off as they walked. "I shocked my father when he realized I could do magic. He wanted to ignore it, but after trying to have the Winterwolf's train me failed he figured the Guardian of the Veil was my last hope to learn control."

While walking backward in front of him, she mis-stepped and fell, but Duncan caught her right before she hit the floor. Their eyes locked as her fingers dug into his forearm. Clearing his throat, he helped her right herself, then moved away.

"Don't walk backward and keep pace with me before you are late for today's lesson," he said, moving down the stairs.

Vandrah waited in the garden. There were magic books stacked on a black iron bench that was set up in the center of a vine archway. Although Vandrah called it a garden, there were no flowers, only twisted black vines and a light mist that hovered just above the ground.

"You're late." Vandrah looked from Onnisha to Duncan before continuing. "Never mind. Let's get started, Onnisha."

Duncan took a seat on the iron bench. The books at his side caught his eye, so he flipped through one while Vandrah started the lesson, gathering magical energy from within. The lesson flew by, but near the end, Onnisha struggled with doing the last spell.

"I can't do it!"

Onnisha exclaimed aloud, falling dramatically to her knees.

Vandrah stood over her. She followed the young female Lycrian's eyes, which were staring at Duncan as he sat cross-legged, reading.

"If you would focus, you could do it. Each lesson, you have complained about and given up and failed because of your lack of focus. I'm not one to waste my time. If you keep this up, I will send you back to your father. I have better things to do than to babysit a pup."

Onnisha jumped up, her anger boiling. "Fine, I don't need your grief or your lessons! You've been annoying this entire time and Duncan is the only one I like here!"

Vandrah's eyes narrowed, then she waved her hand, which silenced Onnisha, stealing her voice.

Duncan, watching the exchange, walked over as Onnisha's eyes glowed intensely and she began to transform.

"Calm down Onnisha. Vandrah, return her voice."

"I am the leader here. You both must be confused. This is my fortress, and I will do as I please. But you know what? I will return her voice," she said, and with a snap of her fingers, Onnisha's voice rang out again.

"You old sorceress bitch!" Onnisha yelled, advancing on Vandrah.

"Don't tempt fate, child. I am as old as the wind that blows between the veil and the mortal world. So, tread carefully." Vandrah stared her down. "Wolf, take your charge and return her to her family. I only agreed to train her because you are her Watcher, but now I'm bored with this."

She left without a backward glance. Onnisha stared at the exit at a loss for words.

"Well . . . shall we?" Duncan said, lifting his hand for her to precede him.

***

Vandrah did not see them off. "Onnisha, do you need a step or help mounting your Drageer?" Duncan asked. "No. I'll be fine," she said, then whistled to the Drageer. It pawed the ground then lowered its two four-foot horns. Onnisha took hold and swung up into the saddle. They rode through the gates in silence as Duncan led the way.

A while later Onnisha pulled her mount alongside Duncan's. "She didn't have to get so angry. My father is going to be so upset with me."

Duncan kept his eyes straight ahead as they rode toward the Mahaven mountains. Onnisha's home was just at the base of them.

They stopped at the tree line of the Gordrick Forest, which was the only way to reach her home.

"Stay alert. As you know, these woods can be treacherous."

Duncan dismounted, and Onnisha did the same. His wolf darted off into the dark while Onnisha led her mount with her into the woods.

They moved through the dense Gordrick Forest; the trees tall and the air thick with the scent of damp soil. Duncan called forth a magical blade and let it hover at the right of his hip.

"What's that for? There shouldn't be anything much in these woods that would attack us," Onnisha said, eyeing Duncan's summoned weapon.

"Being careful is always necessary, and sometimes one needs to engage in close combat."

Onnisha walked beside him, her sharp eyes scanning the path ahead. They weren't far from her home and would reach it in a short time if they kept a steady pace. A sound from up the path and off to the right caught Duncan's attention. He moved ahead of Onnisha and waited.

Suddenly, the forest erupted in chaos. From the shadows, Lycrians charged from between the trees, teeth bared and eyes glowing with malice.

Duncan drew his sword and cast a shield spell to protect them.

"They are from our rival pack!" Onnisha declared, putting her back against Duncan's.

"Onnisha, stay within the shield!" Duncan shouted and charged the first group of beasts on the left.

Ignoring his command, she transformed and joined the fight. She bared her claws and fangs, but the ambushers were many and strong. One of them knocked her to the ground. She snarled and slashed, but more Lycrians surrounded her. Duncan fought off another one, setting it on fire before he ran toward Onnisha.

They had her pinned to a large tree in the center of the woods. While four more attackers intercepted Duncan, a group of them dragged Onnisha off. He fought with all his might, his sword a blur, but they kept coming.

"Let her go!" Duncan roared, casting an ice spell that froze half of the pack—but there were still more, and they surrounded him. Onnisha and her captors had disappeared into the trees when howls from the dark of the woods rang out, catching the attention of the Lycrian that was about to pounce on Duncan. Other Lycrians attacked from the shadows, making quick work of them. Duncan took the opening and pursued the ones who had kidnapped Onnisha.

He plunged into the woods, following the trail of broken branches and trampled undergrowth left by the abductors. Every rustle in the foliage set his nerves on edge. He moved quickly but carefully; his senses heightened. He couldn't afford to be ambushed again.

As he moved deeper into the forest, he saw signs of the struggle. Claw marks on trees, patches of fur caught on branches. They were making their way toward the lower cliffs. He pressed on, determined to get to her before they escaped with her.

Duncan reached the cliff's clearing, stopped, and listened. The surrounding forest was silent, but he could feel eyes on him. He tightened his grip on his sword and stepped into the center cautiously.

"Turn back, Watcher, before we make short work of you," a deep, monstrous voice called from his left.

"Leave her with me and you can disappear back to where you came from. There is no escaping with her."

A massive Lycrian leaped out of the trees at him. Duncan reacted instantly, blocking the attack and swinging his sword in a wide arc. The beast jumped back, the blade just missing its mark. More of them emerged from the dark. They gathered close to him, snarling and snapping.

Duncan's mind raced. He needed to end this quickly. He summoned a burst of light and it exploded from his hand, blinding the group. They howled in pain, giving Duncan the chance to strike. He cut them down one by one until only the two holding Onnisha remained.

She had transformed back into her humanoid form, her clothing nothing but scraps now.

Duncan charged but came to a stop when he saw they meant to jump from the cliff's ledge with Onnisha.

"Duncan!" she cried, but she could not get free from the two Lycrians' grip.

Duncan charged forward, his sword raised high. The Lycrians leaped with her off the edge. With a wave of his hand, he called forth a magical net. He quickly raced to the ledge and floated all three of them back up and over his head, dumping them on the ground. The clearing filled with Lycrians from Onnisha's pack. The last two Lycrians surrendered, bringing the fight to an end.

Duncan helped Onnisha to her feet as the Lycrian general stepped forward, carrying a large fur blanket. He covered his daughter as she hugged him.

"I received word from Vandrah that Onnisha was returning home, so I came out to meet you," the general said, embracing his daughter.

"Does your pack get attacked by that other one often?" Duncan asked, disbursing his magical blade.

"We had a falling out. The leader is my nephew and he and Onnisha were once planned mates, but that was a long time ago. Seems he still wants to claim her."

"I won't ever be with him," Onnisha declared, and then looked over at Duncan. "I want to marry Winterwolf."

Her father laughed aloud. "I think Vandrah has claimed him. And you, my daughter, as it stands, have little hope in besting her in magic, from what I hear," he said, his tone turning serious on the latter.

Duncan cleared his throat and looked away. "I will escort your pack back to your home."

"That is unnecessary."

"As Onnisha's Watcher, it is something I must do."

A WATCHER'S FATE

Duncan left Onnisha and her pack as the hazy sun rose over the Mahaven Mountains. Calling to his wolf mount, he returned to the Lycrian tree.

He entered the throne room. For once, the king sat forward on his throne instead of being covered in shadows.

"Ah, Winterwolf, I see you have ended your position as Watcher to Onnisha? Ran into a bit of trouble, did you?"

"Nothing I could not handle. Though if I had failed to rescue my charge at the cliff's edge, which was an entrance to the mortal realm, I would have had to follow the kidnappers to retrieve her. And that is one thing I would find unpleasant indeed."

"Well, I have good news and bad news for you then."

Duncan came closer to the center of the room as the king continued.

"As I mentioned before, you are to be my grandson's Watcher. He has lost his parents and needs guidance. However, you will go to his location and discreetly monitor him until your help is required, and even then, he should remain unaware of your involvement."

"I don't understand. If he is your grandson, will he not detect my presence?"

The king reached behind him and brandished a black stone that hung from a silver chain. It emanated black smoke from its center as it swung back and forth.

"You will wear this. He will not see, hear, or be able to detect you. When you are not with him, you may remove it, but while on duty, you must wear this. When I give word that he is ready to know of you, then and only then can you remove this stone in his presence."

Duncan took the offered necklace. Low whispers came from the stone as he stared at it, but then fell silent when he looked back at the king.

"Was this the bad news?" Duncan asked.

"The bad news is he lives in the mortal realm, and you will have to stay there as long as he does. He will go through a lot because of what he is."

"Is he not a Lycrian?"

"He is much more. Beings are not always as they seem," King Kalius said, and a smile that did not reach his eyes spread across his face. "It is imperative that you do not interfere directly with his decisions until he comes home."

"When do I leave?" Duncan asked, wrapping the chain of the necklace around his knuckles.

"As soon as you are ready."

"I will gather my things." Duncan said, then turned to leave.

"His name is Caliostro. There is a location stone in your room. Use it. And Winterwolf, be sure to do as I say. Your future and everything depends on it."

Duncan stopped at the exit and listened with a glance over his shoulder.

He left then and prepared to leave for his fated position as Watcher.

"This is only the beginning, Caliostro," said the king, as he leaned back into his throne once more.

OBSESSED

THE
WANTING

Amid a starry, moonlit night, a sticky pile of body parts wriggled and slid about as a blood-soaked hand pushed its way to the surface of the pile. The delicate fingers slipped through deep guts and pieces of torn flesh. Thick, succulent blood dripped down the palm and further down the four arms as it pushed further free.

A dark head of hair emerged a second later, and ice-blue eyes glanced around, smears of blood covering both lids above long eyelashes.

"Mmm. What a yummy and fulfilling meal that was."

"Lady Dalidah!" called an older man with graying hair that was styled in a buzz cut.

Dalidah glanced in his direction, then stretched and pulled herself fully from the sticky mess. Her beautifully shaped body was naked and covered in her meal. She sat atop the pile and folded her legs in front of her.

"My lady, I have clothing waiting for you, and you can take a dip in the lake near here to wash yourself," he said, then presented a large, flat, white box.

Dalidah reached her arms above her head and yawned before jumping off the pile.

"Halvik, can I honestly depend on you to dress me? I mean, your style is very... questionable."

Dalidah looked him up and down. He wore dark, tan pants; a black, button-down shirt with a dark, forest green sweater over it; and black combat boots to finish his monochrome ensemble.

He glanced down at himself and shrugged. "What do you wish to do with the remains, my lady?" he asked, nudging his head toward the pile of corpses.

Dalidah glanced over her shoulder, then back to Halvik.

"I don't care. Whatever you think will do. Also, there's the house to take care of. I've had my fun with this area. I will move on."

She took the box from his hands, then walked through the trees and toward the lake.

Halvik sighed aloud then snapped his fingers, first igniting the pile of bodies, then he set the old log cabin on fire as well.

"Contain and consume," he said with a swish of his hand. A flash of white light domed over the house and bodies as he turned to follow Dalidah into the woods.

***

Ripples of the lake's cool water pushed against Dalidah's body as she swam. After she felt all the blood and sticky meat leave her, she returned to the rocky surface and pulled the red, body-fitting evening gown from the box.

"Well, maybe he knows me after all," she said, a light smile dancing to life on her face.

She smoothed her hands down and around her frame and spun in a circle.

Halvik broke through the trees just as she spun one last time.

"We should leave the area, my lady. I contained the fire, but mortals will find the remains at some point, and we should get moving," he said, looking around nervously.

Dalidah had him by the throat before he could blink. She held him high off the ground and smiled up at him.

"Halvik, my dear. You dare tell me what I should do and when? You know how old I am, child, yet you would think to direct me? Have you forgotten whose blood you feed upon to hold even the small amount of powers that you currently possess?"

"No… M… y La… dy," he croaked out.

Dalidah released him. He went into a coughing fit, then stood, rubbing his neck.

She flipped her hair over one shoulder, then dashed away. He followed, trudging behind, into the night.

The Next Evening~

In the small town of Prixy, close to Drawdic city, Dalidah strolled through a festival. Mortals laughed and walked about, some hand in hand, others with large groups. A family of nine sat at an open barbeque with many others. This family caught Dalidah's eyes, since they all looked happy as she watched them. There was a mother and father, five children of varying ages, and a grandmother and grandfather. She listened to them chat and call upon each other.

One table over, she smiled to herself. "Tonight's dinner will be plentiful."

Once they had eaten and played a few more games, the family piled into their large SUV and a car, then drove out of the festival. The sun had set, and it was completely dark. Dalidah followed them. Running behind the tree line and keeping pace as they headed toward home.

After about fifteen minutes, the SUV and car turned into a large farmhouse off the main road. She waited until the house was quiet and everyone was asleep.

She giggled to herself as she approached the back door of the house. Her lips formed a pout when she found the door unlocked.

"Aww, I wanted to break in."

She stepped inside. The house was pitch black. She listened. The sound of light snores reached her ears from every bedroom, except for the oldest child's room, indicating they were awake.

Dalidah licked her lips in anticipation of feeding on the blood of the youths. Mortal youth's blood made her giddy.

She flashed to the teens' room, who had left the door ajar. Dalidah eased the door open to find the young boy relaxing on his bed, staring at a device, headset covering his ears.

Her eyes lit with fire as she could see his veins pulsating under his skin. She pursed her lips and blew in his direction. He looked over at her as she closed the door. His eyes glassed over, and he stood, coming toward her.

She beckoned him into her arms and sank her fangs deep into his throat. His headset fell from his head, and his arms went limp. She drank her fill until he was dry.

She tossed his lifeless body on his bed and turned his bedroom light off as she exited.

Dalidah made quick work of the younger children, draining each while they slept, though one was missing from their bed. The children's perfect blood filled her veins, giving her power a boost.

Next, she went into the parents' room. Neither stirred as she glided above them. She breathed her vampiric breath into their nostrils. Each opened their eyes, sat up and started making out and tearing at each other.

"Oh, what fun," she said, watching them.

They were naked in minutes. The husband entered his wife, and she moaned aloud. He pushed into her repeatedly, making her tremble against him.

Dalidah approached the husband and pulled his head back toward her by his hair, exposing his neck. She bit into his pulsating vein, where his shoulder met his throat. He continued to ravish his wife, the sucking of his blood intoxicating. After his body stopped moving, she jammed her hand through his wife's stomach. With a firm grip on her entrails, she pulled some free and sucked on them. Her eyes flashed, and the wife returned to awareness. She screamed and fell off the bed, trying to escape her dead husband's body and her own pain. Her intestine pulled free as Dalidah continued to suck and lick upon them. The woman had crawled to the door, smearing blood along the way, but died from the pain and blood loss soon after.

Dalidah fed on her warm blood before leaving the room and going back to the first floor where the grandparent's room was. Upon reaching the last bedroom, she felt other vampires in the area, fast approaching her location.

"Fuck."

Her desire to finish the entire family outweighed her senses, and she stayed.

With a swift kick, she burst into the grandparents' room and placed one hand at the top of the grandfather's mouth and one at the bottom and ripped. Blood splattered all across her face and she licked her lips. Her beguiling was strong, so the female did not awaken when Dalidah lifted her into her arms. She cleared the fog from the old woman's mind and let her awaken as she broke her back over her knee, then threw her to the floor.

The old woman cried out in pain and shock; she could not move as Dalidah crouched over her and leaned in. Fear made the woman's eyes open wide and her mouth gaped open as a heart attack gripped her. Dalidah could hear the erratic beating of her heart, then the slowing. She bit into the grandmother's left cheek and pulled back flesh, then spat it across the room as she leaned back in to suck on the wound she had left.

Dalidah sat up from her meal. She could feel the other vampires. They had reached the house.

She got to her feet and listened for the last mortal child that had been missing from their bed. The youngest of the five kids, the most flavorful of them all. She could feel him. He was back upstairs, but it was too late.

The house filled with the eight vampires she had felt earlier.

"Dalidah, you will come with us."

She wiped the back of a blood-soaked hand across her already blood splattered mouth, smearing more of it on her skin. A smirk, showing four of her eight fangs, was her greeting to them.

"Finally caught up to me, have you now? Well, it is of no matter. I still intend to do as I wish, whether your little vampire council deems it permissible or not so . . . kindly disappear from my sight," she said, with a dismissive wave of her hand.

A male in an all-white, three-piece suit and black necktie dashed like a shadow an inch from her face.

His golden eyes flashed blue, and his eight fangs protruded as he hissed down at her.

Dalidah did not give a care and just checked her nails and folded her arms over her ample bosom, glancing around at the other seven vampires who were all dressed like him. They stood back and waited silently.

She sneered and looked pointedly at the leader.

"Do you all shop at the same store, or is this a new fashion statement?" she said, and broke into a heavy fit of laughter.

"Vasca, retrieve the child upstairs and prepare to clean. Leave no sign that this was the work of one of our kind."

The only female of the group with long, bright red hair disappeared to the second level.

Dalidah closed the last inch between her and the leader.

"The child belongs to me!"

"You shut that mouth of yours," he said.

"Who the fuck are you, anyway?"

"My name is shut the fuck up and do as you're told," he said, grabbing her by the arm and biting into her neck. She could not best him as he sucked her blood to nearly empty in a second. She fell to her knees at his feet.

Vasca returned with the small child under her arm. Dalidah stared at the unconscious child's form.

"Mine . . . ," she moaned, reaching her hand toward the child.

"Vasca, I will leave the rest to you. You should make it look like an accidental fire and burn the bodies to ash. You know what to do about the next few days of cleanup," he said, then lifted Dalidah up into his arms.

One of the other vampires put a half-mask on her face, covering her mouth. Despite her exhaustion, she was conscious enough to feel the burning of the mask against her skin.

Dalidah was placed in a white van. Her vision blurred as two vampires jumped into the back with her and a third got behind the wheel. The vehicle jerked forward just as she passed out.

***

Dalidah was lured awake by the powerful scent of innocent blood. She jolted upright to find she was bound by unbreakable cuffs.

Shiny, black dress shoes filled her view. She followed the long legs up to a narrow waist, to wide shoulders and tight muscles in a wine-red suit. Upon those shoulders was the head of a male with Egyptian god–like features. His red, ocher skin shimmered in the room's glow. High cheekbones sat well above his chiseled jawline. Golden eyes framed by long lashes stared down at her. The wavy mahogany hair upon his head was slicked back and fell past his waistline. In one hand, he swirled a wine glass full of blood.

The intoxicating scent wafted down to her again, and her eyes glowed brightly with hunger.

"My lovely Dalidah, we haven't had a formal introduction yet. I am the leader of the vampire council. Thothius Duran, at your service."

Dalidah said nothing and kept her eyes glued to the glass in his hand. His eyes followed her line of sight and he chuckled.

Stooping, he swirled the liquid in her face. "A one-track mind you have there. I like it."

He smoothed his free hand over her head, from the crown to the nape of her neck, then took hold of her hair, twisting until her head tipped back.

"Open your mouth," he commanded.

She could not resist. The thought that he would give her the contents of the glass overruled any thought to defy him. Her lips parted.

His mouth curled up at the corners; then he poured half the blood down her throat. He released her, and she moaned. The fresh blood heated her skin to its mortal tone.

"Good girl. I will have you tamed in no time," he said, downing the rest of the blood before standing.

Dalidah stared up at him once more in renewed defiance.

"If dreams come true. However, I won't be tamed."

Her tongue darted out to lap up the last drop of blood on her bottom lip.

"We shall see my beauty. We shall see."

DEFIANT IS MY NAME

They gave Dalidah only small sips of blood each evening during the first seven days of confinement. Then, at midnight, she would be taken to Thothius Duran's. Each night, he would try to make her beg for more blood, but she would not.

When the eighth night came and went with no sip of blood offered, she knew starving was next. She had heard stories of other vampires who had faced the wrath of the vampire council. If they did not give in to the demands or face their crimes, as the council deemed them, they would starve until they gave in.

The room they had kept her in was nice, considering she was a prisoner. A large, king-size bed, silk sheets and velvet draped walls. No windows, like she liked. But she could never hope to break through the door locked with magic, as she had no blood to fuel her escape, nor any of her magical trinkets.

On the tenth night, she was brought before the council. They gave her a small amount of blood so that she would be within her mind for most of the proceedings.

Someone pushed her onto the black marble floors before the council. They dressed her in a black evening dress with spaghetti straps. Her long, black hair had been combed but left loose.

When she looked up, there was a table over twenty feet long where the twelve council members were sitting. Thothius Duran sat in the center, his fingers interlocked together under his chin, his elbows resting on the table, and watched her with an unblinking stare.

"Dalidah, we will list off your most recent crimes in the mortal realm. One: feeding and leaving evidence of your killings. Two: sloppy kills. Three: Feeding too much

389

in one area in a short period. Four: not following any of the council's rules in the veiled realm or in the mortal realm. And these are just a few of your crimes. What do you have to say in your defense?" asked the council member with long, dark brown hair and who sat at the far-left end of the table.

Dalidah laughed aloud and shrugged, then changed her position on the floor from sitting on her side to her favored tailor sitting position.

Thothius smiled and kept his eyes trained on her.

Another member cleared their throat. A female spoke this time, one with snow-white hair and dark brown skin. She lifted her thin, pointed nose in the air and looked down at Dalidah as she spoke.

"If you were to be released from here, will you follow the ways of the council?" the female with her nose pointed in the air asked.

"I'm not sure what the issue is here. I ate food. Mortals are our food. Not sure what the problem is with eating. Am I to starve? Oops." She looked at each one of them, then continued. "I supposed that is the point, since you are literally starving me."

"You will be in confinement without nourishment until you agree to follow the ways of the council. You are one of our stronger bloods, so you need to act accordingly. Not this savagery you have been playing at for centuries," another with long, black hair chimed in.

"What say you, Thothius?" asked the one who had read off the list of crimes.

"I will get her to comply. Worry not. Council dismissed." The two guards that had brought her in took her back to her room, sealing her in once more.

***

One month later~

A soft knock came at her door one evening. She barely registered if it was real. Her mind was not intact without blood, so sounds came and went, as did voices and illusions of feeding daily.

She heard a soft voice, yet it was also deep in tone. Then someone put a glass to her lips, and she drank. When the glass disappeared from her mouth, she clawed at the thigh of her would-be savior.

"Who?"

The face that stared down at her while lifting her head was the face of Thothius Duran, but yet it was different. The face was softer around the edges, and he was not as tall as Thothius.

"My name is Horustia. I have been watching their treatment of you. I do not think it is fair, and I wish to help you."

He lowered her head back to the pillows as color returned to her lips for the blood he gave.

"I have to go. I will do what I can when I can."

Before she could say anything, he left and re-sealed her room.

The next night, Thothius showed up.

"Why are you here?" Dalidah asked, after he entered her room.

"It seems starving you has yet to break your will," he said, and took off his suit jacket, throwing it over the back of the nearest chair.

Dalidah stayed seated in the center of her bed, watching as he approached the bottom. Next, he undid his tie.

"I have no plans to break anything . . . well, maybe your neck at some point." She said.

"I never tire of that sassy mouth of yours."

She watched as he removed his shirt, showing off his muscular body. He was hard and sculpted in all the right places. Dalidah could not help licking her lips.

He moved to the side of the bed. His eyes traveled down her body and back up again.

"If you just give in to me, I will make you mine and none will question anything you do," he said, leaning toward her.

His lips were a few inches from hers. Dalidah leaned in as well, then quickly reared back and collided her forehead with his. Then she jumped on him and bit into his neck, gulping down as much blood as she could drink before he tossed her off. In a blink, he had her pinned under him.

"You dare to drink from me without permission!?"

He returned the bite and sucked the little blood she had gained, leaving her nearly empty once more.

Thothius's gaze fell on her parted lips when he leaned back. "As much as I want to claim you here and now, I will wait until you beg for my touch."

With all her energy drained, she did not notice when he left. She laid in the same spot on the floor until the next day, when she dragged herself back to the bed.

***

Horustia paid her another visit. It had been weeks from what she could tell since he had last come to her. This time he did not bring a sip of blood, but offered her his own instead. He crawled into the bed and snuggled close to her, pressing his neck to her parted mouth.

"Dalidah, I'm here. You will eat this night. If you would take from me, then I will give what I can."

His hand moved up and down the back of her head, coaxing her to drink. She would not deny him.

Dalidah leaned away and stared at the soft flesh on his neck. Four of her fangs grew in anticipation.

A long moan slid from his mouth the moment her fangs pushed into his flesh, followed by her own. She drank and drank until he pulled her mouth away and kissed her.

Dalidah pushed him into the mattress as she kissed him back, straddling him. She could feel that he wanted her, and she moved against him in response. A groan in his throat made her smile. He flipped her under him, pulled back, and stared down at her.

"What do I need to do to have you as mine?"

She grinned and locked her arms around his neck, pulling him back down to her. This time, she bit into his tongue while they kissed, sucking his blood again.

Horustia undid his pants, but she stayed his hands.

"We cannot do this here. Thothius will know and then what will become of me? Of us?" she asked.

His hands fell away, and he sat back.

"He is away but will return tonight and he'll know someone has fed you. So why stop? Let us run from here."

She took his face between her hands.

"He won't because you will take back most of what you gave me, leaving me with enough so I can walk on my own. Can you do that?"

He looked at her in confusion.

She sighed aloud.

"Tomorrow I must go before the council once more for my sentencing. When I am being sent back to my room, you can get me out then. That's how we can be together, my Horustia."

She leaned in and pushed her lips to his. Their kiss heated as he laid her down on the bed once more. Dalidah turned her neck to his lips, and he bit into her, drinking what she offered until she said stop.

He left her with their plan in the forefront of his mind.

Dalidah laughed as she closed her eyes and let a light sleep take her into the bosom of the dawn.

The next evening, she was brought before the council once again. This time, they listed her offenses on the side of the veil.

She listened, but kept her gaze locked on Thothius, as his was locked on her.

"Have you anything to say about your crimes, Dalidah Masterson?" the council members asked in union—all but Thothius.

"Well, I don't count any of the things you have stated as crimes, but only my nature."

The member who had listed her crimes previously stood up.

"You have violated almost all our laws, and you care not—as if you are a fledgling!"

Dalidah gasped.

"Are you saying I left some laws unbroken? Well, I will get the list of laws when I leave here and break them as well," she said, followed by an evil grin.

Thothius held his hand up to silence the room.

"Dalidah, if you agree to be my mate, I will wipe your record clean, and all will be forgotten."

The other council members stayed silent, but the disagreement on their faces said it all, though they dared not contest him.

"What do you say? Do you agree? Because I will not force you. But you only have two choices. Be mine or stay as you are now for as long as you can survive."

"I will think on it and get back to you tomorrow . . . how's that?"

"That's fine by me, my beauty. Take your time. I have eternity, after all."

Dalidah's guards came in and led her back to her room. On the way, right before they reached her door, Horustia killed both guards. Dalidah danced in gleefulness as he took her hand and they fled through the underground tunnels of the Vampire Consulate. Once out, they sped to the mortal world through the veil.

TASTE OF THE END

On the run in the mortal world, Dalidah contacted the witch she knew at the magic guild to request masking magic that would temporarily hide her trail and a few pieces of defensive jewelry. She took Horustia to one of her many homes. Her servant, Halvik, was there waiting.

When she walked in, he ran and groveled at her feet. "Oh, my lady, I thought you would never return!"

"Yes, yes. At least you did as I told you."

"Of course, my lady. I waited here at this precise location until your return. When you were gone for years, I feared you may never come back."

"I was not gone that long. There was no need for panic."

Halvik turned his gaze on Horustia, who walked ahead of them, looking around. He moved closer to her.

"And who is he, my lady?"

"He will stay with me. We will not be here long. I plan to move around until things cool off. The losers from the vampire council will definitely pursue me since they didn't let me go."

The house had ten rooms and seven bathrooms. It was nestled nicely in the mountains. Though secluded, she would have to leave after a few days and travel to one of her other locations.

"Horustia?" she called.

He turned at his name and smiled at her. She took hold of his hand and led him to the second level and to her bedchamber.

They entered together. She left the lights off as he kissed her there against the door. His passion had peaked. He lifted her into his arms and carried her to the bed and sat her on it, but before he joined her there, she leaped up and wrapped her legs around his middle.

"Dalidah . . . there is something I have to tell you."

She put one finger to his lips.

"It can wait."

***

They stayed in her room for the next few days, and only sounds of passion and drinking of each other's blood seeped from the space. Dalidah decided it was time to move to one of her other locations, and time for a deep hunt.

Going back to her old habits, but with a new partner, made things more exciting for her. Horustia was younger than her by a few centuries, and he had never slaughtered an entire mortal family.

So, as a surprise for him, she found a nice family they stalked for a few days. One night, they broke into the family's home and murdered all three of them and set the house ablaze after they had their fill.

The two of them ran away from their destruction in laughter and hungry for the next kill.

Horustia was a fast learner in the enjoyment part of the feedings. He reveled in it, following Dalidah's lead perfectly.

A few weeks after one of their many kills, they had sex in the bloody remains of their victims. A group of hikers had been in the woods near one of Dalidah's many homes, and the group had been camping when she and Horustia came across them.

As they lay under the stars, Horustia rolled over her and looked her in the eyes.

"What is it?" she asked.

"I need to tell you… I am the heir to the lead council seat."

The smile on her face died, and she sat up.

"Thothius Duran is my father. My full name is Horustia Duran."

"I see. Then why did you help me escape?"

"Because I love you. And I didn't want to watch my father hurt you anymore. Please don't hate me. I never want to return there. I enjoy living this existence with you."

She kissed him and they made love continuously throughout the woods all night.

***

Over the next few weeks, Dalidah contemplated how to ditch Horustia.

I cannot have him stuck at my side. They will never leave me be if he is with me.

"Let's have a big feast tonight," she said.

"You mean?"

"Yes, Horustia, an entire family! It's been over two weeks since I have had the thrill of hunting and eating a family. It's one of my favorite things to eat," she said with a giggle.

"I don't know. If we bring too much attention to ourselves, my father could…"

"Stop! I will do what I want. Fear and caution be damned."

"I didn't say I was afraid, just that it could happen; that we'd get caught."

Dalidah grabbed a cape and walked to the exit of her four-story townhome.

"There is a family I have scoped out. You coming or not?"

He hurriedly caught up to her as she sped down the street to parts unknown.

Soon she led the way to a house that rested on the edge of town. It was late at night and a family that consisted of a mother, father and three children sat down to dinner.

Dalidah smiled while staring through the window. Her tongue darted out. Licking her lips as she watched them. Horustia leered at them next to her.

"How do you want to do this?"

She turned and smirked at him, then walked to the front door and kicked it in. Piercing cries rang out, and Horustia followed her lead. Dalidah went after the children as their mother yelled for them to hide. However, Horustia interrupted her words by ripping her throat out and then attacked the father, who aimed a shotgun in his direction. He tore the man's arm clean from the socket and jumped on him.

The screams from the children died out, and Dalidah returned to the main room to find Horustia feeding on the father. She pulled out a long silver blade that was strapped to her thigh and plunged it into the back of his neck and pulled it side to side, almost severing his head.

She smiled down at his body, jerking about when something from the side knocked her into the far wall.

Dalidah looked up to find Thothius retrieving the long dagger that was still embedded in Horustia's neck.

Blood pooled on the floor beneath Horustia as the wound slowly closed on each side. A group of Thothius's vampire flunkies scuffled in, grabbed his body, and left.

Dalidah recovered and jumped at Thothius. He captured both of her wrists and kissed her hard on the mouth. She bit his tongue when he pushed it into her mouth.

But she moaned and fed on his blood when it awoken her blood lust. He lowered her wrists and let her drink her fill. Before she could react, he pinned her to the far wall.

"You see, you want my blood. And I want yours." He slid his tongue down the side of her throat and bit into her shoulder. She locked her legs around his waist and gripped his hair, locking his lips and fangs into her flesh.

He tore her panties free and took her there against the wall while they drank from each other.

After he lowered her to the floor, he pressed his forehead against hers.

"You know now that you are mine, Dalidah. My son is foolish and confused about who you belong to, but you and I understand that you're my mate . . . no one else's."

His vampire guard appeared as he turned his back to her.

"Take her away."

"What? No!"

She could not fight the two off as they took hold of her.

"These are my most trusted and most powerful guards. You are no match for them, even at your strongest, Dalidah. Now bring her."

***

A prisoner once more. Dalidah waited for Thothius.

I will be no one's pet.

She gripped the necklace she'd purchased from the witch from the magic guild when she was in the mortal realm.

"I was saving this for a special occasion. I suppose there is no time like the present," she said.

Her throaty laugh filled the room as she stared down at the stone.

A few days passed before Thothius came to her. But when he did, he arrived smug and relaxed.

"So, are you ready to give me your answer? Though I am sure it will be that you agree."

"Yes, so I don't understand why you had to lock me up in here again if you already knew?" she asked with a light shrug.

"I had to see if you would give in now or fight longer."

Dalidah walked over to him and pressed her body to his, leaning them against the door at his back. She kissed him and wrapped her arms around his neck.

"Yes, I give in, I like the idea of the power you promise so there's no need to lock me up anymore."

He turned, lifted her onto the bed, and undressed her. They kissed as he pulled her under him. She rolled with him until she was on top and took over. Their strength and power matched in their lovemaking throughout the night. When he finally slept, Dalidah slid from the bed and away, putting her back against the wall.

After a few moments, Thothius felt the space next to him and found it empty. He partially sat up.

"Dalidah?"

"Yes?"

"Come back to bed."

"No, I enjoy watching you from here."

She wrapped her hand around the gem and released the magic. In a blink, her form turned into a Lycrian. Her wolf-like head almost touched the ten foot high ceiling.

He flipped up from the bed, but it was too late. She had her maw around his neck.

"You bitch!"

A deep laugh erupted from her transformed throat.

"It will take more than a Lycrian to destroy me! Even if you take my head, I will return, and you will pay."

Her mouth closed, snapping his head from his shoulders. His limp body fell to the floor. With a burst of speed, she crashed through the wall of the room. Vampire guards flooded the halls in an effort to stop her. She made quick work of any that dared cross her path. Just as she reached the exit, she smelled Horustia's scent and turned to find him staring after her from down the hall.

She ran off into the night and toward the veil line, not looking back to see if she was being pursued.

Upon crossing back into the mortal world, she knew she'd require the protection of someone powerful. The only other vampire old enough to combat the vampires of the council was Cordaglen. She returned to her regular form, the power of the stone fading.

"I'll need to go into hiding for a little while and then make a deal with the leader of the hunter's guild. Whatever he wants, I will do."

A sinister smile inched to life on her lips.

"But first, a meal."

That night, the street ran red with the blood of the innocent, as Dalidah's hunger knew no end.

LYDRAGA

CREATED

Rain poured. The heavy droplets soaked into the ground and formed slick mud.

"Please! Ah! Just a little farther."

"Alessandro! Come back! Let us take it out of you!"

She looked over her shoulder but pushed forward, her heavy belly dragging her down, rain-soaked clothes making each step harder.

"Ahhh!" she screamed as a contraction hit, bringing her to her knees. Mud and blood stained the tan-colored dress she wore. A quick look down solidified what she felt. The baby would soon come.

Alessandro got to her feet and trudged on.

"The veil. I must reach it. Please . . ."

Her nails dug into the tree that she used for leverage, once again looking behind her. The two men chasing her were getting closer.

Alessandro pushed herself into a full-on sprint as more blood poured from between her legs. She heard them calling her name as she broke through the line of the veil. They couldn't follow her beyond the veil. No living mortal could.

She surveyed the area. It was nighttime; only the moon and stars lit her way. Ahead, she could make out a large, old tree with nothing around it but grass for miles. She stumbled forward, holding her belly, when a sharp, piercing pain shot through her stomach.

Alessandro lurched forward but twisted, falling onto her back. Blood sprayed from her gaping mouth. Bone and guts burst from her torso.

Her left hand reached for the mangled lower half of her body as tears streamed down her cheeks.

The cries of a baby filled her ears. A smile eased to life on her blood-stained face, her pupils dilating.

The sky was clear, and the night was quiet, though the sounds of new life filled the dark moments later. Alessandro's remains bounced and wiggled about the ground. The newborn baby no longer cried. It feasted, filling its small tummy with its mother's entrails.

***

Twenty-Nine Years Later

"Out of the way! Move! Move! Move!"

Maverick Kendall shoved people out of his way as he chased the lowlife who had eluded him earlier in the day. A quick jump and a hop over the bus stop bench landed him his target.

"Stop struggling, you piece of shit!" he said, pulling the man's arms behind his back, straddling him.

"Let me go! I didn't do a thing. And you're not a cop, so fuck you!"

"Just shut up."

Maverick lifted the man with little effort and started back the way he had come, holding the man's handcuffed wrists. Tightly.

People watched. They recorded and took pictures with their phones, whispering as he made his way through the crowd. Thankfully, his black pickup truck was around the corner.

He loaded his target into the back seat and then slid into the driver's side. The man banged his feet on the cage between him and the front seats.

"Just sit tight back there. We will be at your new home soon enough."

***

Maverick counted his bounty, then returned to his truck. "Not a bad day," he said, starting the engine.

On the way home, he stopped and grabbed some beer. His apartment was in the heart of Drawdic City. It wasn't much, but it was his. The fifteenth floor had sounded good when he bought it—but not when the elevator was out.

"Damn it!" he said, pressing the elevator button again and again.

A silver sign stood near the doors. It read: OUT OF ORDER.

He made his way up the stairs. By the time he reached the fourteenth floor, sweat covered him and seemed to pour from every orifice. He stopped, pulled off his brown bomber jacket, and pushed his dark brown, shoulder-length hair back.

"What a great thirtieth birthday this turned out to be," he complained, holding onto the banister for support.

Guess I'll have to wait for the beer to get cold again, he thought, peering down at the bag that held the six-pack.

Maverick stepped on the last landing, when a burning filled his belly and sharp pain shot through his left eye. He instinctively covered it, dropping the bag with his beer. Before he could retrieve them, both his feet flipped backwards and reformed into beast like paws. Blood splattered the wall behind him, and he fell down the stairs. Mid-fall, his spine broke, splintering through his skin. He could hear his own screams as new ribs replaced his old ones.

"Please! Someone! Help ME!"

He begged no one and everyone. From the center of his muscular back, silver hair sprouted. Long hair grew from the tip of his hairline to the new, short tail he now had. His eyes were also silver when they had been chocolate brown. Sharp claws dug into the tiled floor beneath him. His entire body was bulging muscles; silky and slimy. A howl emerged from his long muzzle, making the walls vibrate.

His eyes dashed about when the creaking of a door from above caught his attention.

"Hello, is someone there? Do you need help?" asked a voice from the landing above.

Maverick bounded up the stairs, pouncing on the unsuspecting neighbor. His long maw clamped around the man's throat, severing his head. Blood gushed out and cascaded down Maverick's beastly form. His maw widened and enlarged, taking the man's body into his oversized throat. A sizzling sound emanated from within his neck; the remains dissolved as he devoured them. An inhuman light beamed from Maverick's eyes and pores, making all the blood evaporate. His body reshaped and transformed back into what it once was.

***

Maverick awoke minutes later, naked. He grabbed his brown jacket off the stairs, throwing it on, before sprinting for his apartment. Luckily, he didn't encounter anyone on the way. He showered, though his body was spotless.

"Was I dreaming? What the fuck happened? I couldn't have . . . eaten." He paused, pulling on a black t-shirt and jeans. "No, it had to be a nightmare. Did I pass out? And what happened to my clothes?"

He rubbed his hands up and down his midsection and over his upper arms. Everything was normal. He smacked his lips and clicked his tongue. Tasting.

A taste of sugar and salt caressed his taste buds. Built-up saliva slid down his throat, and a thirst he had never felt came over him. He rushed into his small kitchen and rummaged through the fridge, pulling out a glass container of water. With three large gulps, he emptied it.

"Fuck!" he shouted, downing three other bottles of water.

The front of his T-shirt was soaked through with spilled water, and his breathing became labored.

"What's happening to me?"

His vision blurred, and a splitting headache rumbled to life behind his eyes. In the other room, a faint buzzing caught his attention.

Unsteady steps led him to his brown leather couch. He flipped over his cell phone. The screen said *Dad*.

"Yeah?" he answered, scrunching up his nose as the pain in his head worsened.

"You, okay? You sound terrible," said his father, his voice laced with a nervous undertone.

"Well, I've been better."

He sat down and rested his forehead in his hand. "What's up? You never call this late."

"It's not that late, Mac. I had a feeling something was… off."

"Dad, I'm fine. Look, I'll give you a ring tomorrow. I need to get some rest, okay?"

"… Sure, talk to you then."

Maverick tossed the phone next to him onto the couch and leaned his head back, keeping his eyes closed. The soft glow of the city lights from the buildings across the way were the only illumination in his otherwise dark living room. He fell asleep there in the cold, unsure and hungry.

***

The sound of crunching bones seared his ears, and the fresh scent of blood caressed his senses. Maverick jumped from his sleeping position on the couch and landed, crouching and ready to fight. A quick survey of his surroundings calmed him. Sunlight filled his eyes, making him turn away from the beaming glow.

He grabbed his cell phone. It was 8:15 a.m., and he was late.

"Shit! Shit!"

He ran into his bedroom, shrugged on a button-down shirt, and grabbed his brown bomber jacket before heading for the door. With keys, wallet, and cell phone in hand, he left the apartment. He stopped in front of the elevator that was still out of order. His gaze fell on the door to the stairwell.

"Nothing happened. It wasn't real," he said, looking through the door's small glass window.

After an uneasy breath, he pushed it open and charged down the first set of stairs. He froze mid-stride, looking back. The landing above closed in, making him sprint down the next two flights. He kept a jogging pace until he reached the bottom.

***

Throughout the day, Maverick found he had boundless energy. He caught and took in three bounties. His hunches had all been right. Before the afternoon, he

418

had taken on four more bounty jobs. It was 2:20 p.m. when his father called.

"Hey, Mac, you have time this evening to drop by?"

"Yeah, what's up?" Maverick asked, sitting down in a booth at his favorite diner.

"There's something I need to tell you."

"Can't you spill over the phone?" he asked, waving the waitress over.

"No, I need to see you and explain a few things."

"Can I get the afternoon special and an iced tea, please, Martha?" he asked, grinning.

"Hey, you listening to me?"

"Yeah, Dad, I hear ya. I'm trying to get lunch. Look, I'll see you tonight after work . . . okay?" he said, hanging up and putting his cell phone away.

Ten minutes later, the waitress placed a double cheeseburger, fries, onion soup, and an iced tea in front of him.

He picked up the burger and took a generous bite, chewing a few times. An overwhelming need to regurgitate followed the first swallow he took. He spit the rest out and looked nervously at the fries and soup. After trying each, the same reaction followed.

Maverick's brow beaded with sweat as a deep-seated hunger took hold. His eyes moved around the room. He could see veins and muscle tissue under the other patrons' skin. Scents from all around him filled his nostrils. He jumped to his feet and ran for the door.

"Maverick, wait! You didn't pay!" shouted the waitress.

With a look of distress, he took out two twenty-dollar bills and threw them on the counter as he rushed out the door.

"Wait! That's . . . too much."

He heard her but ran for his truck. Once he was behind the wheel, he took deep breaths, leaned back, resting his head for a few minutes.

"What's wrong with me?"

His cell phone buzzed in his jacket's left pocket. He pulled it out and answered without checking the caller ID.

"Yeah!"

"Son, are you okay? What's happening?"

"Dad?" he said, his brow scrunching up in confusion.

"Come home now. I know what's wrong with you. Just come home."

The line went dead. Maverick looked at the black screen for a moment before he started up the truck and headed out of the city to his dad's old cabin in the woods.

***

Fifty minutes later, Maverick banged on his father's cabin door.

"Dad, open up."

The headache had returned, and his stomach was on fire. He raised his fist to bang once more, but the door opened. His father stood back so he could come in. He hadn't seen his father in over six months. He looked much older somehow. The edges of his dark brown hair were now gray. His tanned skin had wrinkles where it was once smooth. He was a tall man, standing at six four, but now he hunched a bit, making Maverick's height of six three look to be more.

"What are you staring at, boy? Come on in, already."

He moved into the warmth of the cabin. Old memories danced to the forefront of his mind. The wooden stairs to the left of the entrance had been his area of play. He was yelled at a lot as a child to not run up and down them. A smile inched its way to life on his face as he made his way to the living room. The same old brown fabric couch and loveseat sat against the walls facing each other, and the woodstove's light in the far-left corner burned bright. The newest addition was the sixty-inch TV off to the right side of the room.

"What did you need to tell me you couldn't have over the phone?" he said, sitting.

"No 'nice to see you, Dad,' huh?" his father asked, running his large hand through his long brown, shaggy hair.

"Nice to see you, Dad."

"Yeah, sure. Look, I'm going to cut to the chase. You won't be able to eat regular food anymore."

Maverick had been rubbing at his temples to ease the headache but froze at his father's words.

"What are you talking about?"

"Your awakening has happened, hasn't it? Did you hurt anyone?"

The events from the night before flashed before his eyes. "No, no. None of that was real. It was a dream," he said, standing.

"Afraid not. It's time I told you the truth about your mother and me."

"What do you mean?"

"I'm not from here, nor am I mortal. Your mother was, but after she nearly died, a Dagaru worm took control of her, and she became something else."

"What do you mean, not 'from here' . . . 'nor mortal'? And that Mom was what? You're freaking me out, Dad."

"It's best if I just show you the real me . . ."

His father stepped back. Crackling, popping, and breaking of bone ravaged his father's body. His head reshaped and became elongated. Dark brown fur covered him, and his legs bent and became like the hind legs of an animal. He was taller. A howl burst from his monstrous throat as his silver eyes stared down at Maverick.

With utter shock, Maverick stumbled back, then ran for the kitchen. "What the fuck!" he said, putting the large kitchen table between himself and the beast.

His father stared. His body re-formed, turning back into his mortal-like self. He stood before Maverick, naked and silent.

"Dad . . . what the fuck are you?"

"We are Lycrian—or rather, I am—and you are half Lycrian and half Dagaru-Slave, due to your mothers change," he said, walking back into the living room and grabbing a blanket from the back of the couch.

Maverick leaned back against the stove, his mouth gaping open. "Are you saying I'm a wolf beast? What I thought was a dream the other night happened?"

"First, you're more than that. And whatever happened last night was real."

Maverick came to stand before his father, who had sat on the couch with the blanket wrapped around him.

"Sit down, boy. You need to know what you really are and what you will have to do to survive."

Maverick sat on the loveseat across from his father. He rubbed the palms of his hands nervously up and down his thighs, the burning hunger gnawing at him.

"Like I said, you are a mix of your mother and me. Your mother was a freed Dagaru slave."

"And what is that?"

"A Dagaru worm is a creature that usually lives on the other side of the veil, where beings like our family live, away from mortals. Your mother was once possessed by a Dagaru worm but was freed. That means it changed her. We met, fell in love, had you and so your kind is rare, but others like you exist."

Maverick swallowed deeply and leaned forward. "And what am I?"

"You are a Lydraga. You're a fusion of Lycrian and Dagaru. I had hoped that maybe you would awaken as only a Lycrian on your thirtieth birthday, but it seems you are a Lydraga. I felt it last night, and that's why I called you."

Sweat beaded on Maverick's brow and upper lip. His skin was burning, and the palms of his hands continued to itch.

His father's eyes narrowed, watching him. "You feel the need to change, don't you?" He sniffed the air. "As a Lydraga, you can no longer consume mortal food. You must eat their flesh to live."

"I can't be here. I can't listen to any more of this," he said, jumping to his feet.

"You know, everything I have told you is true. It would be best to accept what you are and embrace it."

Maverick stopped with his hand over the knob of the front door.

"You should know I'm leaving and have no plans to return. I've lived among mortals long enough. The pack is calling, and the other side of the veil is where I belong. It's also where you belong."

"I don't even know what the veil is."

"When and if you're ready, or if things get too hard, follow my scent out to the back of the cabin. Change, and you will find the entrance to the veil."

Maverick left without another word. He drove back to the city, his mind confused and his hunger surrounding him.

GIVING IN

It was late at night when he drove down the street his apartment building was on. He parked and was about to head inside when a scream came from behind the building.

He casually walked around the side and peeped around. A man and woman wrestled on the ground next to a large green dumpster. The man yanked the woman up from the ground and towards him. She pulled away, continuing to scream.

"Stop! Let me go!"

"Just shut up and come on!" he yelled, yanking her behind him.

"She said stop, so you should let that hand go."

Maverick looked down at the man, who was much shorter.

"Mind your business and get the hell out of my way," the man said, stepping around Maverick.

The woman looked at him, her gray eyes pleading.

Maverick grabbed her other wrist, which made the man pulling her look back.

"I think she doesn't want to go with you. Right, miss?" he asked, looking down at her.

"No, I don't. He'll kill me if he gets me alone. Please?"

The man pulled a combat knife out and slashed at Maverick, letting go of the woman.

He pulled her behind him, dodged, and grabbed the man's wrist. With a twist and bend, the man dropped the blade.

"Give it up and be on your way," he said, then pushed him away.

The man stumbled forward, pulled a gun, and shot. The bullet hit Maverick in his right shoulder. He bared his teeth as the man took off at a dead run.

"Are you okay? Oh my god what should I do?!" the woman asked, hysterical.

"Go inside the building and wait for me." Maverick took off after the man. His blood was boiling, hunger once again filling him. Scents moved and swirled about, lighting up the night, in reds, blues, greens, and more. The man was not far ahead. Maverick entered a garage. Parked cars were on either side of him. It was dark, save for a few wall lights against the gritty stone structure.

"I know you're in here. Come out!"

He sniffed the air. His mouth watered at the man's scent of fear. He stooped, moving closer to the smell. Behind a large, blue pickup truck, the man ducked, gun in hand.

Maverick felt burning pushing at his flesh. He ducked his head and let the change take him.

"I'm so hungry!" he said, his last words distorting.

Within seconds, the change consumed him. He charged the man, whose eyes filled with shock and fear.

His claws ripped his prey's arms from the sockets. He lifted him above his head as the man screamed. Maverick's maw sucked at the blood-soaked opening where his victim's right arm once was. His throat contorted and devoured the man and his muffled screams whole. Light filled the space, evaporating all leftover blood.

After turning back, he left the garage and kept to the shadows.

***

Maverick went over to his truck, dug through the storage case in the back, and put on the spare T-shirt and jeans he always kept there. He smelled the woman from before as he stepped into his building, coming to a stop.

"He won't be bothering you anymore, miss," he said, not looking in her direction.

She moved from behind the wall to his right, approaching him.

"Thank you."

He turned towards her. She was beautiful. Dark brown hair rested on her thin shoulders. Her high cheekbones sat under large almond-shaped eyes, one of which was swollen shut. The light-green jeans and white, form-fitting T-shirt she wore were dirty and yellowing.

Maverick walked over to the elevator, pressed the button, and waited. He felt her standing behind him but said nothing.

They got into the elevator. He pressed his floor, then glanced at her. "Which floor?"

She didn't meet his gaze, casting her eyes down.

"Same as yours."

"Okay."

Maverick stared straight ahead, but he could feel her gaze boring into his back. She smelled of peppermint and cherries. A vein jumped in his neck, and he clenched his fist before closing his eyes. He listened to her breathing and imagined sinking his teeth into her neck and ripping it out.

I can't be hungry again.

The elevator dinged, and they stepped out. Maverick stopped in front of his door, and so did the woman he had saved.

"Why are you following me?" he asked, facing her.

She smiled at him and waved a hand over her swollen eye. When she lowered it, smooth skin replaced the purple-and-red mark.

"Maverick, it's time to lead your people."

"I don't know who the fuck you are but stay the hell away from me."

"I'm Collette Bridges, and we have a lot to talk about. I know how your mother died."

"Get the fuck out of here, I have warned you." He unlocked his door with the spare key he kept in the wall light.

"Do you also know you were born on the other side of the veil?"

Maverick froze. "Come in, but if you try anything, don't expect to walk out of here."

She brushed past him. He closed the door, turned on the lights, and led her into his living room.

"Make it quick," he said, throwing his spare key onto the couch.

"You don't know how long we have all waited for you to awaken."

"Look, Collette. I don't know who this 'we' are, but again . . . make it quick."

"Do you know how your mother died?"

"She died in childbirth."

"Yes, because you ate your way out. We tried to help her, but she ran and gave birth to you on the other side of the veil."

The words "ate your way out" played over and over in his head.

"I need you to leave, now," he said, walking back to the front door.

She made no move to follow and stared after him.

"We are here to serve you, Lord Maverick. We have all waited a long time for your awakening," she said from the living room.

"I'm only going to ask you once more to leave, or I'll make you."

He pulled the door open and waited. Collette smiled and shuffled out.

"We will be watching. And I hope you enjoyed my earlier offering."

His eyes enlarged and the savory taste of the man he had devoured returned.

"That man wasn't really trying to hurt you, was he?" he asked, anger rising.

She smirked and glanced over her shoulder. "Maybe he would have. What matters is that I feed you."

Maverick slammed the door in her face.

"You can't change who and what you are, Lord. We accept you as you are. I will return soon."

Maverick listened until he heard her footfalls fade away. With his back against the door, he slid down to the floor and rested his forehead in the palms of his hands. A deep sigh rushed from him, then he walked into his kitchen. He eyed his refrigerator before retiring for the night, thinking heavily on his next move.

3

EMBRACED

The next morning, Maverick called his father.

"Damn it," he said, in frustration, hanging up. "I need to know if what that crazy woman said is true or not. He would choose now to leave."

Maverick completed bounty after bounty. The day dragged on, and his hunger nagged at him. The last job of the night was a guy who had a record of beating his ex-girlfriends and ex-wives. A warrant was issued, and a bounty called in.

Maverick stepped out of his truck and looked at the motel room door, number 476. He had checked with the front desk clerk, who didn't care about giving out info on their customers.

With his left booted foot, he kicked the door in. His target jumped and ran for the bathroom window. Maverick grabbed him and threw him to the floor. He cuffed him and put him in the back seat of his truck. Halfway down the road, the man kept kicking the door.

"Stay still back there, or we're going to have a problem."

"Fuck you!" the man said, spitting at the cage.

Maverick slammed on the brakes, jumped out, and pulled his passenger out on the side of the road. It was the middle of the night and no traffic passed by. The hunger within him boiled to the surface, and he changed right before the man's eyes.

"What the fuck are you?" he shouted, getting to his feet and ran into the field along the road.

Maverick caught up to him in seconds. Claws and teeth sank into the man's back as he fled, knocking him to the ground.

"Ahhh, no!! Ahhhhhh!"

Blood gushed and covered the grassy ground beneath them. Maverick's right claw dug between the man's shoulder and neck, splitting his body diagonally. His eyes rolled into the back of his head as liver, lungs, and entrails plummeted to the ground. Maverick lapped up the insides and consumed all the remains, leaving nothing to the wild animals of the night.

***

"He deserved it. If I only eat those who do wrong, it won't matter."

Maverick peeked at himself in his rearview mirror before looking back at the road.

He parked in front of his building and saw Collette getting into a silver car. He started his engine back up and followed at a distance.

They drove for over an hour until they turned off onto a dirt road outside the city limits. Maverick stopped and got out, following them by foot. There were no lights except the silver car's headlights, but he could see a house in the distance.

After Collette and an unknown man entered the house, Maverick made his way up the front steps. It was an old cabin with a wrap-around porch. He looked through an open window from which light streamed. Inside, he saw a circle of people in red hoods. In the center, a large, eight-foot statue of a wolf-like beast had been erected. They all bowed to it, then turned towards

Collette's direction. She walked around to each red-hooded figure, cutting their offered wrists, filling a bowl with blood.

"Oh, great Lydraga Lord, grant us the power to live forever, and we will feed you in abundance."

She set the bowl onto the beast's altar, turned, and looked directly at him through the open window. He ducked to the side and jogged back down the steps.

"Bunch of fucking nutbags. I'm getting the fuck out of here," he said to himself, but stopped in his tracks, looking back at the cabin.

"So, they worship what I am, huh?" He ran back to the house and ripped the door off the hinges. All the hooded people turned towards the interruption. Collette smiled and lifted the bowl of blood from the altar, walking up to him.

"This is your offering, my lord. I am a witch of the magic guild, and I have gathered many followers for you. We will serve you well," she said, lifting the bowl higher.

Maverick lowered his head. Though he had only eaten hours ago, he felt famished. He knocked the bowl she offered out of her hand and grabbed her up by the throat.

"You will serve me well for dinner," he said, changing.

Collette had no chance to reply or protest. He squeezed and her head was detached from her body. Her remains plummeted to the floor as Maverick caught her head, swallowing it whole. His focus turned to the screaming and retreating worshipers. Blood covered the interior of the cabin. Cries of sorrow echoed throughout and deep into the dark.

***

His body was clean as he walked back to his truck. The last conversation with his father brought realization. He drove to his father's cabin.

The sun was high in the sky by the time he pulled up to the front of the house. He walked around to the back and sniffed the air, his eyes surveying the surroundings.

He knelt, placing his open palm against the chilled, grassy earth. His father's earthy scent led him. He trotted, following it deep into the woods. The smell became stronger as he entered an open field.

~ **Change and you will find the entrance to the veil.** ~

He let his true form take over. Muscles pulsated and burst through his skin. Silver fur and claws emerged. His shiny, slimy new skin covered his enormous body.

There, only a few feet in front of him, was a misty wall. His eyes focused on it, and he ran towards his new home, where he belonged. When hunger struck, the mortal world would know him now only as Lydraga.

About the Author

D.L. Tillery, "The Mistress of Horror" is known for her short horror tales and poetry. Homeschooled during her formative years fed into the imaginative person she is today. D.L. Tillery was first published at the age of nineteen and worked as a freelance writer for Carpe Nocturne before starting her Fiction Writing career. She currently resides in MD in the USA with her daughter, two brothers and mother, where she was born and raised. The message she loves to leave for all her readers is to "Stay Scared."

Upcoming Stories & Novels

Caliostro Book 2: Fading of the Veil 2025

The Children Of Nana Series: When The Night

Cries 2025 -2027

Beyond the Veil: Horror Collection 2025

Contact Information

Website: www.authordltillery.com

Email: Authordltillery@gmail.com

Instagram: https://www.instagram.com/authordltillery/

Facebook: https://www.facebook.com/AuthorDLTillery

Twitter(X): @Authordltillery

.

Made in United States
North Haven, CT
30 July 2025